# The Divine Finalisation

**The Divine Zetan Trilogy, Volume 3**

Martin Lundqvist

Published by Martin Lundqvist, 2019.

This is a work of fiction. Similarities to real people, places, or events are entirely coincidental.

THE DIVINE FINALISATION

**First edition. April 19, 2019.**



Written by Martin Lundqvist.

# Chapter 1: Prologue

(The prologue is a summary of the events in The Divine Sedition. If you have already read The Divine Sedition, you can skip the prologue.)

The year is 2872 AD. Keila Eisenstein, a young Martian rebel with supernatural visions and premonitions, is on the run from the Terran Council. The Terran Council is brutal dictatorship representing the mightiest corporations on Earth. Keila is on the run from her nemesis, Rear Admiral Bjorn Muller, who is the son of the Terran Council leader, Joachim Muller. During the pursuit, Keila's escapes and she crashes down on the asteroid Eden, the home world of her deceased mother, Susanna. Keila finds out that Eden is an artificial Bronze Age society, dominated by its malevolent god-king Abraham Goldstein. Keila kills Abraham and befriends Metatron, one of Abraham's super-soldiers. After that, Keila fakes her own death and tricks Bjorn Muller to stop pursuing her.

Once Bjorn Muller has left Eden, Keila and her ally Metatron, are in control of Eden. They modernise the Edenite society so that they can use Eden as a base of operations. From Eden they stage covert operations against Terran Council, weakening the Terran Council from within.

The modernisation of Eden faces a problem. It angers Adina, the granddaughter of the late Abraham Goldstein. Adina uses her abilities with the Zetan mind-control technology to attack Keila and Metatron. They both survive Adina's psionic attacks, and Keila retaliates. Keila forces Adina out in the open, where she can incinerate Adina using orbital laser cannons.

After securing her leadership on Eden, Keila seeks ways to fight the Terran Council. Keila realises that she can use Eden's secret technologies to travel to the Divine Dimension. Once in the Divine Dimension, Keila finds advanced alien technology to aid her in her quest. With her new-found technologies, Keila believes that she can win a Martian war of independence against the Terran Council.

Keila needs to reverse-engineer the Zetan alien technologies to enable mass-production. To reverse-engineer the Zetan technology, Keila needs to find skilled scientists. A prominent Terran Council scientist, Markus Bauer, offers to defect to Keila's side. Markus condition is that Keila helps him escape from the Proxima Thule research station. Metatron fears a trap, but Keila's visions tell her to trust Markus Bauer. Using her Zetan alien technologies, Keila defeats her Terran enemies on the Proxima Thule research station. After that, she brings back the scientists to Eden as forced recruits.

Back on Earth, Bjorn Muller's father, Joachim Muller, is angry with Bjorn's lack of progress. To punish Bjorn, Joachim Muller puts him under the command of the genetic mutant Alicia White. Joachim sends the duo on a mission; to find out who attacked Proxima Thule and to investigate whether Keila is still alive. Bjorn Muller and Alicia White travel to Eden to investigate the rumours of Keila Eisenstein's survival. Metatron distracts Alicia through having sex with her, and Keila escapes undetected.

A while later, Alicia gets frenzied from drugs and engage in rough sex with Bjorn Muller. Alicia in her frenzied state, almost kills Bjorn. This causes a diplomatic crisis between House Muller and House White. Alicia and her group go into hiding to avoid punishment.

A couple of months later, Markus Bauer manages to reverse-engineer the Zetan technologies. This means that the Zetan technologies can be mass-produced for war with human technology.

During the same time, Keila finds out that she is pregnant with Metatron. This is a complication for her revolutionary plans. Keila has a vision indicating that she will give birth in two years. To fulfil her vision, Keila has an embryo removal, and she put the foetus in suspended animation for future use. Keila's action upsets Metatron, who ends their romantic relationship. However, they remain amicable, sharing the power of Eden.

Keila uses a Zetan technology, The Zetan External DNA modifier, to alter her appearance and DNA signature. Keila travels incognito to Mars, hoping to meet with Hellas Petrakis, the president of the Olympus Republic. Keila wants to meet with him to discuss a Martian revolution against their

Terran overlords. On the way to Mars, the infamous space pirate Morgan Henry attacks Keila's passenger ship.

Morgan's attack terrifies Keila and Rangda offers to help her, in exchange for temporary control of Keila's body. Keila is wary of Rangda but she sees no other option. Possessed by Rangda, Keila butchers Morgan's crew and finishes off Morgan Henry, by tearing out his heart and eating it. Keila sustains injuries during the altercation, but they are only superficial. Keila lands in the Olympus Republic and local police brings her in for questioning.

Meanwhile, Bjorn Muller arrives to investigate the mysterious woman that killed all the pirates. Bjorn analyses bloody-stained bandages in the medical room, and he realises that the mystery woman is his nemesis, Keila Eisenstein. Bjorn destroys the evidence of Keila's resurgence to save his own image, as he was the one who declared her dead, one year earlier.

In the Olympus Republic, Keila convinces Hellas Petrakis, of her real identity. They agree to join forces, and Keila goes back to Eden to bring more Zetan technology, as well as her personal strike force. Before Keila leaves, she inserts a mind control technology chip into Hellas' brain, to make sure that he stays loyal.

After Keila's departure, Bjorn arrives at the Olympus Republic, asking Hellas Petrakis about the woman that killed Morgan Henry. Hellas denies any knowledge, and Bjorn doesn't want to press the issue as he doesn't want the truth to come out. During Bjorn's visit, Hellas sets Bjorn up with Martian prostitutes and secretly films the encounter to have leverage against Bjorn.

The next few months, Keila performs covert attacks on Terran Council member installations. Keila plants fake evidence, causing the Terran Council members to fight among themselves. This weakens the Terran Council's hold of the solar system. Eventually, Keila leads a successful attack on the Terran Council mines on Mars. After this, Keila reveals that she is alive and that her faction, The Martian Humanist Alliance, has returned. House White responds by orbital bombardments of Martian settlements. This furthers the resentment towards the Terran Council among the Martian population.

Sometime later, Keila launches coordinated surprise attacks on the Terran Council bases on Mars. The Terran Council defenders are not prepared for the alien Zetan technologies, and Keila defeats them. Keila gets injured during the battle for the North Pole. Thus, she must sit out the decisive battle, the attack on the Terran Council's Phobos base.

A colossal wave of oppressed Martians, led by Melchior Dorevitch, is heading towards Phobos. Bjorn Muller won't let them conquer the base to gain their independence. Instead, he redirects the fusion thrusters on the Phobos Moonbase, setting it on a collision course with Mars. On impact, this would melt the surface of both Phobos and Mars, killing everyone in an instant.

Keila wakes up, and she sees what is happening in a vision. Despite her injuries, Keila sets out to stop her nemesis, Bjorn, and she faces him near the thrusters of Phobos. Bjorn shoots her twice and leaves her for dead, and then he takes off in his spaceship. Keila doesn't die from her wounds, however, as divine intervention from the True Maker temporarily heals her wounds. The True Maker grants Keila enough strength to change the direction of Phobos fusion thrusters. This redirects the Phobos Moon onto a collision course with the Sun, away from the Martian surface. Keila chases after Bjorn, and they both crash on Mars, on top of Olympus Mons mountain.

Bjorn gets out of his spaceship. Bjorn is gravely wounded, and Keila's appearance shocks him, as he thought he killed her moments earlier. Keila states that Bjorn is under arrest for his crimes. Bjorn asks her what the point of that is, since they are both dying in the wilderness. Shocked, Keila drops to the ground, with her previous wounds coming back. Bjorn professes his everlasting unrequited love for Keila. Keila is cold towards Bjorn and calls him out for kidnapping her, and forcing her to become his sex slave. Feeling heartbroken, Bjorn throws himself off a cliff. This is to kill himself and to make sure that Keila won't put him on trial.

A few days later, Keila is recovering from her wounds and gives a speech where she declares Martian independence. Keila hopes that she can negotiate a peace treaty with the Terran Council, as they cannot invade Mars anymore, having lost the Phobos Moon.

The Terran Council, led by Joachim Muller, has other plans though. Following the defeat against the Martians, the Terran Council members stand united and are ready to strike back. As they have lost Phobos Moonbase, Joachim Muller orders the redirection of a giant asteroid, Asteroid B600, to crash with Mars. The Terran Council sends a black operations team to the rogue asteroid B600. The mission is top-secret, and Joachim is unwilling to let his own brother, Supreme Commander Matthias Muller know about the plan. Instead, Joachim lies to Matthias and commands his fleet to protect the giant asteroid from Martian interference. Knowing that Matthias Muller is a reasonable man, Keila sends a delegation to negotiate with Matthias. During the negotiation, one of Joachim's agents assassinates Matthias. The agent makes it look like the Martians were behind the murder.

Running out of options, Keila asks Rangda for guidance. Rangda tells Keila to use Zetan technology to change her appearance to that of Alicia White. Furthermore, Rangda instructs Keila to travel Earth and open portals hidden in pyramids scattered around the planet.

A high-ranking Terran officer, Hilda Muller, questions Keila, who is posing as Alicia White. Hilda doesn't see through Keila's ruse, and they socialise and drink wine together. After that, Hilda gives Keila clearance for entry to Earth. Once on Earth, Keila sets off to activate the portals in the pyramids, but nothing seems to happen. Eventually, House Rashid forces arrests Keila for vandalism. This is a blessing in disguise, as they believe Keila to be the prominent Alicia White. The soldiers take Keila to a Terran Council conference in the city of Rashidium, to sentence her for her crimes.

Meanwhile, Hilda Muller meets Markus White and tells him about her drinking session with his cousin, Alicia. Markus exposes that "Alicia" must be an imposter, as the real Alicia White is allergic to alcohol. Together, they rush to the meeting to stop the imposter, Keila Eisenstein.

Keila, posing as Alicia White, has surrounded herself with Terran Council faction leaders. Keila uses this golden opportunity to massacre her enemies by releasing a nerve agent that she had hidden in a fake tooth. Once the Terran Council leadership has fallen, Keila orders the diversion of asteroid B600 towards a collision with the Sun. After this, Keila watches the sunset behind the distant glowing pyramids, feeling at peace with her impending death.

Hilda reaches the meeting room and she tries to breach the door. Before Hilda breaches the door, Keila observes a bright blue light as the portal to the Divine Dimension opens on top of the Cheops Pyramid. A massive horde of Xeno beasts arrive through the portal. The Xeno forces butcher and eat the unprepared House Rashid security forces, and approaches Rashidium. Eventually, Keila stands face to face with Rangda, the evil Xeno queen, who Keila has only seen in her visions. Rangda knocks Keila unconscious and carries her back to the portal to the Divine Dimension.

# Chapter 2: Desperate Moments

Hilda Muller, Markus White, and a group of House Rashid security guards exited the lift at the top level of Rashidium Tower. They walked towards the courtroom where the sentencing of Keila Eisenstein posing as Alicia White, took place.

Hilda Muller saw Ibrahim Rashid through the doorway at the end of the corridor. Ibrahim Rashid was scolding the imposter Keila Eisenstein for vandalising the Cheops Pyramid. Hilda Muller gave the signal to follow her, and the group headed towards the courtroom. 'Alicia' noticed the approaching troops, and she jumped towards Ibrahim Rashid. Once on top of him, she pushed his hand towards a control panel, to close the courtroom door. Hilda realised that there was no time to lose, she rushed towards the door to get in, but she was too late.

Hilda's skin burnt from colliding with the force field that protected the bullet-proof glass door that sealed off the room. She had got there too late, and the madwoman Alicia was holding the Terran Council leaders' as hostages. What Hilda saw next shocked her and her crew. The Terran Council leaders collapsed, and 'Alicia' transformed into the infamous Keila Eisenstein!

"Get those doors open now!" Hilda exclaimed, and the security guards requested reinforcements with appropriate equipment. Hilda looked at Keila. She noticed that Keila was activating The Terran Council Blood Encryption machine. This machine was rarely used, and Hilda could not figure out what the damn terrorist intended to do with the device. Regardless of what it was, it wasn't good news!

Hilda kept studying Keila. Keila had managed to access the Blood Encryption Machine, but Hilda wouldn't know what Keila had done until she had access to the machine herself. Hilda watched, as Keila bashed the skulls of the unconscious Terran Council leaders with a metal sculpture. Considering the amount of brain matter on the floor, it seemed unlikely that they would be able to resurrect any of the fallen leaders.

"We'll break through the doors in 20 minutes", one of the Rashid soldiers said. "Good, make sure to wear protective equipment, we don't know what gas she has released in there!", Hilda replied.

Hilda examined the situation. It would be a public relations nightmare, to explain how Keila had accessed a Terran Council meeting and murdered all the faction leaders. There was a risk for potential uprisings among the civilian population, in the chaos that would follow. This event would put the power of the Terran Council into question, for the second time in just a couple of months.

But in the situation, there was also an opportunity for Hilda. Hilda had suspected that Joachim Muller had something to do with the assassination of her father, Matthias Muller. Hilda had lacked the proof, and she wouldn't accuse the leader of her faction without any evidence to support her claims. With Joachim Muller and Benjamin Muller lying dead on the floor, things were looking better for Hilda's position in House Muller. With the two of them dead, Hilda was second in line to leadership after Joachim's third son Michael Muller. Michael Muller was an unambitious family man who did not seem to care much about power and ambition. Hilda was confident that she could persuade Michael to give up his position to her, as long as he could live in wealth and abundance.

Hilda stopped her succession planning when an intense blue light appeared on the horizon. The blue light was so intense, so it blinded her temporarily. When Hilda had regained her eyesight, she saw something that shocked her. A blue portal had opened on top of the Great Pyramid, and out of it came a massive horde of alien species.

A severe migraine struck Hilda, and the world became blurry and stopped making sense to her. This was because the Xeno invaders had brought stolen Zetan technology. Some of the Zetan technology disrupted the bionic microchips that Hilda had in her brain. Hilda could hear unintelligible chatter on the soldiers' transistors.

Hilda realised that her bionic microchips had broken as she could no longer understand Arabic, the language of the House Rashid soldiers.

Fortunately, Hilda had learned some English using her brain, and she spoke to the petrified Markus White.

Hilda Muller, speaking with a firm German accent:

- Stay close to me, Markus. We are under attack by alien life forms.

Markus White:

- What are those things? We are all going to die!

Hilda Muller:

- No, we are not. The army will get here shortly and sort out this mess. Fight to stay alive until then!

Markus White:

- Fight with what? We don't carry any weapons.

Hilda Muller:

- The Rashid soldiers will have to give us weapons!

Hilda Muller tried talking to the Rashid soldiers to get weapons for her and Markus. This didn't work as the Rashid soldiers only spoke Arabic, and they were too agitated to make any sense.

Suddenly, Hilda heard a thundering shriek and turned around. The scream had scattered the fortified glass to the boardroom. Hilda studied the source of the howl. A two-metre tall humanoid-like monstrosity with shiny purple eyes. Several three-metre tall beasts accompanied the monstrosity!

Rangda, knocked Keila unconscious, grabbed her, and jumped out of the building. The other beasts, however, attacked.

Hilda pulled Markus towards the floor, and thus, saved his life when a Xeno beast jumped towards her. The Rashid soldier behind them was not as lucky, and he got decapitated by the fearsome creature. The panicking Rashid

Soldiers shot towards the Xenos but to a limited effect. The Xenos had ballistic energy absorbers and thick skin that was hard to penetrate with the weapons that the guards carried. "Use your plasma knives!" Hilda shouted to the Rashid guards. But the guards didn't understand her. Instead, they panicked and the Xenos decapitated them one by one with their razor-sharp claws.

Hilda picked up the plasma knife from one of the fallen soldiers. She took a leap and saved Markus White through piercing the skull of a Xeno Beast with the plasma knife, slaying the beast. Hilda dragged Markus to the boardroom where the dead Terran Council leaders were lying on the floor. Since they were at a high altitude, the room was very windy. Hilda and Markus ran to the window.

There was no way out. They heard the Xenos behind them roar. The beasts had killed off the Rashid guards, and they had turned their attention towards Hilda and Markus.

Markus White:

- What do you say, Hilda? Should we end our lives jumping off the building, or would you rather be alien food?

Hilda Muller:

- You do whatever that pleases you. I am a soldier; I'll stay and fight.
- Get down!

Hilda pulled Markus to the ground and behind them came their salvation. It came in the form of a House Muller combat helicopter, that blew the remaining four Xenos to shreds with their autocannons and rockets. Hilda grabbed the Blood Encryption Tablet and got on the aircraft.

Hilda Muller:

- The city is overrun with Aliens. Let's get out of here!

Helicopter Pilot:

- Hilda! What about Joachim and Benjamin?

Hilda Muller:

- They are dead beyond resurrection. Murdered in cold blood by Keila Eisenstein. Now let's get the fuck out of here before those monsters come back!

Helicopter Pilot:

- Jawohl Fräulein Muller!

As the helicopter left Rashidium city, Hilda studied the carnage that the Xeno invasion had caused in the city. Reinforcements would arrive, but it was too late to save Rashidium's inhabitants from the destructive alien invasion!

# Chapter 3: Hilda Muller Seduces Markus White

Hilda Muller was back in the relative safety of her luxurious apartment in the Europeum Tower, located in Hansstadt. She was looking at the exhausted Markus White, who was sleeping on her couch in the lounge area. While she could have housed him in one of the many guest apartments in Europeum Tower, keeping him near was a crucial strategic decision.

While sleeping seemed to be a good idea, to relieve the stress, Hilda wouldn't have it. The Xeno invasion at the Terran Council meeting in Rashidium city had left all the Terran Council factions, leaderless. There was a lot of opportunity for someone with ambition to advance their own position. Hilda knew that in the upheaval that would follow, there would be a lot of knifing to come. Hilda would much rather be the one holding the knife, than being the receiver.

Since the assassination of her father, Matthias Muller, a few months earlier, Hilda had seen her power diminish. Matthias' death had put Hilda out of reach to the leadership of the House Muller. Officially, Martian rebels had killed Matthias, but Hilda had never believed in that ploy. After all, why would the Martians send assassins after her father, who was the most likely to listen to their pleas? Instead, Hilda was certain that it was her cousin Benjamin Muller who was behind the assassination. But Hilda had kept quiet. It would have been risky for her to accuse Benjamin, the son of the House Muller leader, Joachim Muller, without any hard evidence.

But now, both Joachim and Benjamin were dead, and the way lay open for her to contend for leadership. Joachim's youngest son, Michael Muller, would be first in line. However, Hilda doubted that Michael would have any interest in command as he preferred living a comfortable, careless life in luxury.

Hilda would need allies to secure her claim, both on the inside and on the outside. Hilda glimpsed at the sexy, half-naked body, of the sleeping Markus White. It was time to combine business and pleasure.

Hilda went back to her bedroom and got changed into a sexy dress. Hilda admired her own body in the mirror. This felt a bit strange as she saw herself as her father's daughter, a strong military woman and not as a seductress. Then again, to play the game of politics, she needed to be able to do both! Hilda sprayed herself with a potent pheromone perfume and approached Markus White.

Hilda Muller:

- Markus, darling, wake up.

Markus White woke up with a twitch, and he looked at Hilda in confusion before he spoke:

- Hilda? What's happening? Where am I?

Hilda touched Markus' face gently and spoke again.

- So, so. You are safe here with me in Europeum Tower.

Hilda smiled seductively and waited for the pheromones to influence Markus' body. The pheromones worked slower than Hilda had anticipated due to shock and stressful circumstances. However, a while later, they both participated in an extended orgasmic sexual trance. Once the sex was over, Hilda fell asleep in Markus' arms. She felt relieved of sexual tension and was happy to have a potential ally for the coming months!

# Chapter 4: Metatron Finds a Surrogate Mother for Sabina.

Metatron was watching the news about the massive incursion of Xeno alien species. Tears were running down his cheeks. "Oh, Keila, what have you done?" He said to himself. He had supported Keila's idea to take the appearance of Alicia White, and kill the Terran Council leaders. But Keila had never filled him in on the plan to open portals and let giant man-eating aliens attack Earth. Metatron watched imagery of dismembered corpses, and the images would always haunt his eyes. It wasn't the carnage itself that scared him the most. After all, the Terran Council's synthetic virus attack on Pamshal city on Mars a few years earlier had generated similar images. No, what terrified Metatron was that humanity was no longer on the top of the food chain.

Metatron worried about the future of humanity. When humans killed other humans, Metatron knew that our species would always survive. But with the carnage caused by this alien invasion, who knew what the future would hold?

Metatron tried contacting Keila via the Divine Technology, but there was only static. This didn't mean anything, as Earth and Eden were too far apart to establish a connection with the technology. Yet, to Metatron, it confirmed his fears, that Keila had died among the thousands of fatalities in Rashidium city.

Metatron looked at the calendar. He got up and visited the medical bay, where the frozen two-month embryo of his and Keila's future child was in suspended animation. What would he do, now that Keila was gone?

Metatron knew what he wanted, He had wanted to raise a family with Keila, but her fiery nature had stopped her from settling down. Metatron had loved Keila's passionate nature, although it was also what stopped them from having the future he dreamt of.

Metatron studied the vitals of the embryo, it was in suspended animation, and it hadn't changed since his last examination. According to the DNA scanner, the foetus had excellent A-grade genetics. Martin studied the simulation, based on the foetus DNA, showing how Sabina would look at different ages. She would look a lot like her mother, Keila, and this made Metatron miss her even more!

Metatron elevated himself from his state of self-pity. Keila was gone, but through her daughter, Sabina, she could live on. She had to live on, why else had he already given this small lump of genetic material a name? But Metatron didn't want to cultivate the foetus in a synthetic womb. He didn't want to create a copy of himself, so he needed a surrogate mother. There was a knock on the door and one of Metatron's Edenite employees, Melissa, entered the room.

Melissa gave Metatron a worried look and spoke to him:

- Master Metatron, you haven't eaten for two days? I am concerned about you.

Metatron tried to force a smile, but it failed, and his watery teary eyes exposed him:

- I am okay. But I am not feeling hungry.

Melissa:

- Come on now, Metatron. You have already admitted that you are human and not an angel. All humans need support from time to time. Let me be your pillar of support for once, as you been to me so many times before.

Metatron studied Melissa. She had a rather plain Edenite appearance, but her heart was pure as gold. As Melissa hadn't opted to have her Divine Technology "human" chip removed, he could see her every thought. Could he ask her to do what he wanted? He could command it, but Metatron didn't believe in forcing people unless it was necessary for the common good. It was vital for him to find a surrogate mother to give life to Sabina, but he couldn't justify it with the common good. Metatron decided that he could ask her for a favour and spoke up:

- There is something you could do for me, something far more important than fetching me lunch.

Melissa looked at him with a reassuring smile:

- Metatron, you don't need to be shy around me. Just tell me, and I will be happy to help.

Metatron:

- Thanks, Melissa. I am depressed because of Keila's death.

Melissa:

- Mistress Keila is dead? That's terrible! Are you certain?

Metatron:

- I am as sure as I can be.

- But that is where you come in. I want you to give birth to mine and Keila's daughter.

Melissa:

- But she is dead? How can one woman bear another woman's child?

Metatron:

- I can explain the science to you later. Is it something that would interest you?

Melissa:

- It would honour me to carry the child of you and Keila, who will be the Messiah of our people.

Metatron:

- Thank you, Melissa.

- Stay here in the medical bay, and I'll explain the procedure more in detail before we go through with it.

Having said this, Metatron gave Melissa a scientific explanation of the procedure. Melissa, being an Edenite, didn't understand science, but it didn't matter, and soon she was pregnant with Metatron's and Keila's child.

# Chapter 5: Dissatisfaction in Victory.

Melchior Dorevitch was at the presidential palace of the Olympus Republic. He studied a political map of Mars. Despite winning a total victory, with the remaining enemies begging him for peace, he wasn't happy. In fact, he was deeply unsatisfied.

Melchior's problem was that Keila received all the credit for the Martian victory, while his contribution was not recognised. Thus, the temporary power that Keila granted him before going on her mission to Earth was now contested. There were many other contenders for leadership, both on Mars and in the Olympus Republic. The Olympus Republic was a de jure republic and an election would take place to replace Hellas Petrakis who had fallen in the war.

But Melchior wasn't going to give up his power. He would never live to serve some Martian or worse yet, go back to Eden, governed by that wimp Metatron. Melchior had tasted the intoxicating feeling of absolute power, and he would never give it up. And why would he?

Melchior walked up to a mirror and studied his face. There was a large scar on the right side of his face with his outer ear missing. Melchior's tinnitus kept beeping, and his constant migraine made his days miserable. Melchior's doctors had offered him advanced gene therapy to heal his wounds, but Melchior had rejected the treatment. His injuries made him who he was, and they fuelled his rage and ambition.

Melchior Dorevitch considered himself, the true hero of Mars. The general who had soldiered on despite immense pain, to lead his troops towards the final decisive victory against the Terran Council. Meanwhile, the supposed heroine, Keila Eisenstein, sat out the final battle and then claimed all the glory. Melchior didn't believe that Keila had stopped Bjorn Muller from crashing Phobos onto the Martian surface! It was all lies and deception.

Melchior made up his mind, he wouldn't strive to rule by being popular, he would rule through fear. Melchior's implanted "God" microchip allowed him to terrify his subjects and opponents.

Melchior clenched his fist and watched in joy how he killed his opponents, one by one, using the powers of the Divine Zetan Technology. Having murdered the last contenders for the presidency, he laughed maliciously. After that, he summoned a few courtesans to brutally fulfil his other needs.

# Chapter 6: An Unpleasant Awakening.

Keila woke up after what felt like a lifetime. She was standing up, and despite the pain in her legs, she couldn't fall to the ground. An invisible force field was encapsulating her, preventing her from moving at all, except for her eyes. She gazed around the room, and she saw a reflective surface, where her reflection showed. What she saw shocked her.

Keila's eyes were glowing purple, and the texture of her skin had changed completely. She had wrinkled skin like that of a 100-year-old and thick and grey like the skin of a reptile. Her body was in pain, particularly her legs, which were burning with lactic acid. Keila heard a door open, and things weren't improving as the Xeno-Zetan hybrid Rangda entered the room.

Rangda:

- Hee-Hee-Hee-Hee!! We meet at last. Apologies for the lack of formal introduction on Earth, but I had limited time for such ploys!

Keila:

- Apologise for taking me prisoner instead. I opened the portals on the Cheops Pyramid like you've asked me to! How long have I been here?

Rangda:

- You are not a prisoner yet. I have detained you to ensure you are no danger to yourself or others. Although I must admit, you might have outlived your usefulness!

- As for the time passing since you fell unconscious, not much.

- The change in your physical appearance is a side effect of the ritual, which I used to absorb your psionic powers into the corrupted Zeto Crystal.

- But don't worry; neither the aging nor the ritual will kill you here in the Divine Dimension. Unless I intend for it to happen.

Keila:

- What are you talking about, you hideous and wicked creature?! I helped you. If you are going to kill me, do it now instead of dragging things out!

Rangda:

- No! That is not going to happen. You see, I need you. The ritual that powers up my dark crystals kills Zetans outright. But since you are a Human-Zetan hybrid, I can continually drain your energy without killing you.

Keila:

- So, what do you want?

Rangda:

- Well for starters, I want revenge for my mother through wiping out the Zetans species that betrayed her.

- But ultimately, I want what the Zetans strived for but could never achieve. I want to reach godhood; I want to replace The True Maker as the almighty deity of the universe!

Keila:

- The True Maker?! That's insanity! How would you achieve that?

Rangda:

- You shall see sweet sister, you shall see. But for now, it's time for you to sleep!

After saying this, Rangda blasted Keila with a powerful psionic blast that knocked her unconscious. After that, performed the ritual with the corrupted Zeto Crystals, which radiated with darkness, to drain Keila's body even more. Rangda studied how Keila's body was twisting, and Rangda laughed burst of twisted, diabolical laughter.

# Chapter 7: Melchior Turns His Gaze to Eden.

Melchior Dorevitch was celebrating his overwhelming victory in the Olympus Republic elections. The fact that all the other contenders had died mysterious deaths days before the election didn't bother him. The kill-switch feature in the lower tiers of the Divine Technology microchips wasn't common knowledge. Even if it was, who would be foolish enough to stand up against him in the Olympus Republic?

Melchior studied a political map of Mars. It was very fragmented with hundreds of factions. Although the Olympus Republic was the most powerful nation on Mars, it still only controlled 5% of the Martian surface. The myriad of small countries on Mars had been a strategy by the Terran Council to keep the Martians divided and make them easy to rule. Keila Eisenstein had united the Martians. Equipped with Zetan technology, they had sent their previous Terran masters' running. But with Keila missing, the Martians had turned on each other, and the situation on Mars was worse than ever before.

The Martians needed a strong leader that united them. Melchior was confident that providence meant for him to be this leader. He summoned his brother Dov Dorevitch to discuss his strategy.

Dov arrived at Melchior's office in the Olympus Republic presidential palace. Melchior studied his brother with well-hidden contempt. Dov, despite being younger than Melchior, looked older due to his beer gut, smoking habits, and unhealthy lifestyle. While Melchior disliked his brother's lack of discipline, he needed loyal allies, and no-one was a more dependable ally than his younger brother!

Melchior smiled and spoke to Dov:

- Welcome to Mars and the Olympus Republic, dear brother. I hope your trip from Eden was comfortable.

Dov:

- I can't complain. Since Abraham Goldstein died, I have lost fate in the Edenite society. But I would have preferred to travel in comfort on a civil carrier, rather than on a military ship.

Melchior:

- Well, all public transport has ended due to the war. But rest easy, peace with the Terrans are coming any day now. They have more significant problems to worry about.

Dov:

- Yes. I don't know how Keila did it but releasing those aliens onto the unsuspecting people on Earth was both a stroke of genius and a terrifying act of evil.

Melchior:

- Yes, although she was crazy with her visions, she still pulled everyone together and got things done.

- Now I want to follow in her footsteps!

Dov:

- I have heard you are progressing well. Congratulations on your victory in the "elections."

Melchior:

- I didn't rig the elections!

Dov:

- But it was very convenient that all your competitors died, the day before the elections?

Melchior:

- Yes, it was! Praise Yahweh for intervening and helping me, when the Martians couldn't comprehend that I was the right candidate!

Dov:

- Seems more like a Divine Technology kill-switch to me! How did you pull it off? I thought Keila gave you an Angel chip.

Melchior:

- No, she gave me a God chip, so that I could lead the attack on the Phobos base. She must have forgotten about it because she never mentioned it when she headed to Earth to infiltrate the Terran Council.

- Whatever the reason was, it was a lucky coincidence, and since I don't believe in coincidence. It must have been the divine will!

Dov:

- I see. So why did you summon me? I doubt it was for catching up.

Melchior:

- I need you. Together we can fulfil grandmaster Abraham's visions but on a much grander scale. Together we can rule Mars as its rightful god-kings!

Dov:

- But, didn't you pledge allegiance to Keila after she overthrew and killed Abraham.

Melchior:

- Yes, but one should never let ideology get in the way of opportunity. Now that Keila is gone; opportunity is ours.

- I need to take the Olympus Republic army to Eden to confront Metatron and make him hand over the Zetan technologies to us.

- I need you to stay here and rule in my stead.

Dov:

- It would be an honour to assist you, my brother. I have dreamt about spreading Abraham's religious dogma, to the wretched unbelievers on Mars!

Melchior:

- Good. Connect to that medical unit. It will remove your Human chip and replace it with a God chip.

Dov:

- Are you going to put me to the same level as yourself? There shouldn't be two God chips ruling the same nation.

Melchior:

- How would I expect you to rule in my stead, if you are not equipped with the highest tier of Zetan technology? I need you to be able to kill dissidents with your mind. Now scram, before I change my mind!

Melchior watched Dov as he entered the medical unit. It pleased him that Dov had seen things his way and agreed to help him doing the right thing. Dov would stay loyal, and if he didn't, the fat bastard would suffer so much so he'd regret ever being born. Pleased with the situation, Melchior called his generals and ordered for the fleet to travel to Eden.

# Chapter 8: Metatron Confides in Melissa.

Metatron studied Eden through the windows in the reception area of the Divine Control Centre. He had been busy modernising Eden and housing the influx of refugees that had come because of the widespread war and unrest in the solar system. While Metatron hadn't proclaimed Eden to be a haven, he didn't turn away desperate people that came his way. As a result, the population had swelled from 8000 to over 20,000.

The population increase had caused several problems. Metatron had tried solving these problems by keeping the original Edenites and the new-comers separate. As Eden had a surface area of over 20,000 square kilometres and perfect conditions for agriculture, it was easy to house and feed everyone. Yet the problem remained, Metatron would have to integrate the refugees into the Edenite society.

Metatron leaned back into a comfortable armchair. Oh, how he missed Keila and real sleep! Being raised into Abraham's Angel program, Metatron had never known real sleep for the first 120 years of his life. Metatron had only experienced accelerated sleep or extended sleep being cryogenically frozen. In neither of those sleep states had he experienced dreams. When Keila had killed Abraham and set Metatron free, he had finally experienced dreams.

Now that Keila was gone, Metatron had returned to sleeping in the accelerated sleep pod. This was because of his self-sacrificing nature. Metatron felt guilty sleeping when the Edenites needed him. But now, Metatron was at his breaking point. The lack of dreams had deteriorated his soul, and he felt like he did when he was a slave to Abraham's will. He felt more like a machine than like a human.

Metatron realised that he needed to sleep and dream, to regain his sanity. But the problem was that he had forgotten how to sleep. Metatron felt drained, but his body was still too energised for him to fall asleep. Metatron realised what he needed to do. He felt guilty about it, but he had to do it anyway for his own sanity.

Metatron summoned Melissa, the surrogate mother who was pregnant with his and Keila's unborn child.

Melissa studied Metatron. He didn't look well, and he looked a lot older and more burdened than usual, albeit a lot younger than his real age. Tentatively, she approached him and spoke:

- Master Metatron. You summoned me. Is everything alright with
you?

Metatron tried to smile, but it fell flat and instead, he responded in a sombre tone:

- My state is no longer that important. The main thing is, how
things are with you?

Melissa:

- Don't say that. You are important to all of us. If it weren't for
your tireless efforts, Eden would collapse, and we would all perish.

Metatron:

- That's the core of my problems. That I have been too self-sacrificing and given up what I want.

Melissa:

- So, what do you want?

Metatron:

- I want to have human desires. Human impulses for good and
evil.

- Abraham bred me to serve him, and I did so for over a century. I helped a villainous madman doing evil deeds, because I knew of nothing else. Then Keila set me free, and I started to feel human feelings. But now she is gone, and I am yet again a soulless servant. Trying to make up for my evil deeds by serving the Edenites!

Melissa blushed and then stuttered:

- Is this your way of telling me that you want to have sex with me?

Metatron:

- No. I am after something far more critical. I need to sleep natural sleep so that I can dream again.

- I have never slept natural sleep on my own, so I need you to sleep next to me.

Melissa:

- It would honour me to sleep in your bed, Master Metatron.

Metatron:

- Thank you, Melissa.

- You don't need to call me Master. You and I are friends and equals, helping each other out in times of need.

- Let's go to my bedroom, I am exhausted.

Metatron and Melissa headed to Metatron's bedroom, and in her embrace, he immediately fell asleep. Metatron didn't have the dreams that he wanted, as his dreams tormented him.

In the dream, Metatron saw a beastly alien with glowing purple eyes, tormenting an ancient-looking woman. Despite the tortured woman's hideous appearance, he could sense her soul, and he knew that she was Keila. "Save me! Save humankind!" Keila shouted out with a weak and weary voice. Rangda knocked Keila unconscious with a psionic blast and turned to Metatron. She stared him down with her glowing purple eyes and hypnotised him in a state of paralysed fear. Metatron screamed his lungs out, and he woke up, with the bed soaked in cold sweat.

Melissa looked at him with a worried face and spoke.

- You look terrified! is everything alright?

Metatron:

- Come with me to the medical bay. We need to remove your Divine Technology chip immediately.

Melissa:

- Sure. But why?

Metatron:

- Keila spoke to me in a vision. Darkness is coming, and we'll need to remove all Divine Technology microchips to stay safe!

Melissa:

- If you really think so. There is no time to waste! Let's go.

They hurried to the medical ward to remove Melissa's microchip. After that, they devised a plan for how to remove the chips from the other Edenites.

# Chapter 9: Hilda Muller Prepares to Seize Power.

Hilda Muller was preparing her speech for the first Terran Council meeting since the catastrophe in Rashidium. It had been six chaotic months, but on the bright side, it had strengthened Hilda's position and claim for power.

Before the defeat against the Martians and the terrifying Xeno invasion, The Terran Council was all about commerce. For the Terran Council, the army was support functions to protect trade. As the population felt threatened by the Xenos, they were calling out for more protection. This benefitted Hilda as she had claimed the vacant Supreme Commander title after her father's death. Hilda was not satisfied though. Hilda did not want to be the lackey of some hedonistic plutocrat; she wanted to be the top dog herself. Hilda aimed to be the new chairman of the Terran Council, ruling over Earth.

Hilda had an excellent claim to the position. As the leader of the military forces, she had planned and reorganised the army to successfully counter the new threat. After the initial Xeno attacks, the military had pinpointed the locations of the portals, so they could avoid surprise attacks. The army had also adapted their weaponry to their new enemies. They had replaced all their ballistic guns, with energy-based and melee weapons. Hilda had ordered fleets of space warships in low orbit over every identified portal. Hilda's actions had turned the tide of the war; discouraged by their losses, the Xenos had stopped attacking Earth.

Hilda spotted Markus White in the corridor. Unfortunately, he had not reached a prominent position in House White, but he could be useful for other purposes. Hilda called him over, and he entered her room.

Hilda:

- Oh, Markus how nice it is to see you again!

Markus:

- Hi Hilda! Thanks again for saving my life.

Hilda:

- It was my pleasure. Especially the night that followed saving your life!

Hilda winked at him before continuing:

- So, do I have your support for the Chairman position of the Terran Council?

Markus:

- Yes, I would vote for you. But unfortunately, I am not the one calling the shots, so I can't guarantee you the support from my faction.

Hilda:

- I know Markus. But you can help me with something else!

- I want you to fuck me as good as you did when we came back from Rashidium.

Markus:

- Are you crazy? We are on the level where the meeting is taking place. What if someone comes early and sees us?

Hilda:

- Then let them. I will be their boss, and I am going to show them
that I am not intimidated by what they think. Quite the contrary!

Having said this, Hilda released some pheromones, which made Markus
irresistibly horny. Shortly afterwards he fucked her roughly from behind.
When they had finished, Hilda wiped herself and smiled at the exhausted
Markus. She spoke to him as she left:

- You stay here and relax, lover boy, while I take control of the
Council.

Satisfied and confident, Hilda walked to the meeting room. It was a great
relief to have sex with a human again; she had played with droids for the last
few months. Not that Hilda was unattractive but being powerful didn't have
the same sex appeal for a woman as it had for a man. While a man in power
could use his influence to have sex with anyone he wanted, society expected a woman in command to keep monogamous. But Hilda didn't want to be
monogamous. She wanted to be independent and follow her desires, including the sexual ones. Hilda promised herself that once she seized control, she
would do what she wanted, regardless of what her male peers thought about
it!

The leaders for the other factions entered the boardroom, as did Hilda's
cousin, Michael Muller. Hilda studied Michael. Michael had shocked the rest
of House Muller when he chose to step down to Hilda without a fight, but
she had anticipated it. Michael was a man who enjoyed wealth but hated
power and encumbering responsibilities. Michael didn't even want to be on
the board, but Hilda had convinced him to stay and follow her lead. Michael
was perfect where he was, as he gave Hilda credibility while not arguing with
her.

The other factions represented were House White, House Cheng, House
Bolivar, and House Goldstein. House Goldstein was among the five most
-powerful factions again due to the downfall of House Rashid.

Watching the group of foreign dignitaries, Hilda took a deep breath and
prepared to speak.

# Chapter 10: Hilda Muller Becomes the Leader of the Terran Council.

Hilda Muller was looking at the gathered dignitaries in the meeting room of Europeum Tower. As always, the top-level meeting had two representatives from each faction. Hilda didn't recognise many of them, as they were all new due to the massacre at the Rashidium summit. This suited Hilda well, as it would be difficult for her to claim power if all the old faction leaders were still around. As it was now, Hilda had the best claim to authority with a proven success in repelling the Xeno invasion.

Hilda Muller began to talk:

- Dear delegates. Welcome to the Terran Council meeting for March 2875. We have many things to discuss, but we start off with a formality. You are to verify my position as chairwoman for the Terran Council as well as Supreme Commander for the Terran Council Security Forces.

The delegates sat dumbfounded and didn't know how to react. They had anticipated more pleasantries and formalities before discussing this sensitive topic. Eventually, Ping Chen spoke up:

- Miss Muller. My apologies, but you have misunderstood how the Council works. The Council strives to mediate between the leading factions. You haven't made a case for your claim yet.

Hilda smirked sarcastically towards Ping Chen before she replied.

- I don't think you know who I am. I was at Rashidium when the Xenos first struck. I was one of the few survivors, and do you know why?

- Because I struck back. I killed several of those beasts on my own before I evacuated the city.

- I have saved us by repelling the Xenos and securing the perimeters to the portals.

- THAT is worth more than whatever financial achievements the rest of you claim to have.

James Goldstein joined the conversation:

- While the situation is dire, it's good to have my faction back on the Council. I recommend that we DO NOT choose another House Muller candidate, as Joachim Muller's leadership led to disastrous results. Joachim caused the loss against the Martians, and the unpreparedness for the alien invasion.

Hilda Muller:

- Silence, you fool! The Goldstein's have been infighting for decades, and under your "leadership" we would have fallen to the Xeno invaders.

- The people need and want a strong leader that can keep them safe. I am at that leader. The last thing they need, is another money counter.

James Goldstein:

- Since when do you dictate what the people need?

Hilda Muller:

- I don't, but you must know what is going on with the common man. Who do they turn to? It is not the banks!

- I'd win if it were the popular vote.

Ping Chen:

- That might be, Hilda, but the popular vote means little as this is not a democracy!

Hilda Muller:

- Six months after the defeat on Mars, and you still discount the popular will. Where would you run if the people turn against you?

Enrique Bolivar had heard enough of the quarrel. His territories had been severely affected by the Xeno invasions from the Central American portal. Enrique knew why his people were still around, and it wasn't the size of his vault that had saved him.

Enrique Bolivar:

- Dear delegates, I have heard enough. I lost my father Santiago in Rashidium, and most of us lost loved ones in that attack.

- What we need right now is security. We cannot achieve that by focusing on commerce. That is why I cast the votes of House Bolivar on the one who saved us, Hilda Muller.

Jordan White joined in:

- I also cast my votes on Hilda. My cousin Markus told me about her incredible feats of bravery when she saved him from the savage alien attack. This is what we need in these challenging times.

James Goldstein:

- From what I have heard, "saving" him wasn't the only thing she did to him.

Hilda Muller:

- Whatever you are implying is irrelevant. I got the majority vote now.

James Goldstein:

- So, it would seem. Such a sad day, when a promiscuous woman becomes the leader!

Hilda Muller:

- It's not the Bronze Age anymore. Let your buddy Abraham know that if you see him!

- Anyways. Thank you, Enrique, and Jordan for voting for me. Now let me tell you how I plan to take the fight to our enemies.

After this, Hilda gave a detailed account for how she planned to fight the Xenos and what contributions she required for the war.

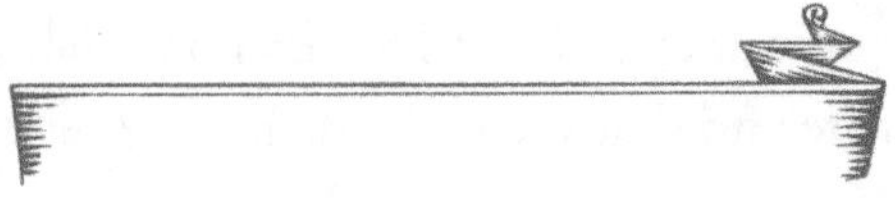

# Chapter 11: Sabina is Born.

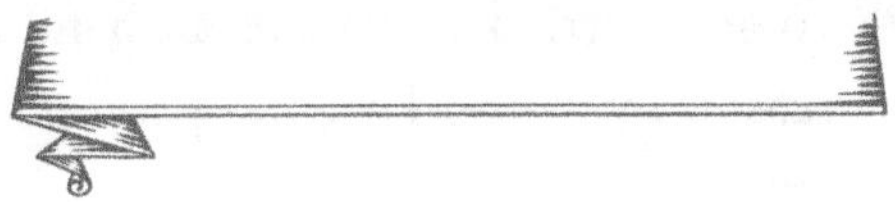

In July 2875, Melissa gave birth to Sabina, Metatron's and Keila's daughter. Sabina was a healthy child despite the procedures on her embryo. When Metatron studied the lively gaze in her light green eyes, he felt her soul. Metatron was happy that a surrogate mother gave birth to Sabina, instead of using a synthetic womb.

Metatron visited Melissa as she was recovering from childbirth.

Melissa:

- She is beautiful, isn't she? The daughter of you and Keila.

Metatron:

- Sabina is our daughter, Melissa. I want her to feel that way when she is growing up.

Melissa:

- But she can't be? We haven't had intercourse.

Metatron:

- That is true. But I don't want her to find out the truth. That her mother died while releasing man-eating monsters devastating Earth. Also, because of Keila, Melchior Dorevitch is terrorising Mars with his army of mind-controlled soldiers.

Melissa:

- So, what do you want us to do? To pretend to Sabina that we are husband and wife and that she is our daughter?

Metatron:

- No, I want us to get married, so we are husband and wife. For all the essential reasons, you and I are her parents. That is if you would like to marry me?

Melissa:

- I would love to marry you, grandmaster Metatron.

Metatron:

- I am happy to hear that, Melissa. I will make an announcement to make it official, and then we will invite all the Edenites to the ceremony!

- I got to go back to work. I'll come by a bit later.

After leaving the room, Metatron retreated to his private bedroom, locked the doors, and cried. He had decided to finally give up on Keila and move on with his life. Metatron had to move on, he had a child to look after, and he could not raise a child obsessing over the child's dead biological mother.

A lie and a new beginning were the best solution for everyone. In due time, Metatron was confident that he and Melissa could form a happy family. Melissa was a perfect woman: loyal, obedient, loving and hard-working. But she lacked the beauty, the passion, and the drive that made Keila extraordinary.

Metatron decided that he wouldn't tell Sabina the truth about her mother. It was better for everyone if Sabina grew up to be a good Edenite woman. In this way, Metatron was old-fashioned. While he hadn't approved of Abraham's tyrannical ways, he had agreed to the basic premise. Metatron believed that people needed to be part of a society with well-defined roles and rules.

In such a community, everyone carried out their allocated lot in life to improve society.

# Chapter 12: A Marriage and a Baptism.

A few weeks later, it was time for the wedding of Metatron and Melissa and the baptism of Sabina. The ceremony took place on Mount Sinai, the holy mountain for the Edenites in the centre of Eden. Metatron's former rival, the angel Samael, led both the marriage ceremony and the baptism.
Samael:

- Metatron, do you swear, on your honour as a servant of the great
  Yahweh, to take Melissa as your wife and be fruitful.

Metatron paused. He had hoped that Samael wouldn't mention Yahweh during the wedding. Yahweh had been dead for millennia, and Metatron didn't want to proclaim himself the servant of Yahweh. Yet, Metatron was a supporter of Yahweh's ideology, so in that sense, Samael honoured him with his words. Metatron found an answer that suited him better.

- As a great supporter of Yahweh's values, I promise to honour my
  marriage commitment to Melissa. I promise to love Melissa, and
  if it's my destiny to be fruitful with her.

Samael gave Metatron a sceptical look. Officially, Metatron had already been fruitful with Melissa, so why did he say those last words? Samael decided to go on as if nothing had happened.

- Yes, you have already been fruitful with Melissa, and we pray that
  Yahweh will give you more blessings to come!

- Melissa, do you promise to honour and obey Metatron until the
  benevolent Yahweh ends your days?

Melissa:

- I do.

Samael:

- Good. Then I proclaim you husband and wife.

Samael took out two beautiful rings with expensive gemstones and put them on Metatron's and Melissa's fingers. The gathered people were cheering. After a while, Samael lifted his hand, instructing them to stop. He then commenced his speech.

- Today is a blessed day for two reasons, as we also welcome a new member to our Edenite family. I present to you Sabina, daughter of Metatron and Melissa, blessed by the great Yahweh himself. May this holy water protect you and forever keep you safe. Let the celebrations begin!

Having said this, Samael splashed some water on Sabina, the band started playing, and the crowd danced for hours.

# Chapter 13: Hilda Muller Interrogates a Xeno Prisoner.

Hilda Muller and Markus White were back in the ruins of Rashidium. They observed the bluish light of the inter-dimensional portal over the gilded Cheops Pyramid. Returning to Rashidium was terrifying. What had once been one of the glowing jewel cities of the Terran Council was now a destroyed wasteland. The smell of death and decay still lay thick over the city.

Hilda walked along the abandoned streets of Rashidium when a foul stench overwhelmed her. Hilda heard a faint growl. She turned to her body-guard, Captain Emma Schindler, and spoke:

> - You said that the army has secured the city. So, why can I smell the stench of the Xenos and hear that faint growl from the building over there?

Emma Schindler:

> - I am sorry Mistress Hilda; I will lead you back to safety at once!

Hilda Muller:

> - No need, Captain Schindler. I am not an armchair general. I want to investigate this sound myself.

Emma Schindler:

> - But that's dangerous. We cannot put your life at risk.

Hilda Muller:

- Don't worry about me. The troops that fought and died here didn't back down, and neither shall I. I won't allow myself cowardice.

Markus White stared at Hilda in disbelief and spoke:

- Hilda, come on, don't be stupid. You're not any high-ranking official. You are the leader of the Terran Council, the single most powerful woman on the planet. Let your soldiers do their jobs.

Hilda shrugged off Markus' objection. She was a soldier at heart, and she had killed several of these beasts when Rashidium was overrun. Besides, if she could capture a Xeno warrior, that would be an excellent opportunity to study and communicate with the creatures.

Hilda Muller:

- Markus, you stay here with a few guards. Emma and the rest of you, come with me. I want to interrogate the wounded Xeno warrior. Soldiers, arm your shields and plasma swords. We are entering that building!

They entered the building, and searched it until they reached the source of the stench and the sound. They found a severely injured Xeno warrior lying in a pool of his own blood, missing both legs and arms. But it had been weeks since the last battle. How could the beast be alive with the injuries it had sustained? Hilda decided that she had to find a way to communicate with the incapacitated enemy.

Hilda spoke to the Xeno:

- Who are you? Why do you come to Earth and fight us? What do you want?

The Xeno warrior:

- Sharaz rambu Ramun. Growl, rubut Rangda. Raman rantiz gudu dugu, gandin dinetion.

After saying this, the Xeno warrior started drooling and shaking. Emma Schindler raised her plasma sword to kill the beast, but Hilda told her off:

- What are you doing Emma? This is our first chance to communicate with our enemy and learn about them. You wouldn't waste that opportunity, would you?

Emma Schindler:

- There is nothing to learn from these beasts. They are bloodthirsty mindless monsters, and we already found the a to repel them. Lasers, orbital bombardment and land mines!

Hilda Muller:

- Lucky that I arrived here today! This beast understood what I said. At least it realised that I was communicating to it, and it tried to respond.

- We have quantum computers capable of decrypting any code. Deciphering the Xeno language should be a piece of cake.

Emma Schindler:

- You are right, Chairwoman Muller. I will connect us to the quantum computer at once.

A few minutes later, the quantum computer had analysed the Xeno language. The computer had deciphered what the Xeno warrior said, and created a potential vocabulary for the Xeno language. Hilda uploaded the Xeno vocabulary to the universal translator chip in her brain. When the upload had finished, Hilda spoke to the Xeno warrior in the Xeno language:

- So, Ramun the Xeno Warrior. You can stop following Rangda now because she is not around. Instead speak to me, Hilda Muller of Earth, and tell me what you know and what you want.

Hearing a human speak her language baffled Ramun. Eventually, she replied:

- How can you speak my language human? What kind of sorcery is this?!

Hilda Muller:

- It is not sorcery, it is technology. Travelling through dimensional portals, you should be aware of advanced technology.

Ramun:

- We don't use technology. We rely on the sorcery and the great powers that our God-Queen Rangda grants us.

Hilda Muller:

- You, Xenos, have advanced technology. We scavenged your fallen brethren of the technology you use. Ground-breaking stuff. But once we realised how your technology works, we found a way to counteract it. Something you never seemed to comprehend!

Ramun:

- Yes, my brethren told me that we have had problems with the guile of humans before. You helped the Zetans defeat us in the multi-millennial interstellar war.

Hilda Muller:

- What are you talking about? There is no mention of a multi-millennial interstellar war in human history.

Ramun:

- Humanity followed the vile Zetans like they were your gods. Refusing the one true goddess Rangda in her holy quest to free the galaxy of Zetans' falsehood and deceit!

- Check your religious scriptures, and you'll find plenty of references to the war. Your scriptures would describe it as the heavenly fight between "good" and "evil."

Hilda Muller:

- Interesting, but not very relevant. Tell me about your "god-queen" Rangda. Who is she, and how do I kill her?

Ramun:

- You already know who she is. You saw her during our first attack when we extracted our prisoner Keila. You fought me back then, you defeated me, and that's why I am talking to you.

Hilda Muller:

- I haven't seen enough of you to recognise individual Xenos. Did I do this to you?

Ramun:

- Yes, and now you must finish the job: Kill me and eat me, as is our custom!

Hilda Muller:

- Sure. If you tell me how you survived for six months with these severe wounds?

Ramun:

- I crawled and wriggled using my torso to get here. We, Xenos, are very resilient and recover from almost any wound. But we can't re-grow dismembered limbs.

Hilda Muller:

- But that's six months ago. How can you still be alive if I dismembered you back then?

Ramun:

- Our home planet Xenora is incredibly harsh, and only the fiercest beast can survive there. Besides, "six months" as you call it is only two days on our home planet.

Hilda Muller:

- That's enough for now. You are my prisoner. We will feed you and further interrogate you.

Ramun:

- But you promised to kill me if I spoke!

Hilda Muller:

- I will kill you. But not now. That's not how humans treat valuable prisoners. And that is why we are going to come after your queen Rangda for what she did to us!

Ramun growled and roared, but it didn't matter. Hilda had her prisoner, and she wouldn't let a go of this opportunity to understand her enemy better!

# Chapter 14: Melchior Forces Metatron to Give up the Zetan Technologies.

Metatron was feeding Sabina with a feeder bottle. Melissa was ill, and he didn't want to expose his daughter to virus-ridden breastmilk. Besides, he loved spending time alone with Sabina, his and Keila's biological daughter. Although Metatron had learned to love Melissa, he did not feel the same way that he had felt for Keila.

When Metatron looked into Sabina's lively green eyes, he saw the Keila he had fallen in love with before Rangda had possessed her. Metatron sighed and felt a bittersweet feeling. On the one hand, he missed Keila, and his daughter reminded him of her. On the other hand, Sabina gave Metatron a sense of purpose that he had never felt before in his very long life.

Samael rushed into the room. Metatron gave him a stern look and spoke.

- Samael, haven't I told you to not disturb me when I am spending time with my daughter.

Samael:

- I know Metatron, but this is important, and it can't wait. The traitor Melchior is here, with a large fleet requesting an audience.

Metatron:

- Melchior? Isn't that psychopath busy tormenting the poor Martians? What does he want from us?

Samael:

- Well, he is from Eden, and some of his family still lives here. I assume he wants to add Eden to his growing domains.

Metatron:

- I won't allow that to happen. I have sworn to lead and protect the Edenites from danger.

Samael:

- How do you intend to scare off a large hostile fleet?

Metatron:

- Samael, do you trust me?

Samael:

- Yes. Why do you ask?

Metatron:

- Because you must follow my lead, regardless of how outrageous it might seem.

- Let's go meet our prominent visitor.

Metatron authorised Melchior's command ship to dock with B528B. Metatron studied Melchior as he disembarked the ship. Melchior seemed to have aged many years, although it was just a year since they last met. And what was the thing with Melchior's eyes? Was he wearing tinted lenses? Metatron decided to find out. He shouted to Melchior:

- Hey Melchior, you got something in your eyes.

Instinctively Melchior rubbed his right eye before he replied.

- No, I haven't, what are you talking about?

Metatron had seen enough. He knew what he was dealing with. During Melchior's eye-rubbing, the tinted lens had moved out of position, revealing Melchior's real eye colour, purple. Two years earlier, When Rangda had possessed Keila, Keila's eye colour had changed to purple, and that had ended in disaster. Now Melchior was under Rangda's evil influence. Metatron decided to tackle the question headfirst:

Metatron:

- How is your old friend, Rangda?

Melchior:

- I don't know what you are talking about!

Metatron:

- Rangda has possessed you. That's why you have turned from an altruistic freedom fighter to a power-hungry tyrant. That's why you wear tinted lenses to hide your real eye colour, glowing purple!

Melchior:

- That is preposterous! Do you think anyone would believe this?

Metatron:

- I have proof. A high-velocity camera took this photo of your iris when you were rubbing your eyes.

Metatron streamed the photo of Melchior's iris onto the large displays in the spaceport of B528B.

Melchior responded nonchalantly:

- Those manipulated photos won't convince anyone. Besides, I am disappointed in your lack of hospitality.

- As an Edenite and soon to be emperor of Mars, I would have anticipated a more courteous reception.

Metatron:

- Don't call yourself emperor yet, there is plenty of opposition to your tyranny, and besides, you never won the presidential election.

Melchior:

- Oh, but I won the presidency fair and square.

Metatron:

- That was because all your opponents died the day before the election.

Melchior:

- What better way to prove that God is on my side? God wants me to rule Mars!

Metatron:

- It only proves you are a murderer and a fraud!

Melchior:

- Look who is talking, the man who helped Abraham to deceive us Edenites for 60 years!

- When I become emperor over Mars, I will rule it with Abraham's rules. But I will use doctrines suitable to the conditions of the 29th century.

- But let's talk about why I am here.

- I am here to take control of Eden and the Divine Control Centre. Being a generous man, I am offering you and the other angels amnesty if you surrender immediately.

Metatron:

- As the leader of Eden, I cannot grant you that request. Instead, I have a counter-offer. Leave us alone, or I will deactivate Eden's atmosphere. This will suffocate everyone, including your parents, your siblings, your nephews and your nieces.

Melchior:

- Impressive! I didn't think you had it in you. Then again, I could have my men shoot you!

Metatron:

- Killing or incapacitating me will trigger the release of cyanide gas into Eden's atmosphere, killing everyone on the surface.

Melchior:

- Okay, so be it. You can keep your Bronze-age colony for all I care.

- But I must have what I came for. I need the Zetan technologies and The Divine Detector machine. Give me those and I'll leave you alone. Refuse, and I don't mind if you kill everyone, including my own family!

- To prove myself, I'll show you what I am capable of.

Melchior streamed a video hologram into the room and continued speaking.

- Do you recognise this woman?

Metatron:

- Yes. It's your mother.

Melchior entered a command on the device on his arm. The video showed how a laser from Melchior's command ship incinerated Melchior's mother.

Metatron:

- Nice try, but I am not falling for that bluff.

Melchior:

- Oh, am I bluffing? Ask the AI for confirmation.

Metatron:

- AI. Did Melchior kill his mother using a laser cannon?

AI:

- I cannot deduce who fired the laser, but a laser did kill Mrs Dorevitch 20 seconds ago.

Melchior:

- Happy now? That's how dedicated I am. Hand over your Zetan technologies or no-one is getting out of here alive!

Fear overwhelmed Metatron and didn't know what to do. He knew that he had the moral duty to stop Melchior by not handing over the technologies. But he was also responsible for the lives of the Edenites. The most important aspect for Metatron was to save the lives of Melissa and Sabina. Metatron felt trapped between duty and love. Love was a dual-edged sword that stopped him from doing the right thing.

Metatron decided to give in to Melchior's demands. Regardless of what he did, Melchior would find a way to steal the Zetan technologies, so it was pointless to resist. Avoiding bloodshed was the best solution, as he had no other options.

Metatron:

- Okay, Melchior, you have proven your point. We will assemble all the Zetan technologies and deliver them on a portable drive tomorrow.

Melchior:

- Wise move! And don't even think about double-crossing me, or I'll expose you to a fate worse than death!

Having said this, Melchior returned to his command ship and undocked from B528B.

# Chapter 15: Melissa's plan to protect Eden from Melchior.

Later the same day, Metatron was seeking advice from Melissa. Melissa sensed Metatron's fears, even though he tried to project a calm exterior. Melissa:

- What worries you, Metatron? Was Melchior threatening you during his visit?

Metatron:

- Melchior came for the Zetan technologies. I don't know if I should give them to him or not. I know that Melchior will cause a lot of damage if he gets hold of the technologies. But if I don't hand over the technologies, he will take them by force, and the people that I care about will suffer.

Melissa:

- I see. But you're not the only one who struggles. Melchior's parents and sisters still live on Eden. Surely, he wouldn't attack risking their lives?

Metatron didn't answer. Instead, he played the video from his meeting with Melchior. Melissa studied the video in shock and spoke:

- What happened to Melchior? He used to be a devout follower of Abraham's teaching, and he loved his family. How could he kill his own mother in cold blood to prove a point?

Metatron:

- Rangda has possessed Melchior. Rangda possessed Keila and caused her to open the portals on Earth, unleashing the Xenos.

Melissa:

- What makes you think that Rangda possesses Melchior?

Metatron:

- Because Melchior wore tinted lenses to hide his real eye colour. I caught a glimpse of his actual eye colour when he rubbed his eyes. Melchior's eyes are glowing purple, the same colour Keila had when her possession started to embellish her.

- I wish I had realised the danger back then.

Melissa pondered what Metatron had said. A plan popped up in her head. Melissa battled with her self-doubts on whether to tell Metatron or not, but eventually, she spoke:

- What about if we imbue the Zetan technology with a Trojan horse?

Metatron:

- A Trojan horse?

Melissa:

- Yes. We pretend to give in to Melchior's demands by giving him what the desires. But unbeknownst to him, we hide a computer virus amongst the technologies. We can activate this virus in the time of need.

Metatron:

- Good thinking, but it would never work. The Artificial Intelligence in Melchior's mainframe would identify the virus, and we'd be in trouble.

Melissa:

- Wouldn't Zetan programming code be foreign software to human-made supercomputers? Zetan code is another programming language. Thus, the AI would consider it as a virus?

Metatron studied Melissa's face, and he realised how blind he had been to her real character. He had believed that she was a dumb peasant and a tool to give birth to his child. At this moment he realised her true potential. Although Melissa lacked education, as she grew up under Abraham's archaic rule, she had still had more wits than most people.

Metatron:

- You are correct, Melissa! If we add extra virus code, Melchior's supercomputers won't be able to tell the difference. Let's infuse a Trojan virus into the blueprints that we will give Melchior tomorrow. This way, we can make sure that he never threatens Eden again.

- Come with me to the Divine Dimension. There is plenty of work for us to do, and time is of the essence!

After saying this, Metatron and Melissa transported their minds to The Divine Dimension. Once they were there, they programmed an invasive Trojan virus and embedded it into the Zetan blueprints. Once they had finished, Metatron prayed to the True Maker that this would be enough to save Eden from Melchior's tyranny.

# Chapter 16: Melchior's Dark Dreams.

A few days later, Melchior was studying the Zetan technologies on his Command Ship, ISS Red Storm. Melchior was happy that he had acquired the advanced Zetan technological artefacts. The artefacts would give him almost unlimited power and would make sure that no one on Mars could stand against him. But Melchior felt annoyed that he couldn't use the technologies until he landed on Mars. Melchior didn't dare to transmit the Zetan technologies to Dov, fearing that the Terran Council would intercept the signal. The last thing Melchior wanted, was for his enemies to access these new advanced technologies.

Melchior opened another Zetan blueprint. The AI tried to block him from viewing the diagram, claiming that the files were a virus. Metatron had briefed Melchior about this when he handed over the records. The AI saw all Zetan codes as viruses by default, as the Zetans had used a different type of coding than human-made computers. Melchior chose to override the AI and opened the enticing top-secret code. He felt uneasy every time he did this. While his experts had advised him that he had nothing to fear, Melchior suspected that Metatron had found a way to outsmart him. This idea lingered like a splinter in his mind, yet he chose to ignore it.

Melchior lost interest in the Zetan blueprints and turned off the supercomputer. He walked to his bathroom and removed his tinted lenses. Melchior stared into the mirror studying his glowing purple predator eyes. He felt powerful studying his terrifying eyes. Melchior's transformation had triggered his hunger for flesh and bloodlust. Melchior desired to eat humans alive, while their hearts were still pumping blood, fresh and loaded with delicious zinc and iron. He desired to stare into his victims' eyes, paralysing them with fear, as they took their last breaths.

But Melchior couldn't fulfil his desires yet. Although Melchior wanted to eat one of his soldiers, he controlled himself. At the moment, Melchior was not powerful enough to kill and eat his own soldiers, without facing serious repercussions.

Failing to satisfy his bloodlust, Melchior felt exhausted. He went to sleep knowing that another night of vivid, violent dreams awaited him.

In the dream, Melchior was on an alien planet, which was very hot and filled with strange plants and animals.

Melchior's vision changed. It became narrow and blood-stained. Melchior could feel how his blood pressure and heart rate increased, along with feelings of excitement and pleasure. He had found his target. A human female was running away from him. Melchior leapt onto the target and sank his vicious fangs into her, drinking her blood. Melchior met her terrified gaze, and he recognised her. It was his mother. In his dream, Melchior felt a terrible sense of guilt. He had wasted his mother's life when he killed her with a laser cannon. The proper way to kill her, would have been as his pray, as her blood was thick, delicious, and satisfying!

# Chapter 17: Rangda Influences Melchior.

Rangda studied the sleeping Keila. She was a costly prisoner to keep, and she hadn't been as useful as Rangda had hoped. When Rangda captured Keila, she had expected to find a way to drain Keila's psionic powers, to power up Rangda's corrupted Zeto Crystals. This hadn't worked. Rangda had tried to energise Keila's psionic powers, and had sent her troops to raid Earth looking for suitable food for Keila. While Keila had gorged on the food, she hadn't cooperated and charged the corrupted Zeto Crystals with her powers. Rangda realised that Keila was too strong-willed, for Rangda to dominate her.

But, Keila had proven to useful for another purpose: to influence Melchior.

As Melchior lacked Zetan DNA sequences, Rangda couldn't influence him via Zetan telepathy. But using Keila as a transmitter, Rangda had found out that she could manipulate Melchior's dreams and desires. Through dominating Keila, Rangda could use Keila's powers to influence Melchior. Rangda studied Melchior. His eyes had turned. Melchior had glowing purple predator eyes, but he feared revealing his true self. This was good. Melchior's fear of exposing his dark feelings would make them grow stronger, and he would succumb to them.

Rangda induced Melchior with another dream. In this dream, he was eating his young niece Elsa, daughter of his brother Dov Dorevitch. Rangda was confident that this dream would push Melchior to insanity. Once his dark desires immersed hem, Melchior would become her slave!

# Chapter 18: A Military Expedition to the Divine Dimension.

Hilda Muller studied the GDP for House Muller territory, as well as the Gross Planetary Product (GPP) for planet Earth. It was a terrifying read. Since the Xeno invasion, The GDP of House Muller was down 70 per cent, and the GPP for Earth was down 80 per cent. It was an unprecedented economic collapse and Hilda had to act to avoid a revolution on Earth.

Hilda led a police state with minimal personal and political freedom. The citizens had remained content, as the Terran Council had ensured that every Terran citizen lived a life in abundance. This was possible due to the asteroid mining stations and the plundering of other planets. Living in abundance, but with minimal freedoms, most people avoided any form of dissent. The average Terran citizen had much to lose and very little to gain from political dissent.

When people were destitute and desperate, things were different. There had been constant warfare and uprisings on Mars throughout the centuries. Hilda knew that the reason was poverty. Even though the Terran Council propaganda claimed it was because the Martians were uncouth and prone to violence.

Hilda needed to improve the economy, but to do so, she needed to deal with the elephant in the room. She needed to defeat the Xenos and find a way to close the inter-dimensional portals.

Hilda had gathered a lot of intelligence from her Xeno prisoner, Ramun. Ramun claimed that the Xenos in their natural state were fearsome but honest and noble. 13,000 years ago, the Xenos had fallen under the dark influence of Rangda, their Xeno-Zetan hybrid queen.

At first, Ramun was furious that Hilda wouldn't grant him death. But he had come around when Hilda had ordered her scientists to use stem cell technology to regrow Ramun's limbs. Now Ramun was Hilda's personal pet living in a secure enclosure at Hansstadt zoo. The zookeepers fed Ramun a variety of live animals, to keep him fed and happy, to ensure his cooperation.

Because of Ramun, Hilda had access to pure Xeno DNA for research. It was time to fight back! Hilda had equipped an expeditionary force with weapons adapted to fight the Xenos. House Muller had also developed viruses meant to be efficient against Xenos.

Hilda met with Emma Schindler, who she had promoted to General. Emma would lead the expeditionary forces on the dangerous expedition.

Hilda Muller:

- Emma, you have specific orders. I want you to lead an expeditionary force through the portal, deep into Xeno territory and kill Rangda. House Muller will equip you with hovercrafts, laser cannons, and battle armours, capable of withstanding a Xeno claw attack. Your troops will fight with plasma swords and diamond shields, as ballistic guns have proven to be ineffective.

Emma Schindler:

- Understood. Do you know where we will find Rangda?

Hilda Muller:

- Our prisoner couldn't answer that question as the Xenos are always on the move. Since the Divine Dimension is an endless, featureless plain, finding them will be difficult. But my scientists have developed a solution. We will equip you with a sensor that can detect infrared radiation from 100,000 kilometres away. Hopefully, this will be enough to find the Xenos.

Emma Schindler:

- And what about the Zetans?

Hilda Muller:

- The Zetans haven't attacked Earth and are not a priority. Try to stay out of their way. If necessary, state your business and tell them to back off. Don't let them enslave you!

Emma Schindler:

- Understood. How do we know that your Xeno prisoner is telling the truth?

Hilda Muller:

- We don't. But we must do something. The portals drain Earth's rotation speed. The length of a day has increased from 24 to 25 hours already. If this continues, we will get endless hot days and long freezing nights. The climate of our planet will collapse, and we will be unable to grow food.

Emma Schindler:

- Understood. Is there anything else that I need to keep in mind?

Hilda Muller:

- Yes. Be prepared for anything, we do not know what is on the other side of that portal. The prisoner says that Divine Dimension is safe, but we can't know for sure.

- The lives of 400 soldiers are on your hands, not to mention the future of humankind.

- You will not be able to communicate with me from the Divine Dimension. Use your best judgement!

- Good luck! I'll see you when you get back!

After saying this, Hilda Muller entered a private aircraft that took her back to Hansstadt.

# Chapter 19: A Lethal Confrontation Between the Terrans and the Zetans.

The Terran expeditionary force, led by Emma Schindler and Wilhelm Brandt, entered the Divine Dimension. Emma's troops needed to examine whether it was possible to move quickly and kill Rangda to end Xeno threat. Hilda Muller had refused to send a significant force as they had no reliable information on what was on the other side of the portal. Hilda thought it was foolish to send in the main army without knowing where the portal would take them.

Emma Schindler were awestruck by the beauty and the tranquillity she faced in the Divine Dimension. Emma checked the sensors. The sensors indicated that the air was safe to breathe. Emma look at her wristwatch; it seemed frozen in time.

Emma Schindler activated the mobile sensor trying to find the Xeno horde. Even though the sensor had a 100,000-kilometre range, the sensor couldn't detect any Xenos. The only things that showed up on the sensor were a group of 20 creatures that Emma assumed to be the Zetans. The Zetans were not far away. Emma turned to Wilhelm to discuss their options.

- None of the Xenos are within range for our sensors, what do you suggest that we do?

Wilhelm Brandt:

- Well, Hilda told us that this is an endless plain. We can't search blindly, or we'll end up out of fuel and supplies in the middle of nowhere.

Emma Schindler:

- Yes, but the only species that are nearby are the Zetans. Our orders are to stay clear of them if possible, as we don't know their disposition to us humans. The last thing that we want is to create more enemies.

Wilhelm Brandt:

- So, what do you want to do? Run back Earth and admit failure, days after our promotion?

- According to our Xeno captive, the Zetans and the Xenos are mortal enemies. I am confident that the Zetans will help us.

Emma Schindler:

- What if the Zetans are hostile?

Wilhelm Brandt:

- Why would they be? There are 400 of us and only 20 of them. I doubt they survived this long being reckless!

Emma Schindler:

- You're right. Let's establish contact with the Zetans and see if they can assist us!

After this, Emma and her troops advanced towards the Zetans in their hovercrafts. Half an hour later, they approached the Zetan Vanguard, led by Thor. Emma Schindler approached the Zetans and spoke into a universal translator. The universal translator translated the message to an array of ancient languages. This was because Ramun had told Hilda that the Zetans had posed as human deities during ancient times:

- I am Emma Schindler, in charge of this Terran Council expeditionary force. We are here to attack the Xenos and their queen Rangda, in retaliation for their attack on Earth.

The universal translator conveyed the same message in a variety of ancient languages. Thor replied:

- No need for a universal translator, feeble human. We have studied you for millennia, and we can articulate your current language.

- We appreciate that you are coming with weapons and vehicles as offerings to us. Leave them here and walk back to the portal, so no-one needs to die.

Wilhelm Brandt intervened:

- We are not here to surrender our weapons and hovercrafts to you. We are here to kill Rangda and the Xenos. Their attacks have caused massive damage to Earth. If you know where the Xenos are, you'll tell us now, and no-one will get hurt!

Thor roared:

- I will not tolerate a lowly human threatening me. Take this!

After shouting this, Thor threw his magical hammer and hit Wilhelm Brandt. The impact sent Wilhelm flying hundreds of meters backwards! Emma ducked for cover, and a barrage of laser beams and bullets rained down on the Zetans. This was to no avail. The Ballistic Energy Absorbers stopped the shots and the Prismatic Reflectors redirected the laser beams to hit the hovercrafts and destroyed most of them.

The Terran fighters didn't give up. Equipped with plasma swords and diamond shields, they charged at the Zetans. A fierce battle ensued where Emma's tenacious troops swarmed the superior Zetans. The humans snatched the victory, after Emma snuck up on Thor and decapitated him with a blow from her plasma sword. Seeing their leader killed, the remaining Zetans ran away from the battlefield. Some of the human soldiers wanted to pursue them, but Emma ordered them to stay back.

After the battle, Emma overlooked the battlefield. It was a disaster. The Zetans had destroyed most of her hovercrafts, and half of her soldiers were dead or injured. Worse yet, Emma had drawn humanity into conflict with another species.

Walking around among the dead, Emma found an injured Zetan, Anumati, and they began to speak.

Anumati:

- Why did you attack us? The Xenos will come soon. You have doomed us all.

Emma:

- We didn't attack, we only responded to the attack from your leader.

Anumati:

- Yes, Thor was overzealous. He still believed himself to be a God to your species. He couldn't accept that times have changed, and we are closer to equals now.

- But we must move. This place is swarming with Xenos, and we can no longer form a psionic barrier that keeps them away.

Emma:

- What are you talking about? We scanned the surroundings with infrared sensors. There are no Xenos within a 100,000 kilometres radius.

Anumati:

- The Xenos can mask their infrared heat signature, but they can't hide their psionic presence. I predict that they will attack very soon.

Before Emma answered, there was a loud scream of pain as the Xenos appeared and attacked an unsuspecting soldier.

Xenos were coming from everywhere. There were thousands of them swarming in on her exhausted soldiers. Emma made a quick decision. She didn't like the concept of abandoning her soldiers, but the council needed to know what had happened. She found a functional hovercraft and dragged Anumati onto it. Emma set her course to the portal. The Xenos heard Emma starting the engines, and a large group of them jumped onto her hovercraft and started tearing it to shreds.

"Just a little bit longer," Emma said to herself as she was approaching the portal. When Anumati saw the portal, she screamed out in angst:

- We can't go through the portal yet. I must eat and drink, as I have no energy left in my physical body. Millennia of starvation will kill me when I leave the timelessness of this Dimension.

Emma:

- I am sorry, but I am unable to feed you right now. Hold tight!

Emma crashed her hovercraft through the portal, and she ended up outside the Cheops pyramid. The Terran automated defences killed the Xenos that had clung on to her hovercraft. When the shooting had ceased, Emma sighed of relief. She had survived the ordeal, and she had a valuable prisoner that could give invaluable insights and technology. Emma turned to Anumati. What she saw shocked her. Crossing the dimensional rift had killed and mummified the Zetan captive!

# Chapter 20: Hilda Muller Covers Up the Disastrous Military Campaign.

Hilda Muller was looking at the corpse of Emma Schindler. The official cause of death would be heart failure. Yet, Hilda knew the real cause of death. Emma had died from a synthetic virus designed towards Emma's genome, which caused a heart attack. After the disastrous expedition to the Divine Dimension, Hilda had to silence her former bodyguard.

Emma had failed the mission and lost her expeditionary force. Worse yet, she had also caused a confrontation with the Zetans. Instead of dealing with the Xeno threat, Emma had increased the threat level by battling another alien species!

Hilda, as Chairwoman of the Terran Council, had forbidden further expeditions to the Divine Dimension. Thus, she needed to find a way to restore Earth's rotational speed. Otherwise, she would face a widespread ecological collapse, when the day-night cycle became too much out of sync.

Hilda's intercom beeped. It was Markus White. Hilda had been busy dealing with the Emma Schindler debacle and had forgotten about her planned meeting with him. Hilda hesitated, but she decided to let him in. Markus was her closest ally, and she trusted him more than she trusted most of her own family members.

Seeing Emma Schindler's corpse shocked Markus, and he stuttered:

- What happened here? Why is your right-hand woman sitting dead in a chair?

Hilda Muller:

- Emma died of a heart attack.

Markus White:

 - A heart attack? So where is the medical staff?

Hilda Muller:

 - They will come here in due time. In half an hour or so.

Markus White:

 - Half an hour? But then she will be dead beyond resurrection?

Hilda Muller:

 - Yes.

Markus White:

 - What is going on here?

Hilda Muller:

 - I will tell you since you are my friend.

 - I appointed Emma to lead an attack on the Xenos. I hoped to kill their queen Rangda who was behind the attacks on Earth. You have seen her, remember?

Markus White:

 - Yes, I am still having recurring nightmares about that day!

Hilda Muller:

 - Anyways, Emma failed. Instead of fighting the Xenos, she caused a confrontation with the Zetans. After the battle, Emma abandoned her army when the Xenos ambushed our troops.

- So, because of Emma, we are not at war with one alien species but two different species.

- As for Emma's death, a military court would give her the same outcome. But we cannot allow this to become be public, that's why I did what I had to do.

Markus White:

- I am sorry, Hilda. But this is too much for me. Why are you telling me all this? You could have kept me in the dark and met me in another room.

Hilda Muller:

- Yes, but you are my ally, my friend, and my love interest. I don't want us to keep secrets between each other.

Markus White:

- Not even dark secrets?

Hilda Muller:

- Not even dark secrets!

Markus White:

- I see. Well, thank you for being honest with me. I must leave now! I'll see you another day.

After saying this, Markus rushed off to the closest toilet and threw up.

# Chapter 21: Melchior Fulfils His Dark Desires.

At the beginning of 2876, Melchior Dorevitch had accomplished his conquest of Mars. With access to Zetan technologies, conquering Mars had been a piece of cake. With his superior weaponry, his armies were unbeatable on the battlefield. With access to the Zetan mind-control technology, Melchior had inserted chips into everyone's brains. This way, Melchior could snuff out any dissent against his rule before it even happened. He had accomplished what no-one before him had achieved; he had unified Mars under one government. Melchior wouldn't rule Mars as the president of The Olympus Republic. No, Melchior would rule Mars as its god-king! Melchior saw himself as a messiah leading humanity into the future. The Martian would have to follow the rules set forth by the almighty Yahweh.

Melchior decreed that the new name of his territory would be the Martian Dominion.

Having access to a Divine Detector machine, Melchior knew the truth about Yahweh. Melchior knew that Yahweh was a long-dead Zetan. It didn't matter, as there was no such thing as objective truth. Words repeated enough times became the truth. Such was the case for all religions, and the only thing that mattered was to become more successful than the other religions!

While Melchior's religious aspirations were still in their infancy, his tyranny had made him the most powerful ruler in the solar system. The terrified Terran Council members sent him gifts and bowed to him, trying to win his favour. Things had certainly changed in the last few years!

Melchior decided that it was time to stop hiding his real self. He invited his brother for drinks.

Melchior poured Dov a glass of whiskey. Dov Dorevitch glanced at Melchior and spoke:

- Are you not drinking whiskey, today, brother? What are you having, Bloody Mary?

Melchior:

- Yes... Bloody Mary.

Dov:

- Okay. You wanted to show me something?

Melchior removed the tinted lenses from his eyes and revealed his purple predator eyes.

- Behold the true me. I have the same gift that Keila had, the purple eyes of destiny. Purple eyes are the mark of anyone that Rangda possesses.

Dov:

- Wow! So, you are as insane as Keila? Who is Rangda, anyway?

Melchior:

- Rangda is the pinnacle of creation. She is a Xeno-Zetan hybrid destined to rule the galaxy as its immortal goddess.

- Rangda has been to Earth, she led the first assault on Rashidium after the portals opened. There are photos of her, although the Terran Council are trying to cover up her existence.

Melchior streamed a hologram of Rangda. They studied the hologram for a while, and Melchior spoke:

- There she is, my goddess and my future queen! Isn't she beautiful?

Dov:

- But she is not even human? She looks like a demon, straight out of a nightmare?!

Melchior:

- Silence! Do not criticise the beauty in something because you cannot appreciate it!

- Anyways, you are here today because I need you to rule in my stead for the next few days. I am going to participate in a ritual to strengthen my connection to Rangda.

Dov:

- But Yahweh's laws forbid demon-worshipping rituals?

Melchior:

- Yes, but I am not going to let the laws of dead deity stop me from acquiring almost limitless power. Let the Martians believe in our doctrines. I made up the dogmas to weaken their minds and to destroy their chances for rebellion.

Dov:

- Understood, brother. I will head back to my office and prepare to lead.

Dov left Melchior's office, and Melchior summoned his secretary Sandra. Melchior had designated her to be his first victim. Sandra felt uneasy when she noticed his glowing purple predator eyes.
Sandra:

- What happened to your eyes, Master Melchior, they look so scary!

Melchior:

- Don't worry, Sandra. I am wearing a pair of tinted lenses that Dov gave me. I need to speak to you in private in the backroom.

Sandra felt uneasy, but she didn't dare to argue with her boss. She followed Melchior into the soundproof room. Once she was in the room, Melchior locked the door and took out the key from the lock. He stared into her eyes and spoke:

- Today Sandra, you'll be a very fortunate woman.

- Today, I'll grant you a favour that most people are dying to have. You'll die for a purpose. A very important purpose.

- You'll be the first human that I eat. Your death is the key to establishing my connection to Rangda, the ultimate being in existence!

Sandra felt terrified, but she wouldn't oblige to the madman in front of her without a fight. Sandra put up a good fight, but Melchior was too strong in his frenzied state. The last thing that Sandra saw was the possessed Melchior eating her alive, ripping off flesh from her body.

After gorging on Sandra's flesh, Melchior felt blissful and satisfied. He felt better than ever, and yet Rangda hadn't materialised. Melchior decided to take a nap. In his dreams, he had a vision of Rangda:

- We finally meet Melchior. You have been very impressive this far!

Melchior:

- I greet you my beautiful goddess Rangda, and I will do your bidding.

Rangda:

- Good! Build up a vast army, and travel to Earth. Together we will wipe out the Zetan filth that has infested the galaxy for too long. Together we will rule this galaxy as its rightful king and queen!

Melchior:

- I will do your bidding, Empress.

Rangda:

- Good. As you don't have ideal genetics for telepathy, you need to eat and kill someone before communicating with me.

Melchior:

- Magnificent! I can't wait to speak to you again, Empress Rangda!

Melchior fell back to sleep. He would stay in this room for a few days. There was still plenty of meat in the room, and it would be a shame to waste it!

# Chapter 22: Metatron Notices Sabina's Amazing Abilities.

A few months later, in June 2876, Metatron was watching the news. He felt guilty and remorseful over giving up the Zetan technologies to Melchior. Giving up the technologies had saved the Edenites and Metatron's family, but the cost for everyone on Mars was too high. With the Zetan technologies, Melchior had crushed his opponents, and now the Martians suffered under his tyranny.

Metatron sighed. The reign of the Terran Council had been evil, but it was nothing compared to the atrocities under Melchior. The Terran Council had ruled over the solar system to satisfy their greed and desire for domination. The Terran Council army had only used real force when someone opposed them. With Melchior, things were different. Melchior and his inner circle tortured and maimed people for the fun of it.

Melchior claimed that his rule over Mars was a theocracy following Yahweh's teachings. But this wasn't close to the reality. Yahweh's instructions were harsh but, in some sense, fair and predictable. Melchior's rule, on the other hand, was a tyranny that made a mockery of the laws in the Old Testament.

Melchior started every Saturday with human sacrifice, cannibalism and demon worship. The Bible, which Melchior claimed to follow, had outlawed all this behaviour. To make things even more gruesome, Melchior sometimes forced his prisoners to kill and eat their own family members!

Hearing about all the atrocities under Melchior, Metatron felt powerless. He wished that he had resisted Melchior and died on that fateful day.

Metatron exhaled and tried to let go. There were always two sides to everything in life, and on the bright side, Melissa had fallen pregnant. In a couple of months, Sabina would have a baby brother. Thinking of Sabina, Metatron decided to spend time with his daughter.

Metatron entered Sabina's room. It appeared like she was talking to someone. But that couldn't be. Sabina was only a year old and could hardly walk, even less so having a proper conversation with someone. But Melchior could her a child's voice. Feeling surprised and curious, Metatron walked towards Sabina. Sabina noticed his presence and turned around:

- Hi daddy. So lovely to see you today.

Metatron froze. Sabina couldn't speak yesterday, and now she spoke like a much older child. Sabina gave him a curious look and spoke again:

- Is something wrong daddy? Come, give me a hug.

Metatron gave Sabina a hug. He looked at her in amazement and spoke:

- I didn't know you could talk? When did you learn?

Sabina:

- A few days ago. I have been speaking a lot to my mother lately.

Metatron:

- Really? Why hasn't she told me about it?

Sabina:

- She couldn't reach you. It's not in your blood to communicate via telepathy.

Metatron:

- Sabina, have you been speaking to Keila?

Sabina:

- Yes, who else? We both know Melissa isn't my real mother.

Sabina's statement stunned Metatron, and he looked into her eyes. They were glowing with a luminescent blue colour. Suddenly, they stopped shining blue, and they reverted to their natural green colour. Sabina spoke again:

- Dada. Peekaboo!!!!

Metatron looked at Sabina. Nothing indicated any superior advanced intelligence, and she had reverted to the one-year-old child that she was. Had he imagined it all? Metatron knew one thing, Sabina needed him. What she needed right now was to play peekaboo, so that's what he would do!

# Chapter 23: Metatron Visits Hilda Muller.

Metatron and Sabina were sitting in the lobby of Europeum Tower waiting for an audience with Hilda Muller. Metatron wondered what had he gotten himself into. Sabina had spoken to him on several occasions. She had told him that she had special abilities which the True Maker had given her. Furthermore, Sabina claimed that it was her destiny to stop Rangda's terror, and that she needed to speak to Hilda. But between these moments of divine intervention, Sabina was a regular child. Regardless, the conversations had convinced Metatron that he had to act, as he felt responsible for how things had turned out.

Contacting the Terran Council was a risky move. They had not been a humanitarian organisation in the past. If they knew that Eden had assisted Keila, coming here was suicide. Metatron believed that the Terran Council didn't know about the Edenite involvement in the Martian uprising. Otherwise, they would have attacked Eden by now.

Metatron entered Hilda's office, and her looks astonished him. Metatron had pictured Hilda Muller as a resolute lady in her military uniform. But Hilda was young and good-looking in an expensive blue dress, laden in jewellery. Hilda smiled at him and spoke:

- You look surprised, Mr Jack Silver, or shall I call you Metatron?

Metatron:

- Metatron is fine.

- Yes, you look so much younger and prettier in real life than you do in your press conferences.

Hilda:

- Yes. When I speak in public, I use makeup to look older. To instil authority, I wear my Supreme Commander uniform.

- But now I am not in the public eye, and like any 32-year-old woman, I like to look pretty.

- But how cute is that child? Is she your daughter?

Metatron:

- Yes, Sabina is my daughter, and this is her first visit to Earth.

Hilda:

- Then let us hope that she has many visits to come!
- She looks familiar. Have I met her mother?

Metatron:

- Have you been to Eden in the past? Her mother, Melissa has never been away from Eden.

Hilda:

- Oh, well then, I must be mistaken. I have never been to Eden. But from what I have heard, you have created something unique there.

- Sorry to be rude, but I am a busy woman, so let's get down to business.

- Have you come to pledge yourself to the Terran Council and incorporate Eden into our territory?

Metatron:

- No, I want Eden to remain a neutral colony.

Hilda:

- I am sorry, but then I don't understand why you have come here?

Metatron:

- I have come to introduce you to my daughter. Sabina is a prodigy child bestowed with superior intelligence by the True Maker.

- With your help, we can deal with Rangda before she becomes a threat to the entire galaxy.

Hilda:

- Is this a bad joke? You are bringing me a toddler, and you claim that I must send my army to stop the Xenos? All of this because of religious superstition?

Metatron:

- Yes. I would like you to talk with my toddler. Let Sabina tell you about her prophetic powers. Why haven't you sent troops through the portal to Divine Dimension? The Xeno attacks have receded, and it's time to counterattack

Hilda:

- Mind your manners. You cannot come here and dictate how to run my faction.

Suddenly, Sabina's eyes changed to a glowing crystal blue, and she spoke:

- Dear Hilda. Please help me stop Rangda and Melchior. Their power is increasing every day. If you don't act soon, it's going to be too late.

Hilda:

- What is going on here? What bionic implants have you put into the child's brain, to enable this kind of unnatural behaviour?

Sabina:

- I don't have any implants. The True Maker grants me the ability to reason on an adult's level.

Hilda:

- AI! Scan Sabina Silver for bionic implants!

AI:

- Sabina Silver doesn't seem to have any bionic implants.

Sabina:

- I would prefer that you use my mother's last name, Eisenstein.

Hilda:

- Are you Keila Eisenstein's daughter?

Sabina:

- Yes.

Hilda:

- Then your mother is the cause of all the bad things that have happened. Keila opened the portal that allowed the Xeno horde to attack us.

Sabina:

- Yes, but she never had bad intentions. Rangda deceived her. As fear deluded Keila, she failed to foresee what was to come. That's why I am here; to set things right!

Hilda:

- So, what would you have me do?

Sabina:

- You know what to do! Send me to the Divine Dimension with the backing of your Terran troops!

After saying this, Sabina lost her connection with the True Maker. Sabina's eye colour changed back to green, and she reverted to the mental status of an average 1.5-year-old child.
Hilda, unaware of the change that took place, screamed at Sabina:

- No! This is impossible, I don't believe you. Don't you dare to tell me what to do!

Sabina, who was back to being a typical toddler, said: "gaahhh, boohoo, mean lady!" Sabina started crying and ran to Metatron for comfort.
Hilda:

- What happened? Why is she acting like a toddler again?

Metatron:

- She is no longer connected with the True Maker. Thus, she is now a typical toddler.

- Anyways. You have seen enough. You know what to do.

Hilda screamed at Metatron, who flinched in surprise:

- Yes. I should have you both executed for your connection with our mortal enemy, Keila Eisenstein!

Metatron:

- If you kill Sabina, you'll doom us all! She is the only one who can save humanity and close the interdimensional rifts!

Hilda:

- Silence! Get away from me. I'll let you live, but never come back to Earth again.

Metatron realised that Hilda Muller wasn't receptive to further communication. He picked up the crying Sabina, and they left Hilda Muller's office in disappointment.

# Chapter 24: Melchior Boards Metatron's Shuttle.

Metatron and Sabina were travelling back to Eden when trouble struck. Several space warships from Melchior's faction, the Martian Dominion approached them and requested to dock. Metatron realised that he could not outrun the fleet, so he surrendered. A short while later, Melchior and his bodyguards entered the shuttle.

Melchior:

- We meet again, Metatron. That must be your daughter? How delightful! What a shame you didn't introduce us the last time we met.

Metatron:

- I don't want to drag infants into politics.

- Besides, you promised to leave me alone if I handed over the Zetan technologies to you.

Melchior:

- Bah, speaking of promises. We discovered that you infested most of the technologies with Trojan viruses, which made them useless. But you failed. The ones that we could use were enough to help us conquer Mars. Whatever devilish plan you tried to set in motion came to naught.

Metatron:

- Is that so? Why do you reckon that I was the one who put the viruses there? They might have been from the start.

Melchior

- Yes, I realised the same thing, and that's why I kept my promise.

- But I never promised to leave you alone. My promise was to stay away from Eden if you gave me the technologies. This promise causes me severe grief, as I'm forced to live separated from my Edenite relatives. You're inhuman, Metatron, forcing a man to stay away from his beloved family!

Metatron:

- Beloved family? You incinerated your own mother to prove a point, you evil monster!

Melchior:

- You forced my hand. I wasn't going to let you blackmail me into staying away from what is rightfully mine.

- Regardless, why are you travelling back to Eden from Earth? What business did you have on Earth?

Metatron:

- I was feeling homesick. I was born on Earth, and I wanted to take my daughter to Earth and show her my roots.

Melchior:

- What a load of rubbish. Bringing a toddler on a long trip to Earth for sightseeing? Ridiculous.

- Unless...

Melchior aimed a DNA scanner towards Sabina, and the answer was what he expected. Sabina was Keila's child.
Melchior:

- Fascinating. You and Keila must have used a surrogate mother before she went on her suicide mission to Earth?

- What did she hope to achieve?

Metatron:

- Keila wanted a part of her to survive after her death.

Melchior:

- Nah, that doesn't sound like Keila. It must have been one of the visions that told her to have a child with you. In that case, we both know what I must do.

Melchior pulled up a stun gun and electrocuted Metatron. Then he grabbed the crying Sabina and studied her carefully.
Melchior:

- Fascinating. She is the spitting image of her mother.

- But why would you go to Earth with Keila's daughter? What do you hope to achieve?

- Are you collaborating with the greedy cowards in the Terran Council? Why would you bring your daughter to such a meeting?

Melchior looked at Metatron who was cramping after the electrocution. Melchior gave a signal to his bodyguards, to get Metatron back on his feet, and handcuff him to a wall. When Metatron had regained consciousness, Melchior spoke again:

- I have realised that I will never find out why you brought your daughter on this dangerous trip to Earth. And I don't even care why. This is my opportunity to get revenge for what you caused me to do to my mother.

Melchior smiled a sinister smile, stared into Sabina's eyes, and took a small bite into her shoulder. The toddler screamed a heartbreaking shriek of pain as Melchior took a gulp of her blood.
Melchior turned to Metatron:

- You should thank your daughter, Metatron. Because she is the reason that you'll get out of here alive. You see, witnessing what I am going to do to her is worse than dying, and I want you to suffer!

Melchior took another bite of Sabina's arm and then threw her roughly into the wall, knocking her unconscious.
With Sabina's blood dripping from his mouth, he walked up to Metatron to mock him. Metatron didn't respond. Instead, he head-butted Melchior who fell to the floor. Melchior got up. Smiling like a madman, he spoke:

- Ah, pain. Why do people avoid it when it is the purest form of pleasure?

Melchior knocked the chained Metatron unconscious with a flurry of hard punches. He turned to, Sabina who had regained consciousness, to finish the gruesome murder. Rangda appeared as an illusion and stopped Melchior.

- Stay clear of Keila's daughter, Melchior! I sense that Sabina has a lot of untapped psionic powers. I want her to grow up so that I can capture her and drain her power. Sabina's powers will make us even stronger if we give them time to grow before we kill her!

Melchior:

- But Empress Rangda, this girl is my prey, and she is delicious.

Rangda:

- I'll let you eat her later. But first, she must grow up and face me. After I have drained her psionic powers, she is all yours.

- I command you to let Sabina and Metatron travel back to Eden.

Melchior:

- Arrrgh...! Yes, Empress Rangda. I will do your bidding.

Melchior ordered his bodyguards to patch up Sabina's and Metatron's wounds so that they could go back to Eden safely. After that, he went back to his command ship. There, Melchior picked up a huge rat, crushed it with his hand and drank the blood to quench his unquenchable thirst. But this was to no avail. The rat's blood was not what he was after.

Melchior was furious with Rangda for denying him his prey, but he would obey her for now. After all, he still needed her as she had a lot to teach him!

A while later, Sabina approached Metatron with her eyes shining bluer than ever:

- Are you okay daddy? I am so sorry that I couldn't stop those men from hurting you.

Metatron:

- I am your father; I am the one who should protect you.

Sabina:

- Yes, but you are only human, so I can't expect you to do everything. How are your injuries?

Metatron:

- A bit swollen but I'll be alright. I am more worried about the bites he took off you.

Sabina pulled off the bandages that Melchior's bodyguards had put on her shoulder and on her arm. There was not a scratch, and the wounds had healed like they were never there. Sabina spoke:

- Don't worry about me. Be a good father for Sabina when I am not around.

- I don't usually use my healing powers on humans, but I'll make an exception today.

Sabina put her tiny hands on Metatron's bleeding wounds. Metatron felt a short burst of intense serenity and calmness. When he got back to his senses, his injuries and his headache were gone. Sabina was back to her usual self and she hugged him:

- Daddy, I am scared. Bad men hurt me. Boohoo!!

Metatron:

- The bad men are gone and won't hurt you again, my sweetheart. Let's go home to mommy Melissa and tell her about our fun trip to Earth!

Having said this, Metatron returned to the pilot seat on his spacecraft and set the autopilot to destination Eden.

# Chapter 25: Hilda Muller's Dilemma.

It was New Year's Eve; 2876 was about to end. Hilda Muller excused herself from the New Year's celebration, and she withdrew to her private level of Europeum Tower.

Hilda had changed after Metatron and Sabina had visited her, six months earlier. What had happened that day? How had the child changed eye colour and spoken like an adult? Sabina had urged Hilda to attack the Xenos, but had reverted to a toddler moments later. Hilda couldn't comprehend it, and she didn't know what to do.

Hilda had studied the video footage with her scientists, and no-one could explain what had happened. Hilda wondered whether she had experienced a divine intervention. By why had God used the daughter of her enemy, Keila Eisenstein, as the vessel? And what would Hilda do?

The toddler had urged Hilda to lead her army to the Divine Dimension, but would she do this? If she was unlucky, Rangda could be the one possessing Sabina. Rangda had possessed Keila, and if she possessed Sabina as well, returning to the Divine Dimension was a trap.

Hilda felt frustrated by her own fear and indecisiveness. She decided that she had to do something. As it turned out, that something was someone, one of her bodyguards, Melanie Weber. While Hilda preferred men to women, it was interesting to try something different, and she had grown disillusioned with men. They either feared her for her power or tried to seduce her to dominate her and steal her power. Markus White had been different, but he was too weak to stomach the brutal reality of power.

Hilda had done the right thing murdering Emma to cover up the disastrous military expedition. If Markus White had been the right partner, he would have seen things Hilda's way and supported her. Instead, he had added to her burden when he left her alone with her guilt over murdering Emma.

But in Melanie Weber, Hilda had found what she needed. Melanie was loyal, secure, discrete, and she was more than happy to help Hilda with her every need. Hilda studied Melanie as she entered the room. It was a shame to hide such a beautiful woman under an ugly bodyguard uniform. But it would be too conspicuous to dress one of her bodyguards different from the others, besides the clothes wouldn't stay on for long.

Melanie:

  - Melanie Weber reporting for duty!

Hilda:

  - Melanie, you are my only guard on duty tonight, I need to keep you near, very near, to protect me.

Melanie:

  - And who is going to protect you against me?

Hilda:

  - I am more than capable of protecting myself against you.

Melanie:

  - Is that so? Then wrestle me to the ground!

Hilda:

  - With pleasure, you'll be under me in no time.

After that, the two of them started a rough session of wrestling, and a while later, Hilda was on top of Melanie.

Hilda:

  - I still got it!

Melanie:

- Yes, Mistress Muller, you still got it!

Hilda moaned in pleasure. In Melanie's embrace, Hilda could disconnect from the anxiety and fear that clouded her mind.

# Chapter 26: Melchior Reveals His True Form.

In August 2877, Melchior was studying his military forces. The Martian military strength had increased as Melchior had ordered the redirection of all resources to the army. They would soon be ready to travel to Earth to face the Terran Council and make them bow to their will. Melchior smiled. In his visions, there were so many beautiful places in the universe, planets that were ripe for Martian expansion. When Melchior had finished, he would rule the entire galaxy. Every intelligent living being would have to bow him and serve him.

Melchior fell to the ground with tremors. He was in immense pain. Melchior had been too busy working on his plans, so he had forgotten to eat for several days. Melchior felt how hunger made his entire body ache. Since Rangda possessed him, Melchior had adopted the Xeno way of eating, i.e. biting chunks of meat off an alive victim. Eating this way, he could eat 10 kilos at once and stay full for days as meat digests slowly.

Melchior got up, and he studied his reflection in the mirror. His ashen grey thick skin was cracking up everywhere, and he was bleeding from multiple wounds. He needed to eat straight away! He called his brother Dov:

- Dov, bring me a prisoner right now. I am starving.

Dov:

- Which prisoner? There are plenty to choose from.

Melchior:

- Bring anyone.

A while later, Dov brought a female prisoner, imprisoned for abortion. Melchior forbade abortion, not because he valued life, but because he was against killing without eating. Thus, it was legal to give birth to a baby and then eat it. But Melchior didn't allow abortion since it was "unnatural".
Melchior studied the woman and spoke:

- Ah, delicious. What crime did she commit?

Dov:

- She had an abortion and wasted the meat.

Melchior:

- Heinous! Well at least her end will serve a useful purpose.

Melchior leapt at the woman and tore pieces of flesh off her with his sharp teeth. Dov had gagged the woman to stop her from screaming in agony, as he couldn't stand hearing the screams of the murder victims. Dov left; knowing that half an hour later, his brother would lie on his couch like a lion after a big meal.
Half an hour later, Dov came back, and he spoke to Melchior:

- What is happening to you, brother? You don't look human anymore.

Melchior:

- So, my experiment is working? Thank you.

Dov:

- Your experiment? What have you done?

Melchior:

- Rangda gave me a Xeno DNA sequence in a vision. She said that I can become immensely powerful if I become a human-Xeno hybrid.

Dov:

- But when would you have done this? You can't change your DNA when you are awake? You can only do it when you are in suspended animation.

Melchior:

- That was what my doctor said. He said that the pain from such as procedure would kill any human from the sheer shock.

- And he was telling the truth. I found that out when I tested the procedure on him!

- But I realised something. That my doctor was a mere human, a weakling not destined for greatness, while I am destined to rule the galaxy.

- So, I did the experiment on myself, and it works. I am in immense pain, but instead of running from the pain, I embrace it, and it gives me strength.

Dov:

- So, you turned yourself into a man-eating monster in constant pain, for what? Power? You are already the mightiest person in the solar system.

Melchior:

- Your small-mindedness annoys me! Yes, I was powerful, but I was still a man. A bullet through my brain could end me at any time, and if nothing else, time would take its toll.

- Now I am something more. I am a hybrid of the most powerful races of the galaxy, and when I am united with my queen, we will rule everyone!

Dov:

- About that. There is a critical problem affecting our military build-up. Ecological destruction of Mars is destroying our harvests. We will starve in a couple of months.

Melchior:

- Well then. We better cull the population, so we have fewer mouths to feed. Our soldiers shall kill and eat the leeches in our society.

Dov:

- Most of our soldiers follow us out of fear. Forcing them to cannibalism will push them against us.

Melchior:

- Bloody weaklings! But you're right, Dov. We need to move now. Prepare my fleet for departure to Earth. I'll bring most of the army there. You'll stay behind and rule Mars in my place.

Dov:

- But brother, we are not ready with our military build-up. We cannot conquer Earth, yet.

Melchior:

- I know. But I will give them an offer that they cannot refuse.

After that, Dov left the room to carry out Melchior's orders and prepare everyone for departure.

# Chapter 27: Enemies at the Gates.

Hilda Muller was lying naked in Melanie Weber's embrace. What Hilda had intended to be a short fling and an experiment to get over Markus White had turned out to be something else. Hilda's relationship with Melanie gave her both joy and pain. Melanie made Hilda feel protected and appreciated. But her relationship with Melanie would be political suicide if it became public. As a mighty leader, Hilda could have several flings on the side and no-one would care. But her official partner needed to be someone important, and not her bodyguard.

There was a beep on the intercom. Hilda's cousin Michael Muller, the second most prominent leader in House Muller, requested an urgent meeting. This was very odd. During the two and half years that they had overseen House Muller, Michael rarely approached Hilda with any urgent matters. As a matter of fact, Michael preferred letting Hilda make difficult decisions.

Hilda got dressed and met Michael in the lounge room. Michael appeared stressed and irritable.

Michael:

- How was the tryst?

Hilda studied Michael. How could he know about her and Melanie? Hilda decided to dismiss Michael:

- My sex life is none of your business.

Michael:

- That is correct. I wouldn't give a shit that you fuck your bodyguard if you could pick up the phone when I am calling you. We are in the middle of an emergency.

- Tell Melanie to come out. I need to speak to her!

Lost for words, Hilda didn't know what to say, and she agreed to her cousin's demands. A few minutes later, Melanie Weber came out to greet Michael. He spoke to her with a direct tone:

- Melanie. Thank you for looking after Hilda so well. But I cannot allow a bodyguard to be in an ongoing romantic relationship with our chairwoman. You're relieved of your employment as a bodyguard for House Muller!

Hilda was going to protest, but Michael raised his finger to show that he hadn't finished talking:

- As your severance package, I'll give you 10,000 shares in the Muller Corporation. This is enough to attend our annual general meeting. I also offer you the position as the General of our $57^{\text{th}}$ army division.

Hilda Muller:

- Wait. There is no $57^{\text{th}}$ army division.

Michael Muller:

- There is now. Believe me, Hilda! If Melanie has been loyal to you for almost a year and kept your secret, she is worth her weight in gold.

- You cannot be in a relationship with your bodyguard. But partnering up with a prominent and wealthy general is an acceptable solution.

- Now, Supreme Commander Hilda Muller, and General Melanie Weber, we have a serious problem to deal with.

Hilda Muller:

- I am listening.

Michael Muller:

- The madman Melchior Dorevitch, has arrived with a large fleet. They are hovering 200 kilometres above Hansstadt and threatens our capital. He requests a meeting on his command ship.

Hilda Muller:

- What? How did he get this close undetected?

Michael Muller:

- He must have used Zetan stealth technology to mask his ships. There has been a tremendous technological advancement on Mars since their independence.

Hilda Muller:

- Scheisse. Can we beat him?

Michael Muller:

- I hope so. Our analysts believe that Melchior moved early due to the catastrophic harvests and looming starvation on Mars.

- However, with Melchior this close to our capital, any major confrontation would level the entire city.

Hilda Muller:

- We cannot risk that. I guess I have no choice but to meet this madman on his terms.

- You stay back with our army on full alert. If something happens to me, we cannot let this lunatic conquer our territory. Attack him with full force if he tries anything.

Michael Muller:

- Understood. I will head to our underground command bunker and coordinate our forces.

Hilda Muller:

- Good. Now Melanie...

Melanie Weber:

- Yes, Mistress Muller?

Hilda Muller:

- Hurry up and pick up a General's uniform.

- You're coming with me. I need you by my side when I am facing this Martian menace.

Melanie Weber:

- Acknowledged Mistress Muller. I'll get changed and meet you at the starport.

Hilda Muller:

- You can call me Hilda now. Michael just made you one of us. Now hurry up!

Hilda hurried to get dressed and made her way to the starport. On the way to the starport, she experienced a mixture of fear and a sense of relief. Hilda feared for her upcoming meeting with the wicked Melchior. But Hilda felt relief knowing that if she got out of this alive, she would be able to partner up with the woman that she loved.

# Chapter 28: Hilda Meets Melchior.

An hour later, Hilda Muller, Melanie Weber and a few bodyguards docked with Melchior's command ship. The sight of Melchior's lobby shocked Hilda. In the centre of the hall, there was a large fountain that was pumping out blood. Human hearts ornamented the fountain.

Melchior's imperial guard covered the edges of the room. They looked terrifying. The guards had covered themselves in black armour, filled with blood-stained spikes. Hilda feared the mutated Martian guards, but she pulled herself together and stayed strong.

Hilda shouted:

- I am Hilda Muller from the Terran Council. Where is Melchior Dorevitch? What kind of man invites people to his command ship without being there to greet them?

A gigantic beastlike guard, who was almost three meters tall, approached Hilda. She stared in terror at guard, who wore an iron facemask and fear-some-looking armour. The monstrosity spoke:

- I am Peter Belovic, the chancellor of the Martian Dominion and Melchior's right-hand-man.

- I require you to surrender your weapons before Melchior grants you an audience.

Hilda:

- This is an outrage. I am the chairwoman of the Terran Council, not some low-ranking officer. I require you to show your real face before coming with demands like these.

Peter Belovic:

- I am hiding my face to do you a favour. Seeing the terror that lurks behind this mask would terrify you!

Hilda:

- Nonetheless, it is customary to see the face of the one you negotiate with. Show your face, or I will leave, and you have wasted everyone's time!

Peter:

- As you wish, Madame Muller. But don't say I didn't warn you.

Peter Belovic removed his helmet, and revealed his terrifying face. Seeing Peter's face, Hilda flinched and almost fell over. Melanie grabbed Hilda's arm and helped her regain her balance.

Hilda studied the man, or rather, the ghastly and horrifying monster in front of her. His petrifying eyes were blood-sprained, and the optical nerves were glowing red. His skin was ashen, thick and lizard-like. There were large jagged cracks and crusts on his skin, exposing his muscle tissues and veins. Most of Peter's front teeth were missing. The teeth that remained were sharp fangs, and he was drooling and panting like a hungry beast.

Hilda:

- You better put that mask on! What happened to you? You do not look human!

Peter:

- My master tried to make me stronger by injecting me with Xeno DNA. As it turned out, my genes were not strong enough to merge with foreign DNA. The pain is unbearable, and I only have a short time left to live. As I die, my brethren shall consume my flesh to make them stronger.

Hilda:

- Forget that I asked!

- Guards! Surrender your weapons to our hosts. It is time to meet Melchior Dorevitch, leader of the Martian Dominion.

Hilda and her bodyguards surrendered their weapons, and Peter called Melchior over the radio. 30 seconds later, Melchior entered the room.

Hilda studied Melchior. He had the same ash-grey thick lizard-like skin that Peter had. But unlike Peter, Melchior's skin had fused together, and his scars had healed. Melchior's eyes were glowing purple, unlike Peter's sickly blood-sprained eyes. Melchior's eyes gave Hilda a déjà vu. Keila Eisenstein had the same eyes when she had killed the Terran Council leadership in Rashidium.

Melchior approached Hilda and spoke:

- Thank you for accepting my invitation. I am sorry for not shaking your hands, as my sharp claws make handshakes difficult.

Hilda studied Melchior's hands. Large claws were extending from the top of them, and small sharp thorns covered his palm. She nodded in acknowledgement but said nothing. Melchior continued to speak:

- How do you find our centrepiece, the blood-fountain over there?

Hilda:

- I am sorry, but I don't like it. What is it anyway?

Melchior:

- It's a blood fountain. Underneath the fountain sits synthetic bone marrow that creates human blood. The fountain pumps the blood. The hearts of my enemies are beating with the aid of electrical electrodes attached to the bottom of them.

Hilda:

- The hearts of your enemies? So, the hearts are not grown in the lab, but the actual hearts of people that you have killed?

Melchior:

- That is correct. The soul resides in the heart, so keeping the heart alive is the best way to torment an enemy after death.

Hilda struggled with her fear and terror. She had anticipated that meeting Melchior Dorevitch on his command ship would be unpleasant, but she had never imagined it to be this bad. But Hilda had to keep herself together. She was the leader of Terran Council, and if she cracked, there was nothing to stop this evil madman from destroying her beautiful planet, Earth.
Hilda stammered:

- Okay, but I am not here to discuss your religious beliefs. You have travelled all the way to Earth, and you have requested a meeting. What do you want?

Melchior:

- Hahaha! I will get to that in a moment. But first, have a drink with and cheer with me to the future. That is a Terran tradition, right?

Hilda:

- Yes. That is correct, but I don't see any champagne glasses around.

Melchior:

- Oh, how rude of me. I forgot the glassware! Wait a second.

Melchior snapped his fingers, and a servant approached him with two jugs made out of baby craniums. Melchior took the skulls, walked to the fountain and filled the skulls with blood.

Melchior

- In the Martian Dominion, we don't drink alcohol. But share some blood with me. It's rich in nutrients, especially iron, perfect for women in their fertile age.

Hilda:

- Disgusting! I'll pass on the offer!

Melchior had a sip of blood, stared into Hilda's eyes before licking his lips and talking:

- Oh, but you misunderstand. The drinking of blood is not an offer but a rite of passage of my ship. I would consider it very rude if you don't follow through with it.

Hilda lost her calm and yelled:

- I will not let you poison me! If you harm me, the entire Terran Council army will attack you!

Melchior shrugged his shoulders and spoke:

- There is nothing toxic in the blood, as you can see, I am drinking it myself. If I wanted to kill you, I would blow up your fancy tower from orbit before your army had the time to react!

- Now drink the damn blood before I get angry. Trust me, you don't want that to happen.

Hilda felt compelled to drink the blood, and she managed to finish the bowl without spewing. Melchior studied her for a while and then he spoke again:

- Good, you have proven your value. Now, let's discuss why I am here.

- I have decided to help you with the portal problem. I intend to lead my army to the Divine Dimension and wipe out the aliens that threaten mankind. All I need is your approval and support to the cause.

Hilda stared at Melchior in disbelief and spoke:

- You are putting me through this, and now you are offering your help. What is going on and why do you want to help us?

Melchior:

- My motivations are none of your concern. All you need to do is answer this question. Do you prefer to: A. Give us your blessings and support us with fuel, food and materials, or B. Die here today, with most of your capital levelled in the process?

Hilda:

- That sounds a lot like blackmail.

Melchior:

- Is that what you call it when we reverse the roles? What did you call it when the Terran Council forced the Martian nations to pay to keep electromagnetic field running?

Hilda bit her lip. The tables had turned, and she knew what fate had befallen the ones that resisted the Terran Council's power in the past.
Hilda:

- I choose A. I will grant you free passage to the portals, and I'll support your expedition with one million metric tonnes of fuel, food and provisions.

Melchior smiled and spoke:

- Good choice. I am happy that I made a "friend" today!

- I will leave a large fleet here to help you keep your promise. The rest of my fleet will gather near the portal and ensure that the supplies arrive.

- Please notify your allies on the Terran Council about your decision. I do not want any confrontations due to unfortunate "misunderstandings."

Hilda:

- Understood. I will convene with the others as soon as possible and make sure that everyone follows our agreement.

After saying this, Hilda and her group headed back to their shuttle returning to Hansstadt. Hilda felt relieved that she had survived visiting Melchior's lunatic asylum!

# Chapter 29: Melchior Discusses the Events with Rangda.

Later the same day, Melchior and his closest men had a feast on the late Peter Belovic. It was a shame to see a prominent follower die that way, but it was the least wasteful way for him to die. Peter's body hadn't survived the Xeno mutations. The only way to help him was to eat him alive while his heart was still pumping. This was a honourable death, better than letting him die and spoil the meat in the process.

One good thing came with Peter's death. It enabled Melchior's telepathic abilities so that he could communicate with his evil Mistress, Rangda.

Melchior:

 - Our first step was a success. I terrified Hilda Muller and she will not pose any resistance to our army entering the portals. She even agreed to help us with supplies.

Rangda:

 - Excellent. And how did she react when she drank the holy blood from the sacred fountain?

Melchior:

 - The blood failed to initiate her hunger. She reacted with disgust when she ingested it.

Rangda:

- That's unfortunate but expected. The weak Earth humans are only vulnerable to the desire for money. They lack a natural thirst for blood.

- Thus, they kill for money and let the dead bodies go to waste. How wasteful and grotesque!

Melchior:

- Indeed, Mistress Rangda. That is why humanity needs a new beginning. And together we will make sure that the new dawn of humankind happens!

Rangda:

- Yes, we will. Together we shall cleanse the Zetan scourge from this universe. The noble Xeno values must prevail. We will become the rulers of the Milky Way Galaxy!

Melchior:

- Yes. But the Terrans are fearful of us. Let's attack and conquer Earth while they are weak? I hunger for it!

Rangda:

- I know you do. But a true general doesn't enter the battle unless it's already won.

- Help me cleanse the Zetan scourge, and we will wipe out the Terran resistance together. Then earth shall be your price.

Melchior:

- Yes, Mistress. I will do your bidding.
- I will see you in the Divine Dimension.
- Goodbye!

The telepathic conversation with Rangda filled Melchior with rage. This was the second time the bitch had refused him his prey. She had stopped him from eating Sabina, and now she'd prevent him from attacking Earth that was ripe for the taking. But he would obey, for now.

Melchior released his anger on one of his weaker soldiers, impaling the victim with his sharp claws and splitting him in half. The others stared at him in shock and Melchior shouted out:

- Still hungry. Eat more men!

And Melchior's beastlike men feasted on their fallen comrade.

# Chapter 30: Nightmares, Concessions, and Contingency Plans.

Hilda was sleeping restlessly with vivid dreams. She had been feeling nauseous since her meeting with Melchior.

Another dream began. Hilda saw herself and Melanie raising their child. Hilda felt how her blood pressure increased, felt a desire for blood, and then she lifted her child and sank her sharp fangs into the innocent child. In the dream, the child uttered a shattering cry of pain before passing away. Blood was dripping down Hilda's mouth, and her purple eyes shone with an eerie, terrifying glow.

Hilda woke up, and she vomited blood. Had Melchior poisoned her? She wouldn't let this affront go unpunished. She looked up, and she saw her private doctor, dr Herbert Braun. He scanned the blood on the floor with a DNA scanner and then he spoke.

- The blood is not yours, which is a good sign.

- The toxicology report shows nothing. You are sick from drinking over a litre of human blood. I have given you medication to excrete the iron from your body.

- You should be fine in a couple of days.

Hilda:

- But what about my dreams? The dreams of eating my future child alive?

Herbert:

- I am not a psychiatrist, but I'd say you have some post-traumatic stress. I will leave that out of your report. I am your friend, and I don't want your enemies to use your mental health status against you.

- I'd recommend a lot of resting for now. Your cousin can do your work until you feel better.

Hilda:

- But who can protect me, when the one I fear the most, is myself?

Herbert:

- Fearing yourself after those dreams is a normal reaction. That means that you are sane and not a monster like Melchior.

Hilda:

- Thanks, doctor. I need to speak to my cousin. Please help me get to the meeting room.

Herbert accompanied Hilda to the meeting room where Michael was waiting. After Herbert had left, Michael Muller spoke
Michael:

- Oh my god, Hilda! You don't look well at all. What happened to you?

Hilda:

- Dr Braun believes that I suffer from iron poisoning and post-traumatic stress.

Michael:

- Yes, Melanie told me what happened. What a monster Melchior is!

Hilda:

- Yes, and the worst part is that we caused that form of evil to happen.

Michael:

- No, we did not. Joachim, Benjamin and Bjorn committed countless atrocities towards the Martian population. But greed drove them, which is a natural human emotion.

- What Melchior is doing is not even human. Drinking blood, eating humans alive while staring into their eyes. It not a human form of evil.

Hilda:

- So, what are you implying? That Rangda controls Melchior?

Michael:

- Yes, that is the only reasonable explanation.

Hilda:

- Okay, but why would he want to enter the portal with his army? It would be easier to instruct the Xenos to attack via the portals, while Melchior's army attack from the sky.

Michael:

- I don't know. Maybe they are after something else? The botched expedition to the Divine Dimension came across another alien species, didn't they?

Hilda:

- Yes, the Zetans. A small group of them killed a large part of Emma Schindler's expeditionary force before the Xenos swept in and killed everyone.

Michael:

- So, can we assume that the Zetans and the Xenos are enemies?

Hilda:

- Yes.

Michael:

- Then Melchior, who Rangda possesses, is leading the Martian army to the Divine Dimension to fight the Zetans?

Hilda:

- That is a likely scenario.

Michael:

- Okay. Then we should let Melchior and his army travel to the Divine Dimension. Once they are away from earth, we send a small force to contact the Zetans and try to form an alliance.

Hilda:

- What if the Zetans butcher this group as they did the last?

Michael:

- That won't happen. I would send someone skilled in diplomacy and avoiding conflict.

Hilda:

- And who would that be?

Michael:

- You are talking to him.

Hilda:

- You? But you have shunned all responsibility and power in the past.

Michael:

- I prioritised time with my family over scheming and greed. I could live a life in wealth and affluence without committing evil deeds. I stayed friends with everyone to avoid stress and fear of people scheming against me. That my friend is diplomacy in its purest form.

- Now I am 60 years old, my children are all grown up, and it's time to step up.

Hilda:

- You are right. I never thought about it that way.

- So, let's do it your way. Let's give Melchior the supplies he wants and give him free passage to the portals. But how do we sell it to the other factions?

Michael:

- We should hide our suspicions about Melchior's allegiance from the other factions. Besides, you don't think it's a coincidence that he threatens our capital, do you?

- The first Xeno invasion destroyed House Rashid. House Cheng, White and Bolivar have all suffered from the Xeno invasions in

China and Central America. And now our capital is under severe threat. That is not a coincidence, Melchior knows what he is doing.

Hilda Muller:

- Alright then. I will speak to Markus White and make him summon an emergency meeting in America. Let's give Melchior what he wants and get him out of here as soon as possible.

Having agreed with Michael, Hilda hurried to her office to contact House White and set up the emergency meeting.

# Chapter 31: Melchior Receives Instructions and Enters the Portals.

A few weeks later, Melchior overlooked his vast army, numbering almost a million men, which was gathered close to the portal in Rashidium. The spineless cowards in the Terran Council had bent over backwards to fulfil his demands. They had delivered enough food and supplies to last for a long campaign on the other side. Clearing the minefields near the portal had been tricky, but it was all done, and his army was ready to move.

Melchior got an overwhelming feeling that he might have forgotten something important. He needed to communicate with Rangda before leading his army into the portals. He summoned one of his captains:

Melchior:

- Captain Rodovic. I need to eat, and my cravings are for a young one.

Captain Rodovic:

- There is an orphanage not far away. We have stayed clear of it to avoid confrontation with the Terrans.

Melchior:

- Good. Go there and bring the children to me. Leave the employees unharmed. I want to avoid conflict with the Terrans for now, but my inner circle and I need to eat.

A while later, Captain Rodovic and his men came back, with a truck full of orphans. Melchior approached them:

- Did you acquire the children without incidents?

Captain Rodovic:

- Yes. We bribed the warden and his staff. 1000 Terran Credits in gold coins per child.

Melchior scoffed back:

- 1000 Terran Credits for a street urchin? Those Terrans are greedy!

Captain Rodovic:

- Yes. But we bought their silence. The employees will cover up what happened until we have entered the portals and left Earth. Besides, what use has gold on the other side? We are not greedy like the filthy Terrans.

Melchior:

- Correct. I'll pick that child for myself. I command you to distribute the other children among the men.

After consuming the youngest child, Melchior was licking the blood off his lips and started communicating with Rangda.
Melchior:

- We are ready to enter the portals, Empress Rangda. I had an overwhelming feeling that I had missed something, which is why I contacted you.

Rangda:

- Good. Trust your feelings. You need to make sure that the portals close behind you. I suspect that the Terrans only want your troops away from their cities. They plan to launch a counterattack, striking us in the back, as soon as they feel safe.

Melchior:

- Why would the Terrans attack us in the Divine Dimension?

Rangda:

- They are no fools. They must have figured out our connection. Thus, they know that you will attack them at some point.

Melchior:

- Yes, so let's attack them now. Commit your Xenos to a full-scale invasion!

Rangda lashed out with a psionic blast and knocked Melchior to the ground. She screeched at him:

- You fool. If I commit all the Xenos to an invasion of Earth, the Zetans will attack my flank.

- Follow my plan, it will work. I have foreseen it, and I have something you lack: Premonitions and foresight.

Melchior spewed up the blood he had ingested, and he spoke with a weak voice:

- Yes, Empress Rangda. I am sorry for my foolishness.
- But how do we reopen the portals if we close them?

Rangda:

- I know how to power up the portals from our end.

- Hurry up and set the portals to close after your men have walked through them. I will transmit the instructions to you telepathically.

After saying this, Rangda transmitted the instructions to Melchior. He would reverse the steps that Keila took when she opened the portals. The portals would close one day after the reversal process. This would leave Melchior with enough time to lead his troops through the portal.

# Chapter 32: Michael Reports to Hilda.

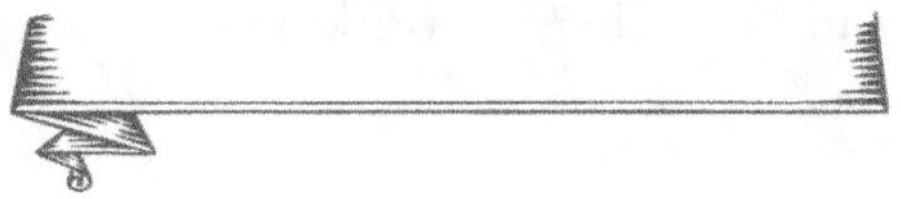

Hilda Muller was sitting at her desk when Michael Muller rushed into her office. Michael's appearance shocked Hilda as she had sent him on a diplomatic mission to the Zetans.

Hilda

- Michael? What's happening? Why are you here? Weren't you meant to form an alliance with the Zetans?

Michael:

- I was. We kept our distance, studying the portals from afar. We intended to move through portals the day the Martian Dominion moved through. We planned to use our cloaking devices, to move past the Martians unnoticed.

Hilda:

- I know the plan. What happened, Michael?

Michael:

- When we woke up, the portal had disappeared.

Hilda:

- Disappeared? We have tried to close those damn portals for years. How did this happen?

Michael:

- Well. You know those rooms with switches in the Central American, Pacific, Chinese and Egyptian pyramids?

Hilda:

- Yes, we had our best scientists working on it for years without any success.

Michael:

- I suspect that Melchior got the sequence to close the portals from Rangda.

Hilda:

- This proves that Melchior didn't go there to fight Rangda but to join her?

Michael:

- Scheisse! What do we do now?

Hilda:

- There isn't much we can do. We cannot send our troops to help the Zetans through the closed portals, and we can't figure out how to open the portals. All that's left is praying.

Michael:

- Praying? I didn't know you spent your time on superstitious nonsense?!

Hilda:

- I didn't use to. But after everything I have experienced, I don't know what to believe.

Hilda broke down and started crying. It confused Michael to see her this way as she usually kept calm. He decided to ask her:

- What's happening? Why are you crying?

Hilda:

- This is all my fault!

Michael:

- No, it's not. You did what you had to do. Our capital and millions of lives were at risk. You had to give in to Melchior's demands.

Hilda:

- I should have acted a long time ago.

- 18 months ago, Metatron, the leader of Eden, visited me with his daughter Sabina.

Michael:

- Why didn't we both take part in this crucial diplomatic meeting?

Hilda:

- Because I didn't expect the meeting to be important. Eden is a marginal fringe world. I am surprised that I even accepted their meeting request.

Michael:

- So, what happened during the meeting?

Hilda:

- Well, I had expected Metatron to ask for protection from the Terran Council, but he wasn't interested in joining us.

- Instead, Metatron was rude. He urged me to send the army to Divine Dimension and fight Rangda. I told him off and warned him about making demands.

Michael:

- Well, in retrospect, Metatron was right. But I wouldn't have listened to him either.

Hilda:

- What happened next have kept me awake for many nights. Sabina's eyes changed from green to a glowing blue shade. Her enchanting gaze glowed with bright light, and she spoke like an adult. She urged me to fight the Xenos.

- I freaked out and asked the AI to scan her for bionic implants, but she had none.

- Sabina claimed that The True Maker was speaking through her and that she was Keila Eisenstein's daughter.

- I freaked out and started screaming at her since she was our enemy's daughter. After this, Sabina reverted to a typical toddler.

- I expelled them and threatened to have them executed if they ever came back to Earth.

Michael:

- I see. Do you have the security footage of their visit?

Hilda:

- Yes, I do. AI, show Michael the security footage from my meeting with Jack Silver on the fifth of September 2876.

Michael studied the security footage, he sat silent for a long time until he spoke:

- Well, I understand why the outcome of this meeting has tormented you. But you shouldn't chastise yourself for what you did.

- All that you knew was that Sabina was the daughter of our mortal enemy and that something possessed her. For all you knew, Rangda could have controlled her.

Hilda:

- Yes. But after meeting Melchior, I realised that a kindred spirit influenced Sabina.

- I failed to do the right thing. I have doomed us all.

- How can I live with myself?

Michael:

- You better work to set things right. Killing yourself or giving up on life is not the right to do.

Hilda:

- But I don't know what to do?

Michael:

- Neither do I. But if The True Maker chose to speak to you, there must have been a reason, so find a way to set things right!

Hilda:

- You are right, Michael. I will set this right or die trying.
- Now, please pray with me.

Thus, for the first time in 600 years, The House Muller leadership prayed to a higher being. They prayed to the True Maker.

# Chapter 33: Sabina Convinces Metatron to Counteract Melchior's Evil

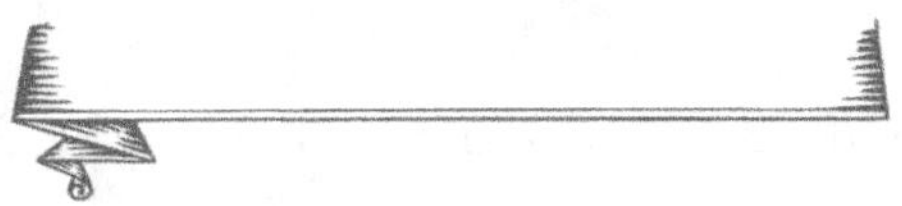

Metatron was watching Sabina play with her dolls when she burst into tears. He tried to comfort her when he noticed something majestic. Her eyes had once again transformed to shining crystal blue colour, albeit this time, her tears dimmed the light. Metatron hugged her and spoke:

- Sabina darling, what is wrong?

Sabina:

- That mean old man, Melchior. He and his bad men entered the portal to meet Rangda. This worries mummy and her friend, The True Maker.

Metatron:

- How come you speak like a child?

Sabina gave him a dumbfounded look and spoke:

- Daddy, I am a child. I am only four years old.

Metatron:

- Oh, I thought that The True Maker possessed you, as your cute little eyes have turned crystal blue.

Sabina:

- Papa, what does possess mean?

Metatron:

- That someone else is in your head, my sweet baby.

Sabina:

- Don't be silly, daddy. No-one else can fit in my head. I am so tiny.

- Anyways, while the mean bully Melchior makes people sad, I want to make people happy.

Metatron:

- That's good. How do you want to make people happy?

Sabina:

- By teaching what the True Maker taught me to other children. I can show them how to make people healthy and happy, papa!

Metatron:

- Okay. We can bring some children here tomorrow, and you can teach them.

Sabina:

- No!
- I want to live on Eden with the children that live there.

Metatron:

- But I am the leader of Eden. I must stay here.

Sabina:

- No, you don't have to, papa. The leader must live with the people. When the leader starts living away from the people, that is when the bad things begin to happen.

Metatron considered what Sabina was saying, and there was a lot of wisdom in it. But how would he rule from the surface? Metatron realised that he shouldn't govern, he should lead by example.
Metatron:

- You're right, darling. Tomorrow we'll build a new house in the village and move to Eden as a family.

Sabina:

- Good. I can't wait to make all these new friends. Thank you, daddy. I love you.

Metatron:

- I love you too, sweetheart.
- Time to sleep. We will have a busy day tomorrow.

Having tucked Sabina in, Metatron had a realisation. That he and most religious people had been wrong all along. They had worshipped the false gods. A proper god would never have lived above the humans, commanding them and forcing their obedience. A decent god, should live among them and guide them in their everyday lives. This was how religious worship had worked among the earliest humans, and this was the correct way of interacting with deities.

As soon as humankind had put their deities on pedestals above them, they also started to act this way among themselves. This caused humanity's leaders to lead with commands and fear. Sabina had shown that a deity could be on the same level as their fellow humans. It was a change to the original human condition, and Metatron couldn't wait to see how things would turn out!

# Chapter 34: A Secret Meeting with Rangda.

A few weeks later, Melchior was meeting up with Rangda in the Divine Dimension. Melchior didn't understand the need for secrecy, but he decided to follow suit and did as Rangda directed. They met in a building next to an unpowered portal. The portal led to a planet that got destroyed in the multi-millennial war.

Rangda spoke:

- Hehehe!! Behold, this is the portal to Proxima Zetani. A beautiful planet immolated in a matter of seconds by our mighty Xenos.

Melchior:

- Interesting, but what relevance does it have to the mission?

Rangda:

- Don't bother!

- You might be wondering why we are meeting in secret when we are leading the two most massive armies around here?

Melchior:

- Yes. I had pictured our first meeting to be a lot grander.

Rangda:

- Yes, marvellous isn't it. Humanity and the Xenos united, fighting against their former oppressors, the Zetans.

- But marvel and beauty don't win wars. Treachery does.

Melchior:

- I don't understand. When we spoke via telepathy, you said that there were only a few thousand Zetans left?

Rangda:

- Numbers mean nothing. A large group of well-armed Terrans got into conflict with a small group of Zetans a few years back. At the end of their battle, most of the Terrans were dead, killed by the Zetans.

- Their ill-fated scuffle helped us as we could move in and wipe out the tired Zetans and absorb their souls. We kept a few of the Terrans alive as prisoners for information about Earth.

- They taught me about the Terran mindset, and that is why I told you to close the portals. The Terrans would have come after us, once their cities were out of harm's way.

Melchior:

- Yes, covering your rear is crucial in warfare. But how do we get back to Earth?

Rangda:

- I can use my primordial Zeto Crystals to power up the portal. But this won't be relevant for many years. We got lots of work ahead of us.

- First, we must fool the Zetans that your army has come from Mars to help them. You need to infiltrate their ranks and become their 'friend'.

Melchior:

- And how would we do that?

Rangda:

- We stage a fight. We make sure that some of your Martians fight some of my Xenos in a battle. The battle needs to be visible from the Zetans fortress, Ultima Zetani.

Melchior:

- But wouldn't this waste our troops for nothing?

Rangda:

- No, it's the only way to convince the Zetans that you have come to help them. Flushing the Zetans out from their fortress Ultima Zetani is almost impossible. They have a defensive psionic barrier preventing us from even approaching it.

- While sacrificing thousands of troops is costly to us, it will convince the Zetans to trust you.

Melchior:

- You are certainly an evil genius. But what do I do once they trust me?

Rangda:

- Well, first of all, you'll need to hide your real face. Our plan won't work if the Zetans detects your Xeno mutations. Use the Zetan External DNA modifier to give yourself a pleasing human appearance.

- You need to convince the Zetans to come out with their army to aid you in the decisive battle against the Xenos. Do whatever you have to do to convince them. Worship them, promise them Mars and the eternal worship of humanity, even let them take command of your army. It doesn't matter.

- The Zetans will lead your army to a final pitched battle against the Xenos. They have waited a decade for this opportunity since my escape from captivity.

- This is when you betray them. Stab the Zetans in the back, lay down a barrage upon them and corner them while my Xenos storm in and wipe them out. They'll have nowhere to run.

Melchior:

- Excellent plan.

Rangda:

- I know.

- I can see myself in you, Melchior. But don't ever consider crossing me, or you'll regret ever being born.

Melchior:

- I wouldn't expect anything less from you, Empress Rangda!

Rangda:

- Good. Choose a dispensable part of your army to face my troops in battle outside Ultima Zetani in five days.

Melchior:

- Yes, Rangda. May it be a glorious battle!

After saying this, Melchior entered his stealth-hovercraft and returned to his army camp.

# Chapter 35: An Honourable Mission.

Melchior approached General George Smith. He would send him on the suicide mission, that Melchior had schemed with Rangda. George Smith and his army, the 13th Reconnaissance Division were the perfect candidates for the task. They were volunteers from the Martian Humanist Alliance, and they upheld the values of the Martian Revolution.

George's values Bravery, compassion and equality, were values that definitely mismatched with Melchior's values. Furthermore, Melchior hadn't infused George's men with any Xeno DNA, and they were still 100 % human. Melchior approached George:

- General Smith. I have an important mission for you.

- I will send your division on a diplomatic mission to the Zetan stronghold of Ultima Zetani. I want you to approach the Zetans about an alliance against our Xeno enemies.

George:

- You have been very secretive these last few years Emperor Dorevitch.

- Why are we here? What purpose does our trip to this strange place have when our enemies are the Terran Council on Earth?

Melchior:

- I am sorry for keeping you in the dark, George. As you know, there are many spies and enemies of the revolution, so I had to keep my inner circle small.

- I plan to ally with the Zetans. Together with the Zetans, we'll find a way to kill the leader of the Xenos, Rangda. Without their leader, the Xenos are mindless beasts. We can take control of them and send them through the portals to Earth to decimate our enemies before taking what is ours.

- I have infused myself with Xeno DNA as the Xenos will only follow other Xenos or Xeno hybrids. Rangda, the current Xeno leader, is, in fact, a Xeno-Zetan hybrid.

George:

- But why won't the Xenos lead themselves?

Melchior:

- They are hive-minded creatures. They share their consciousness with their leader. When they lead themselves, they are primitive beasts leading primitive beasts. The blind leading the blind.

George:

- I see. But wouldn't unleashing the full extent of the Xeno hordes upon Earth cause the death of millions of innocents?

Melchior:

- Yes, and that is our plan. The Terran Council tried to wipe us out twice during the Revolutionary War. It's time for them to taste their own bitter medicine.

George:

- Yes. Sometimes acting evil against evil people is the only option.
- But why am I bringing a whole division on a diplomatic mission?

Melchior:

- To show the Zetans your prominence and importance. Come with a few men, and they'll think you are nobody. Arrive there with 10,000 soldiers, and they'll help you fight the Xenos!

George:

- You are correct, Emperor Dorevitch. I'll get my men ready, and I'll travel there as soon as possible.

After George Smith had left, Melchior pondered what he had told his general. It had been a lie meant to deceive George and send him into a trap, but it was also a real possibility. Melchior didn't care for Rangda, or her mindless hordes of Xenos. If he could throw them into the chopper with the help from the Zetans, that was also a golden opportunity. All that mattered was his own might and power, and Melchior didn't know what the Zetans had to offer yet. Such exciting times ahead of him but for now he had to wait and see. Melchior opened a can of animal blood, and he sipped it while smiling to himself.

# Chapter 36: The Xenos butcher George's army within the Zetans' view.

Odin and Shiva were playing a game of telekinetic chess when Balder approached them with an important message. They woke up from their meditative state, and Odin spoke:

- What is it, Balder?
- I have told you to not disturb me unless it's important.

Balder:

- I'm sorry, Odin. A Martian General is waiting outside our gate, seeking an audience. He must be important as he oversees a large army and is seeking help.

Odin:

- The last time we had contact with anyone outside of our realm, it led to the death of my son and your brother, Thor. What planetary council is he from?

Balder:

- He is from the Martian Dominion, dear father.

Odin:

- Mars. These Martian humans have travelled a long way.
- Hmmm... something is not right. Tell the general to go away.

Shiva interrupted the conversation and spoke:

- No, Odin. We need any help we can get. The Martian humans have brought supplies, fuel, and battle spaceships. Resources that we can commandeer and use against the Xenos.

Odin:

- I don't trust them. I can sense thousands of Xenos hiding nearby. As soon as we lower the psionic shields, the beasts will attack us.

Balder:

- But father, this might be our best chance in years to turn the tide in this war.

Odin:

- Silence! I am your father, and my decision stands. Now tell the Martian humans to leave.

Balder went down and told the Martians to leave. After a while, Odin saw how the Martian army was moving away from the Ultima Zetani fortress.

Odin kept studying the Martians as they left, and he saw how a Xeno army ambushed the Martian army. A brutal battle ensued, and Odin felt guilty over sending their potential ally away.

Odin made a decision. He would not let the Xenos win this battle. He would show them some of his Zetan power and give them hell.

Odin shouted:

- Balder. Assemble my Valhalla warriors! We will save the Martian army and give the filthy Xenos what they deserve!

Balder:

- But father? What about the risk of them ambushing us if we lower down our psionic barriers?

Odin:

- There are not that many Xenos around to worry about. The Xenos are killing the Martian army, which means we must help the Martians.

Balder:

- Are you admitting to being wrong before?

Odin:

- A wise man must be able to change his opinion, in the light of a better outcome.

- Now hurry up and gather our troops so we can help the Martians.

The Zetans lowered the psionic forcefield and opened the gates. Odin and Balder assembled their Valhalla warriors, and they hurried to the battlefield!

# Chapter 37: A Late Arrival

An hour later, Odin and his Valhalla warriors entered the battlefield to aid the Martian army. As it turned out, they came too late. The only thing for them to do, was to battle the Xenos that were busy eating the fallen. The Zetans took the Xenos by surprise and defeated them without any problems.

Odin studied the equipment of the fallen human soldiers. He found it strange that most of the soldiers carried small calibre guns, unsuitable for fighting the Xenos. Small calibre guns couldn't pierce the Xenos thick skin, deep enough to kill the beasts. Why would the Martian military send such an army with unsuitable weaponry to fight the Xenos? The Terrans had repelled the Xeno invasion, so they should know what weapons would work against the Xenos. Odin approached Balder to discuss his findings.

Odin:

- Something is not right here. Look at these unsuitable weapons that the Martian soldiers were using.

Balder:

- Yes, these Martians were not equipped to fight the Xenos. Batons, Tasers and sub-machine guns. All ineffective against the Xenos. It looks like they were going to combat Terran civilians.

Odin:

- I am thinking about the same thing. Weren't the filthy Terrans that killed Thor much better equipped than this?

Balder:

- Yes, but those were from House Muller Special Forces. Look at this emblem: The Martian Dominion.

Odin:

- That's how it seems. Look, their general is lying over there. He looks wounded, but he is still alive. Let's go and save him.

Odin walked over to the wounded General George Smith. A chopped-off Xeno claw pinned the General the ground. Odin approached George and spoke:

- So, you are the foolish General who led your troops into an ambush?

George groaned back:

- Help me. The pain is insufferable.

Odin:

- Coward! The pain shall serve as a reminder of your stupidity.

- Unfortunately, I need to talk to you, and you won't talk much if you're dead. So, I'll give you a new chance at life!

Having said this, Odin pulled out the Xeno claw from George Smith's body. Then he released some Zetan healing powder into the wound, and the pain was gone.

Odin:

- I have helped you with your pain. Now speak and be honest; otherwise, I'll kill you myself! Understood?

George nodded, and Odin continued talking:

- Tell me who you are, and why you brought your army to my fortress?

George:

- I am George Smith. I am a general of the Martian Dominion and I am in charge of the 13th Reconnaissance division. At least I was until this happened.

- I came to negotiate an alliance on behalf of Melchior Dorevitch, The Emperor of the Martian Dominion. He wants to kill the Xenos and put an end to Rangda.

Odin:

- And why would Melchior want to do this?

George:

- I don't know. You better talk to him yourself. I just follow orders. I went to Earth believing that we would fight the Terran Council. Melchior equipped us for fighting urban warfare, not for fighting man-eating aliens.

Odin:

- I see. Go back to Melchior and tell him to bring his army, I'll discuss an alliance with him when he arrives. The Zetans have been fighting the Xenos for millennia, and we help those who are willing to fight the Xenos with us.

- I'll keep the supplies and equipment of your fallen soldiers. I have more use for it than you do.

George:

- Understood. I'll gather the survivors and head back to our camp. Thank you for saving our lives.

After saying this, George gathered his injured soldiers and his decimated division took off. Odin studied the Zetans scavenging the battlefield when Balder approached him:

- What do you reckon, father? There is something fishy going on here?

Odin:

- Yes. But we must take our chances and ally with the Martians. We need them to beat the Xenos. We cannot win the war without them. We have lost too many to the Xenos, and only a few of us remain.

Balder:

- Understood, father.

After the conversation, Odin went back to the fortress to meditate. What a dilemma he was in. Either he would ally with the underequipped Martian expeditionary force, or he would be stuck in this fortress forever.

# Chapter 38: An Alliance Between Melchior and Odin.

Melchior studied himself in the hologram generator. He noticed that he looked handsome, much more appealing than his real Xeno/human appearance. This was because the Zetan DNA modifier had changed his external appearance. Changing his appearance to become more human-like was imperative as the Zetans would never trust him if he looked like a Xeno. The change had one drawback though, he felt starving, and he was thirsting for blood and raw meat. Keeping his urges in check was challenging. It was as difficult as enduring the pain that he had suffered when he altered his genome to become a Martian-Xeno hybrid. But doing so, was Melchior's only option.

Melchior had ordered his inner circle to stay away. He could not change everyone's appearances, and besides he wanted to minimise the risk that the Zetans exposed him.

Melchior studied Odin, who approached him to negotiate. He was an impressive sight, looking like a high technology version of a Norse God. Odin spoke as he approached Melchior:

- You must be Melchior; George told me that you needed our help with battling the Xenos.

Melchior felt irritated, and he desired to kill the pompous-looking Zetan. But then Melchior remembered what Rangda had told him, that the easiest way to coax a Zetan was to stroke his ego.
Melchior

- Yes, we came to save humanity from the fearsome Xenos. Someone with your skills and experience would be an excellent ally.

Odin:

- Good. Since the Zetans created humanity, I will take command of your army. I don't want any more debacles with improper equipment and soldiers running into ambushes.

Melchior was furious with Odin's arrogance and disdain. Apparently, all the Zetans still lived under the idea that they were superior to humans and deserved to be their gods. The notion was wrong. The only thing that the Zetans had done was to alter the human genome roughly 70,000 years ago. They had imbued early Homo Sapiens with alien intelligence to enable a heightened state of mind. After that, the rest had happened by itself. The Zetans had neglected the existence of humanity for almost 65,000 years, until they had decided to become our deities. The Zetans only motive to re-emerge on Earth, was because they needed soldiers for their catastrophic war against the Xenos. Fighting to calm himself down, Melchior spoke with a suppressed growling voice:

- Hmmm.... yes. Letting the Zetans be in control is the best option.
- What is your command, Master Odin?

Odin:

- Our priority is to hunt down and kill Rangda. She is a Zetan/Xeno hybrid, and the only one with intelligence among the Xeno horde. With Rangda out of the way, disposing of the remaining Xenos is big game hunting.

- With the vehicles and fuel that you brought, Rangda cannot outrun us any longer. We will find her and destroy her.

Melchior:

- Excellent plan. And what will be my reward?

Odin:

- Your service to us will be much appreciated, and we will make sure that you get a good afterlife.

Melchior:

- That's very generous of you, Master Odin. I must take my leave and instruct the others to serve you.

Odin:

- Good. Be on your way, human. I'll summon you later.

Melchior was furious with Odin and the rest of the Zetans. That arrogant, self-righteous creature had treated him like dirt when he should have treated him as a saviour. If Odin couldn't see that the Zetans needed Melchior's army more than he needed them, he was blind, and he deserved Melchior's betrayal.

Melchior calmed down. In a way, what had happened was ideal. He would no longer need to worry about which side to follow, now that the choice was so obvious. Odin would regret his smug grin when Melchior stabbed him in the back and then ate him alive!

# Chapter 39: A Mysterious Female Visitor.

The following day, a stunningly beautiful woman arrived at the gates to Melchior's camp. Her beauty mesmerised the guards, so they forgot to consider how she got there in the first place. Captain Rodovic approached her:

- Hello. Can I be of any assistance?

Beautiful woman:

- Yes, I am Helen Barnes. I have an appointment with Melchior. He is expecting me.

Captain Rodovic:

- Melchior hasn't told me about any visitors, are you sure?

Helen:

- Yes. Please take me to him, and he'll make sure that you get rewarded for your duty.

Captain Rodovic:

- Thank you, miss. I will take you to him at once!

At first, Melchior was annoyed when Captain Rodovic disturbed him. But he changed his mind when he saw how beautiful Helen was.
Melchior

- Thank you, Captain, for sending this beautiful lady to me. I'll reward you for your duty.

- Leave me alone with this woman. We have some things to discuss.

Captain Rodovic left the room, and Melchior walked over to Helen and spoke:

- So, tell me, Helen. Who are you and who sent you?

Helen:

- You know who I am.

Melchior sniffed at Helen's body and then he closed his eyes. Melchior:

- Yes

- Whose DNA are you using? Your beauty is so mesmerising, so my captain forgot the absurdity of a stranger approaching this camp.

Helen:

- I am using the DNA of Helen of Troy. She was the most beautiful human female of all times. The Zetans created her as an experiment to see how far men would go, fighting over one woman.

Melchior:

- Pretty far, I suppose?

Helen:

- Yes. One of the biggest wars in antiquity was about her. You can read about it in the Iliad.

Melchior:

- I am not much of reader. But tell me; what do you think a man like me, would like to do with a woman like you?

Helen:

- Copulate?

Melchior:

- Good girl, you know us far too well.

Helen:

- Yes, and it will be an excellent diversion as well. Let's do it.

After that, Melchior and Helen proceeded to have very rough and very loud sex. During the act, Melchior made turned on the public announcement system, so that everyone would know that they were fucking.

# Chapter 40: Odin and Balder Meet with Helen.

Odin was sitting in his command module, making battle plans when his son Balder came in. Odin spoke:

- Greetings, Balder. Have you heard anything from your siblings Frey and Freya yet?

Balder:

- Yes, they are coming back soon. They have travelled around in our space shuttle. They have been able to contact all the other Zetan factions. Ra, Athena, Vishnu, Buddha, and Tlaloc are all coming, and they are bringing their troops.

Odin:

- Tlaloc and the Aztec gods? I haven't heard from them in over a millennium. Are they still violent and blood-thirsty?

Balder:

- Yes, so it would seem.

Odin:

- Excellent, we can use their ferocity against the Xenos.

Balder:

- Yes, there is another thing. Someone has sent a Zetan spy, masked as Helen of Troy to seduce and spy on Melchior.

Odin:

- Yes, I felt an unidentified Zetan presence in the camp. I suppose she was successful? The Helen of Troy DNA sequence is irresistible to human males.

Balder:

- Indeed, she was. They were copulating within ten minutes.

Odin:

- Pfft. Not a very talented spy. She would gain a lot more withholding the sex, driving Melchior insane with desire first. No matter, find her and summon her to me. I'd like to speak to her myself.

Balder left the room, and a while later he returned, bringing Helen back to his father. Helen kneeled to Odin and spoke:

- You summoned me, Master Odin?

Odin:

- Yes. I know that you are a Zetan spy, sent to seduce and spy on Melchior. I need to know who you are working for.

Helen:

- Master Odin, I am loyal to my master, and I will not expose mine or his identity.

Odin:

- I could force the truth out of you.

Helen:

- Yes. But bear in mind that Melchior is head over heels in love
with me. I doubt that he would appreciate that you torture his
bride to be.

Helen showed Odin an exquisite engagement ring that she wore on her
finger, and she dominated him with her cold gaze. Odin winced and broke.
Realising that Helen was not susceptible to his threats, he tried a more diplomatic approach.

- Let's not get carried away. I will leave your secret with you. But
may I ask that you share any information you get with us? We are
in this together, after all.

Helen spoke back to Odin with an arrogant tone:

- I'll share whatever information that I find suitable to share with
you, Master Odin. Now I must leave. I have a private bathing session planned with my fiancée Melchior.

Odin:

- Okay, Helen. Have it your way. But I'll be watching you.

Helen:

- And I will be watching you, Odin. Tread carefully!

Having said this, Helen left Odin's command module, with Odin feeling
ambivalent. It was a good thing that he had a spy near Melchior, as he wasn't
confident that Melchior was trustworthy. But who was she, and who did she
serve? Restless and tired, Odin went to bed, but his worries kept him awake,
bereaving him of any sleep that night.

# Chapter 41: Odin Sends Frey and Freya on a Mission to Earth.

A few days later, Frey and Freya returned to Melchior's army base, and they went to Odin's command module to report. They bowed to their father as they entered, and Frey started talking:

- Great news, dear father. We have convinced all the Zetan factions to join our army for the coming final battle against the Xenos. All of the leadership and most of the remaining Zetan armies are coming, totalling over 5,000 Zetan elite warriors. They are being transported here by Martian transport shuttles as we speak.

Odin:

- Good job, my children. I knew that I could trust you.

- I have another mission for you. You are to make your way to Earth and seek an alliance with the Terran Council.

Frey:

- But isn't the Terran Council the enemy of the Martian Dominion?

Odin:

- Yes, but allying with both the major human factions is an insurance policy against either of them turning against us.

Freya:

- Understood, father. So, do you also have a bad feeling about this Melchior guy?

Odin:

- He is hiding something, but he is our only chance. Besides, the food and supplies he brought have helped us revitalise. Fighting a war, while starving, was never a good option.

Frey:

- You are right, father. But how do we open the portals back to Earth?

Odin:

- Here is a replicated Zeto Crystal. I made it from the supplies that the humans brought. It contains enough power to open the portal for a few minutes.

- To return here, create a new crystal once you are on earth.

Freya:

- Thank you, father. we will be on our way!

Having said that, Frey and Freya kissed Odin on the cheek and said farewell, never to see him again.

# Chapter 42: A Vast Xeno Army en route to Attack the Zetans.

Odin was sitting on a throne and studied the other Zetan leaders that had assembled. It was the first general assembly of the Zetan leadership in seven years. After Rangda's escape from her eternal prison and the emergence of the Xeno hordes, the Zetans had crammed into fortresses. In their forts, the Zetans combined psionic capabilities could create impenetrable force fields. But packing into strongholds, starving and keeping their mental guards up was not a good way to live. So, the Zetans felt relieved when Melchior's army had arrived, and provided the Zetans with food and drinks.

Odin raised his beer tankard and spoke:

- How delightful is this, after 2,000 years of thirsting we can finally assemble again to enjoy food and drinks. Enjoy the Terran wine and beer and rejoice that our luck has finally turned.

A loud cheer broke out, and Ra spoke:

- Cheers that we have all gathered today. Odin, what is our battle plan?

Odin:

- We must unite and kill Rangda. Once she is dead, The Xenos are mindless beasts and wiping them out will be an easy task.

- Any news about the Xeno movements, dear Vishnu?

Vishnu:

- Our spy drones show that the Xenos are gathering their forces. They are preparing for a final battle, and there seems to be over a million of them in total.

- The strange part is that Rangda is missing. Deciphering Xeno conversations, it seems like two Xeno leaders, Gumboll and Dingil have killed her and usurped power.

Odin:

- How is that possible?? I thought the Xenos were loyal to her, and that Rangda had them under her complete domination.

- Regardless, I need to see her body to verify her death. I am not falling for any more of her ploys.

The appearance of a Zetan guard interrupted the meeting:

- Masters, I have urgent news!

- The entire Xeno army, totalling over a million Xenos, is rushing towards us. They are 300 kilometres away running at full speed. We expect them to reach us in three to four hours.

Odin:

- Excellent. This is the day we have been waiting for. The Xenos will run straight into our trap. Once we have dealt with the Xenos, we can finally return to Earth. We'll become humanity's gods yet again! Prepare the soldiers. This will be a glorious day!

After Odin had spoken, everyone left the room in a hurry. There were 5,000 Zetans and almost a million human soldiers so it would take some time to get everyone ready.

# Chapter 43: Helen and Melchior Plan Their Move.

Helen and Melchior were overlooking the Martian Dominion military camp in the Divine Dimension. It would take another one and half hours for the Xenos to arrive at Ultima Zetani, and the battle preparations were in full swing. There was a ring of ruckus, and soldiers encircled the entire base. Most of the Zetan elite soldiers had gathered in front of the main gate where Odin expected the Xenos to hit the hardest. But there were also Zetans present in the dispersed individual army groups guarding the fort. The individual warriors wore thick armour, and lightweight nanotechnology fibreglass shields and they were armed with plasma swords or plasma spears.

Elevated behind the melee formations, Melchior had placed Martian troops with autocannons, laser rifles, and grenade launchers. In the centre of the base, there were large numbers of howitzers firing at the Xenos from afar. Hovering over the base, there were hundreds of Martian aircrafts prepared to wreak havoc on the Xenos from above.

Helen:

- Impressive fortifications. The Xenos must be foolish to attack, such as an impenetrable fortress. Unless of course, they have trump on hand.

Melchior:

- Yes, they would indeed. I am curious about the time of their attack. I thought they would wait a bit longer?

Helen:

- I thought so too, but then I found out that Odin sent his children to forge a secret alliance with the Terran Council. Such an association would make things... unpredictable.

Melchior:

- Damn him! I knew that I couldn't trust him.

Helen:

- I am sure he feels the same way about you.

Melchior:

- I am sure he does.

- The Xenos are within range for our artillery. How do I make our artillery miss, without making it look suspicious?

Helen:

- You don't. Fire at the Xenos. Make it look normal. The Xenos are sturdier than Martian humans, so while direct hits will kill some of them, the shrapnel and the shockwaves won't impede the others.

Melchior:

- As you wish, my beautiful queen!

Helen:

- As I wish, my mighty king. Gather your inner circle. We will make our real move in an hour.

Hearing this, Melchior smiled a sinister smile and rushed off to find his inner circle, preparing for the last step of his plan.

# Chapter 44: Melchior's Betrayal: The Slaughter of the Zetans

Minutes before the battle, Melchior, Helen and Melchior's inner circle entered the Zetan command centre. Odin, Ra, Vishnu, Buddha and Tlaloc were overlooking the battlefield. Odin saw them arrive and spoke:

- Melchior, I must ask you and your bodyguards to leave.

- Helen, I have been expecting you. Have you come to tell us what you found out from spying on Melchior?

Helen:

- That's not why I am here!

After saying this, Helen swiftly threw five plasma throwing knives at the Zetans, burning and injuring them. Melchior's bodyguards rushed in and struck the Zetans with their plasma swords, incapacitating them.
Odin yelled out:

- What are you doing, Melchior?? You doomed yourself and your army, the other Zetans will slaughter you for this outrage!

Melchior:

- I don't think so. You see, I picked the perfect opportunity to take you out.

Melchior lifted a command phone and spoke, his voice echoed out over the base:

- Soldiers of the Martian Dominion. The Zetans are our enemy, and the Xenos are our ally. Attack the Zetans militants with full force. Fire at will!

Once Melchior had broadcast this order, all the Martians fired at the Zetan army from the rear. Meanwhile, the Xenos attacked the Zetans from the front. It was a massacre, and the Zetans couldn't do anything to save themselves. Odin witnessed how the Xenos tore the Zetan army into shreds. Tears ran down Odin's cheeks and he realised that the end of the Zetans was near.

Odin got up and spoke:

- Melchior, why are you doing this?

- You will never be able to control the Xenos. You'll bring doom to humankind.

Melchior:

- I don't think so. I have saved mankind from Zetan enslavement and servitude! I am sure that my queen, Rangda, will be able to dominate the Milky Way, now that Zetans are dead. Or what do you say, Rangda?

Helen deactivated her Zetan external DNA modifier, and Rangda appeared laughing maniacally:

- Ahaha-ha ha-haha!! Odin, I cannot believe that you were as stupid as Brahma! You could sense that I was a Zetan, but despite that, you couldn't realise who I was.

- Zetan leaders, you all thought I was a Zetan spy sent by another Zetan faction. Your mistrust for each other stopped you from reaching the logical conclusion. This was exactly as I expected! Ahaha-haha!!

- You pride yourself as being superior beings compared to all the other life forms of the universe. Yet, you have the same vices and desires as all living beings in the galaxy. Without the Zeto crystals uniting you, there is nothing that sets you apart from the humans or the Xenos!

- The corrupted Zeto crystals that I possess will bind every planet and every dimension under my rule. Under my rule, the innate desire to fight, kill, rape, and procreate is not shunned upon, but encouraged. You are even allowed to eat one another!

Some of the Zetans tried to get up, but they were severely wounded, so Melchior's bodyguards could hold them down. Rangda fetched her corrupted Zeto Crystals. Using the power of the dark crystals, she shattered the souls of her Zetan victims, blowing up their heads in the process. When Rangda had finished, she laughed and spoke:

- Have a feed, men. Zetan flesh is the most delicious flesh in the universe. You have deserved it. Hee-hee-hee!!

Hearing this, Melchior and his bodyguards savaged the headless bodies of Zetans. They had hidden their hunger for weeks, and they were starving!

# Chapter 45: Sabina Breaks Down.

On the 15th of March 2878, Sabina was playing with her younger siblings, Jasmine and Jordan, when terrible premonitions struck her.

Sabina saw all the carnage that had happened in the Divine Dimension, and she felt Keila's agony and pain. The Zetans had fallen to Melchior's and Rangda's evil schemes. With the Zetans gone, there was no-one left that could stand against the combined malevolent powers of Melchior and Rangda.

Sabina sensed Keila's immeasurable guilt and suffering. Keila had acted with good intentions, wanting justice, and freedom for her people on Mars. But Keila had had listened to the wrong guidance, and she had released Rangda upon the world. Keila had promoted Melchior when the Martians were fighting against Terrans, and that decision had proven to be a fatal mistake.

Keila suffered from spending years in captivity with no end in sight. Alone with her thoughts, she lived in constant guilt over what she had caused to her beloved planet and people.

Sabina saw Keila's prison cell. She saw Rangda, feasting on the flesh of a dead Zetan. Rangda turned around, and she met Sabina's gaze. Rangda hissed and laughed menacingly:

- We finally meet, Sabina. I have been waiting for your psionic signal to be strong enough for me to pick it up. You must be growing stronger, day by day.

Sabina:

- What are you doing to my mother? You have used her to reach your goals. Let her move on and die in peace.

Rangda:

- So, you are asking me to kill your own mother? The prophesized girl, the chosen one, is advocating matricide? Hmmm.... interesting.

Sabina:

- I would ask you to let her go, but your evil nature wouldn't even consider that option.

Rangda:

- Oh, but you're wrong, little girl. The moment I release your mother from the stasis she is going to hurt herself or someone else. I am extending her life.

Sabina:

- But keeping her alive is crueller than letting her move on.

Rangda smirked and replied:

- Yes, but it is well-deserved cruelty. Her action caused the death of millions, and more will follow. Mars is dying from the ecological damage caused by the wars and Melchior's environmental destruction. Melchior's genetic experiments have created a new breed, Xeno-Martians. We will overrun Earth when the time is right. I will attack Eden last.

- Because of Keila's actions, humanity as you know it will cease to exist. That, Sabina, is a good reason for your mother to suffer.

Sabina:

- But you manipulated her. You caused all her actions. You are the evil one.

Rangda:

- Oh, am I evil? I am spreading my species over the galaxy. It's called survival of the fittest. A new dawn is upon us all. Gone is the Zetans harmful rules and ideas. Behold the future of my Xeno dominion!

Rangda went over to a dead Zetan and pulled a bit of flesh from its body with her sharp teeth. She stared into the eyes of Sabina and hissed:

- Delicious, but not as delicious as you will be, little girl. I understand why I upset Melchior when I forced him to forfeit you as his prey. No one can resist your delicate skin and tasty flesh.

The paralysed Keila had seen enough. She sent off a psionic blast that knocked herself and Sabina unconscious. This severed Sabina's connection with Rangda, as Rangda could only connect with Sabina using Keila as a host.

Shortly afterwards, Melissa rushed into the room where Sabina lay unconscious. As Sabina woke up, she was inconsolable, and no matter what Melissa tried to do, she kept screaming and crying. Sabina's younger siblings Jasmine and Jordan approached her, and together they soothed Sabina's mind. They healed Sabina with the rejuvenating magic that The True Maker had instructed Sabina to teach her younger siblings.

Sabina:

- Thank you, Jasmine and Jordan, for saving my mind from the darkness.

Jasmine:

- No, we are thanking you. You cannot save everyone on your own, Sabina. We need to work together to protect what matters, the future of the Milky Way Galaxy!

After saying this, they all sunk down in deep trancelike meditation, hoping to find the strength to resist evil. Melissa felt confused, and she left the room, but she understood that her children were in good hands.

Melissa realised that she had unique children. Melissa thanked the True Maker and she was proud over her children, knowing that they would achieve great things.

# Chapter 46: Dov Dorevitch Releases a Deadly Virus on Mars.

Dov Dorevitch, the brother of Melchior Dorevitch, was sitting in his command room on Mars. Various maps and figures were beeping on the displays in the room, and it wasn't encouraging news. With Dov in charge, Melchior's empire was falling apart.

Dov's enemies on Mars had figured out how to remove the Zetan mind-control microchips from the Martian population. Dov's problem was, that while he could connect to his subjects' minds and kill anyone who dissented against him, the workload was too much. Like any human, Dov needed to sleep and rest, and that's when the rebels had the opportunity to strike.

Dov studied the map of Mars and sighed. Six months ago, his brother had controlled all of Mars, and now they had lost most of their territories. Dov's only relief was that the rebels also fought amongst themselves, which stopped them from uniting against him. Yet, his territories were dwindling by the day, and it was likely that the Terran Council would come after him because of what his brother did. Dov knew that House Muller would seek revenge for Melchior's threat to destroy their capital.

There was a knock on the door, and Dov's Chief Scientist Frank Van Stein entered the room. Dov gave him a sullen look and spoke:

- Dr Van Stein, what are you doing here? You are not invited to the upcoming military strategy meeting.

Frank smirked at Dov and spoke:

- Don't worry about the military briefing. As a matter of fact, I have come to tell you to cancel it.

Dov:

- Who are you to give me orders? And besides, you're asking me to cancel a military briefing during an emergency. Are you insane?

Frank:

- We both know that you cannot win this battle with your military might. That ship has sailed. Attend that meeting, and you'll find that half of those commanders will not attend. Some of them have betrayed us and have joined our enemies.

Dov:

- Did you come here to say anything useful, or to spread salt in my wounds?

Frank:

- I am sure you'll find that I have a few aces up my sleeve.

- Melchior predicted that you might fuck up and he told me to work on something that would ensure our control.

Having said this, Frank Van Stein pulled up a vial with a bluish liquid from the pocket of his lab coat. Frank smiled and spoke:

- This vial contains the future for mankind!

Dov was going to say something when a nearby explosion shook the building and knocked him to the ground. Frank stood still in the room, and seemed unaffected.

- It seems like Colonel Slavonic has turned against you, Dov. I'd say you are losing control over the Martian Dominion.

Dov:

- You knew of Colonel Slavonic's betrayal, and yet you did nothing. I should have you executed for treason.

Frank:

- You could. But executing me would also doom yourself. You'll be overrun within days, and then you'll have to make a choice. Stay here and die, or run and face Melchior's wrath when he returns. Which one do you prefer?

Dov:

- I suppose that you are offering me a third option, in exchange for your life?

Frank:

- I am not afraid of dying, but yes, I am offering a third choice to give us a glorious future.

- This vial contains an airborne virus capable of altering the human DNA, and inserting specific Xeno DNA sequences into our veins.

Dov:

- So, are you going to release a virus that transforms our population into a bunch of man-eating beasts? Tell me, how is the Zombie Apocalypse going to benefit us?

Frank scoffed at Dov and looked at him with disdain, before addressing him with a derogatory tone:

- Bah. The Zombie Apocalypse. What a load of rubbish. You should know that zombies contradict all elementary biology. Don't bother me with that rubbish.

- SIT DOWN, and I will explain how this is going to work.

Another explosion rattled the building and the speechless and dumb-founded Dov got seated. Frank spoke again:

- Good! Melchior told me that you would come to your senses.

- The synthetic air-borne virus that I intend to spread is going to revolutionise mankind by altering all our citizens to Xeno-Martians. The Xeno-Martian hybrids are ferocious and powerful like the Xenos. But they are not mindless and have thoughts of their own. After all, your brother had the same mutations, and he still had his wits around him.

Dov:

- Well, he changed though. I never understood the desire for blood and eating his captives alive.

Frank:

- Such is the Xeno way. But don't worry; fearsome as they may be, they are also loyal to their leader, Melchior, and by proxy towards you.

Dov:

- And what about everyone that has incompatible DNA for Xeno-Martian hybridisation?

Frank:

- Oh, I am sure you are referring to Melchior's former chancellor, Peter Belovic?

Dov:

- Yes, among other examples.

Frank:

- Well, true genetic modification always comes at a cost. If we release this vial, a lot of people with incompatible DNA will die painful deaths. But the ones that live on will have superior DNA. Such is the way of nature, and we are living in fascinating times. We are about to get front row seats to the next step in human evolution!

A door got smashed in and a group of armed men stormed into the room. Their commander approached Dov and spoke:

- Dov Dorevitch. We are here to detain you on orders from Colonel Slavonic.

Before Dov had time to respond, Frank pulled up his pistol and rapidly shot the six intruders in their heads before they had the time to react. Frank remarked:

- I guess time is running out Dov. We better hurry to the wind generator so we can release the air-borne virus onto our civilisation.

Dov nodded and said nothing. Together the two men rushed towards the room with the wind generator. Once they were outside Dov opened the door with his DNA signature. Dov took the virus out of the safe, and he put it in the wind generator. Dov tapped on a computer console and fired the deadly virus unto Colonel Slavonic's base.

A short while later, the artillery bombardment ended.

# Chapter 47: The Seven Zeto Crystals.

Melchior was lying in bed exhausted from a session of rough sex with Rangda, posing as Helen of Troy. Rangda had left him to recuperate his wounds after the coitus, as she was not a big fan of cuddles. Melchior could feel the sharp pain from her claws, and he embraced it, as pain was the highest form of pleasure. To his surprise, Rangda came back to the room, carrying two goblets. Rangda hissed at Melchior:

- Get up! We do not have time for laziness. There is a lot for us to do now that the filthy Zetans are finally defeated.

Melchior:

- What do you mean? We have defeated the Zetans; we have all the time in the world?

Hearing this, Rangda ran up to Melchior and punched him in the face, knocking him to the ground. She then hissed at him:

- That was not foreplay, so stay where you are and listen up!

Melchior didn't want to argue with the fearsome Rangda, so he did as Rangda instructed and stayed on the floor. Rangda spoke again:

- We have defeated the Zetans, but that is not the end of my ambitions. I want to rule this galaxy as its God-Queen. To achieve that, I need to find and absorb the powers of the seven Zeto Crystals, spread throughout the galaxy.

Melchior:

- Let me guess. You want me to take my army on a stupid quest looking for useless crystals, instead of invading Earth?

Rangda:

- Useless crystals? You arrogant twat, take this!

Rangda lifted her staff that had a corrupted Zeto Crystal attached to it. Rangda aimed her staff towards Melchior, who started floating and experiencing migraines. Melchior sensed how the essence of his soul was about to shatter. Before this happened, Rangda released Melchior from the corrupted Zeto crystal's power, and he dropped to the ground with a loud thump. Melchior struggled to speak after the experience, and stuttered out:

- I'm sorry for offending you, Empress Rangda.

Rangda:

- I punished you for your insolence while showing you the power of the dark Zeto Crystals. When we gather all of them, nothing can stand in our way, and your friends on Earth will feel our wrath!

Melchior coughed up some blood, and Rangda brought forth a different gem. It was an untainted Zeto Crystal, and it shone with pristine blue colour. Rangda put the crystal on Melchior's head, and his wounds healed. After the treatment with the Zeto Crystal, Melchior felt inner peace. Rangda spoke:

- You are in luck, Melchior, as I haven't corrupted this Zeto Crystal yet.
- Now get up and listen!

Melchior did as Rangda instructed, and she continued her tirade.

- As I mentioned before there are seven primordial Zeto Crystals in the galaxy. I have three of them. The other four crystals belong to The Elves on Elvonia, The Dwarves on Goldonia, The Orcs on Grashdunt, and The Humans on Earth.

Melchior:

- What are you talking about? Orcs? Elves? Those are fantasy creatures that don't exist!

Rangda:

- Oh, is that so? Don't think you know everything, Melchior. The Zetans altered hundreds of species in their image during the Golden Age of their civilisation. This was when the Zetan imbued the Xenos with their intelligence. Being altered in the Zetans image, they have continued to live on their home planets, like humanity progressed on Earth.

Melchior:

- I see, but if one of the primordial Zeto Crystals are on Earth, that gives us a reason to invade!

Rangda:

- Silence, you fool. Stop obsessing about Earth. Who do you rather fight? The Terran Council's army with guns, fighter jets, laser cannons and artillery, or a bunch of elves with arrows and swords?

Melchior:

- So, you want to pick off the easier targets first?

Rangda:

- Of course. Invade some easy targets, and we have enough resources to breed a vast, unstoppable army.

- Now we must move. It will still take months to reach the portal to Elvonia, and I don't want to run out of resources.

Melchior:

- Yes, Empress Rangda. I will alert the army at once!

Rangda:

- Good. I hope you didn't tire yourself too much arguing before. The future god-queen is up for some more copulation!

Melchior:

- It will be my pleasure.

# Chapter 48: Hilda Muller Meets with Frey and Freya.

Hilda Muller were discussing the terrifying news reports from Mars with Michael Muller.

Michael:

- Are you sure that this report is accurate, Hilda? Why would Dov release a virus that turns the Martians into frenzied beasts attacking and killing each other?

Hilda:

- I am certain. I saw people infused with Xeno DNA when I met with Melchior. It's a horrible sight that resembled what we now see from Mars.

Michael:

- That's awful. We must do something to help the Martian citizens.

Hilda:

- I am afraid we cannot approach Mars for a relief effort at this stage. We do not know how the virus works, and the worst-case scenario is that we spread it to Earth if we try to help them. We must blockade the planet and quarantine the Martian population on the surface.

Michael:

- Hold on a minute. We had a delegation on Melchior's command ship. Neither you nor anyone else in the group got infected while you were there.

Hilda:

- I wasn't infected, but my mind got infested. I still dream nightmares about meeting with Melchior. I can't get over how he forced me to drink human blood.

There was a call on the hologram generator from Hilda's mistress, Melanie Weber.
Hilda:

- Melanie, I am in a critical discussion with my cousin, you'll have to wait.

Melanie:

- This trump whatever you're discussing.
- I am accompanied by two Zetan messengers, Frey and Freya.

Hilda:

- You mean like the ancient Norse Gods?

Melanie:

- Yes. They are requesting to meet you.

Hilda:

- Very well. I cannot deny semi-divine aliens a meeting, can I? Bring them in, and bring enough guards to deter them from doing anything stupid!

A short time later, Melanie and three dozen guards escorted Frey and Freya into Hilda's office. Freya smiled towards Hilda and spoke:

- You can send the guards away. If we'd wanted to kill you, there would be nothing your guards could do to stop us. Your girlfriend is beautiful by the way.

Hilda:

- And why would I trust you?

Frey:

- Because Mistress Muller, we have already lost everything, humanity is our only hope.

- My father, Odin, trusted the deceitful Melchior. He believed that Melchior was our ally. Together we would cleanse the Divine Dimension of the Xenos and start a new golden age of civilisation across the galaxy.

- But Melchior betrayed us. Melchior has partnered up with Rangda, and they aim to enslave all the sentient beings in the galaxy, including humankind.

Hilda:

- Hmm. Interesting prospect. We thought of sending an expeditionary force to the Divine Dimension and ally with the Zetans against Melchior and Rangda. But the portals closed in front of us.

Freya:

- Mistress Muller. We can open the portals for you if you promise to send your army to fight Rangda and Melchior.

Hilda:

- But if Rangda has defeated the Zetans, it is too late to send the army after Rangda and Melchior.

- You are welcome to stay as my guests. As a matter of fact; I have someone that I would like you to meet.

Freya:

  - Who?

Hilda:

  - Ramun, a former Xeno General and my prisoner.

Frey:

  - What? How do did you manage to capture a Xeno General?

Hilda:

  - As you'll find out, I am a lot more resourceful than you think. But come, let's introduce you to each other.

Having said this, Hilda got up, and she led her Zetan guests to Ramun's enclosure.

# Chapter 49: An Encounter Between Three Different Species.

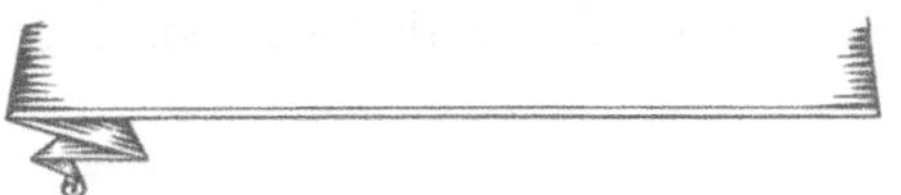

Hilda, Frey and Freya stood outside the secret compound where Hilda kept Ramun. Hilda had kept the capture of a Xeno General a secret from the general population. Knowledge was power, and she wanted to keep power within House Muller. Hilda looked at her Zetan guests, and spoke:

- You better stay outside, I do not want to agitate this prisoner. Take this universal translator device and use it once the coast is clear. Our Xeno prisoner is not very well-spoken.

Frey and Freya nodded at Hilda, and she entered the enclosure. Inside, it was hot as a sauna, and the vegetation consisted of scorched grass. Ramun liked it this way, as it reminded him of his home planet Xenora. Hilda found Ramun sleeping next to the carcass of a cow. She raised her plasma sword with her right hand and whipped him, with the whip that she held in her left hand. Ramun growled as he woke up and he turned towards Hilda:

- Grrrrrr... Mistress Hilda. It has been a long time. How can I serve you?

Hilda:

- I am bringing some guests that I would like you to meet. And as your mistress, I command you stay civil!

Ramun:

- Ramun is happy to follow your commands. Mistress Hilda has been very good to Ramun, providing Ramun with delicious prey animals!

Hilda spoke into her headset, and a minute later, Melanie Weber escorted Frey and Freya into the enclosure. Seeing the Zetans, Ramun started drooling and clenching his teeth preparing to attack. Hilda whipped him out of it:

- Ramun, you promised to be civil.

Ramun growled back:

- Yes, mistress, I did. Ggrrrrhmmm.....

Ramun got down on the ground in a submissive pose.
Freya:

- How did you tame the beast?

Hilda:

- I defeated him in single combat. The Xenos respect someone who can beat them in single combat. Then I used Terran Stem cell technology to regrow Ramun's legs and arms.

Frey:

- Interesting approach. But why would you go through this hassle to make a primitive beast your prisoner?

Hilda:

- That's the reason for the Zetan downfall. Your arrogance. During millennia of interstellar warfare, you never considered capturing a prominent Xeno?

Frey:

- But we created them. We created all the sentient species in the galaxy. We imbued the Xenos with our Zetan intelligence, which caused our demise. We are the supreme species of the universe, blessed by the True Maker. What could we learn from lesser species?

Hilda:

- You could learn what drives them and how to defeat them.

Freya:

- So, what insights do you have?

Hilda:

- Well, the Xenos turn into a violent frenzy when they are hungry, and there are prey animals around.

- Use that to your advantage.

- I can tell that you guys have plenty of catching up to do.

- Ramun!

Ramun:

- Yes, Mistress Hilda.

Hilda:

- I am leaving these Zetans here with you. I want you to communicate and coexist. If you spill any blood between you, I will make sure that all of you will suffer.

After saying this, Hilda turned to Frey and Freya:

- So, Frey and Freya, I am allowing you to do what you should have done eons ago, getting to know the enemy.

Freya looked at Hilda in awe and stuttered:

- But the beast is going to kill us if you leave us here alone.

Hilda:

- No, he won't. If a mere human can tame him, I am sure that two intelligent beings from the Zetan "Supreme" race will be okay. Now I must take my leave. Good luck with your research!

Having said this, Hilda left Frey and Freya with Ramun, hoping for the Zetans to learn something about their eternal enemy.

# Chapter 50: Preparing the Invasion of Elvonia

In December 2878, Melchior and Rangda had led their armies to the portals leading to the Elven homeworld of Elvonia. Rangda studied Melchior, with her desire for power glowing in her eyes. She spoke:

- This will be a historical day, Melchior. For the first time in thousands of years, humans and Xenos will set foot on the Elven homeworld of Elvonia.

Melchior:

- Understood. What do we expect to find there?

Rangda:

- Elvonia is a world filled with tree-hugging hippies. They care so much about their environment so they never became industrialised. Thus, I wouldn't expect them to be a significant military threat.

Melchior:

- So, we can conquer an undestroyed world where we can pillage and set up as much industry as possible before we move on with our mission?

Rangda:

- Yes. Let me deal with their leader myself. The Elves are closely attuned to their Zeto Crystal. Their leader, King Mellron, can use its power to unleash destructive White magic.

- No matter. I have waited for this moment for many years, and that fool won't stop me from taking what is rightfully mine.

Melchior:

- Good. I will lead our army to crush the Elves while you confront their leader in single combat, and seize the crystal?

Rangda:

- Yes, that is my plan.

Melchior:

- Excellent. We will attack tomorrow; these tree-hugging Elves won't know what hit them, and they will be delicious to eat. Haha haha!

After this, both Melchior and Rangda fell into an extended period of diabolical laughter. They rejoiced, realising the suffering that they would cause to the unsuspecting Elves on Elvonia.

# Chapter 51: The Invasion of Elvonia.

Of all the species that the Zetans altered in their image, the Elves were the ones that were the most alike the Zetans. Like the Zetans, the Elves led lengthy lives, had a slow reproductive cycle, and a powerful affinity to the Zeto Crystals. The Elves liked to live in harmony with their environment, which kept their planet Elvonia in a pristine ecological condition. There was one significant difference between the Zetans and the Elves. The Zetans had valued knowledge and science, while the Elves valued tradition and preservation. Thus, the Elves lived with primitive technology, despite being the second most intelligent species in the Galaxy.

The invasion day started like any other day on Elvonia. King Mellron led a prayer to the True Maker, in front of the primordial Zeto Crystal. The peaceful aura of the crystal spread blissfulness and balance to all living beings on Elvonia.

A bright light in the distance interrupted the ceremony. The light came from the long-deactivated portals, and this excited the elves. Had the mythological Zetans, the primordial creators of the Elves, finally returned? Mellron remembered the last time he saw the Zetan goddess Gaia. He had been a young boy, and now, thousands of years later, he was an old man.

King Mellron gathered his court, and they moved towards the forest glade where the portal had opened. If the Zetans had arrived, they deserved nothing less than a royal reception. As King Mellron approached the forest glade, he had a foreboding feeling that something was wrong. Worry surged through Mellron body.

The putrid smell of fire and burnt flesh filled his senses. As Mellron got closer, he could hear the tormented squeals of his brethren.

King Mellron reached the portal and, he realised the terrible truth. The Zetans hadn't returned. The new visitors were something else, something that focused on destruction, evil and demise.

Melchior's Xeno-Martian hybrid soldiers rushed to seize King Mellron. He raised his ornamental staff which contained with the primordial Zeto Crystal to purify their souls and bring them peace. As Rangda had corrupted the soldiers, their bodies couldn't handle the purification, and they dropped dead to the ground.

Mellron studied the fallen combatants and felt sorrow. He had aimed to pacify them to avoid confrontation and instead, he had killed hundreds of living beings. Such a terrible waste of life and Mellron didn't understand what he had done wrong.

Mellron felt a terrifying presence chilling into his bones, as Rangda appeared. She came out from the portal accompanied by a large group of her Xeno bodyguards. Rangda wielded a staff equipped with two corrupted Zeto Crystals. The crystals were so dark and eerie, so they absorbed all the light around them, turning the forest glade into a twilight zone.

Rangda studied Mellron and spoke:

- King Mellron. You have bereaved your people of the light of progress. It is time for a new beginning. Both for the Elves and for the rest of the galaxy.

King Mellron:

- Who are you? What are those dark abominations that extinguish the light around you?

Rangda:

- I am Empress Rangda, god-queen of the Xenos. I am destined to rule the whole Milky Way Galaxy. Yield now and I'll spare most of your people. I'll need them to reform Elvonia to its true potential.

King Mellron:

- True potential? Elvonia is a paradise. Every living being lives in harmony. Once the lifespan of an individual is over, they pass on peacefully, giving back their life force to the Zeto Crystal that granted it in the first place.

- What else could my people want from existence?

Rangda:

- They could want progress, ambition to become better than their fellow elves, greed to fill their vaults with precious metals.

King Mellron:

- That sounds terrible. Giving up on peace to pursue hollow goals that tear communities apart and destroy the natural environment!

Rangda:

- Whatever you say, King Mellron. I am not here to discuss philosophy. I am here to get your primordial Zeto Crystal. Resist me if you must but be wary of the consequences if you do.

King Mellron:

- I don't think you understand, Rangda. The elves and all life forms on Elvonia are dependent on the Zeto Crystal for our existence. If I give it away, I will doom us all.

- I am afraid I'll have to ask you to leave. Go back to wherever you came from and leave us alone. I do not wish any more bloodshed.

Rangda:

- And yet you chose to condemn your entire entourage to a painful death by refusing to cooperate.

- Xenos, Charge!

On Rangda's signal, hundreds of Xeno Warriors charged against King Mellron and his court. In the last second, Mellron conjured a spell that covered his group with a white forcefield. The forcefield repelled the Xenos and set them ablaze. The wailing of the burning Xenos filled the forest glade. A short while later, most of the Xenos were dead or dying, scattered around the grove. Rangda studied Mellron, smiled, and spoke:

> - Feels good, doesn't it? The sight of your enemies dying in front of your eyes? The only sad part is wasting of the flesh. But I sense there is a lot to eat on this planet so we can afford to be wasteful!

> - Their deaths won't be in vain. The Xenos will hail them as heroes!

King Mellron:

> - And why is that?

Rangda:

> - Because their deaths drained your Zeto Crystal, while my corrupted Zeto Crystals remain charged!

After saying this, Rangda aimed her staff with the corrupted Zeto Crystals towards Mellron's entourage. The crystals drained all the light, and the whole sky became black. Mellron's followers screamed in agony as their heads exploded with their headless corpses falling to the ground. Rangda smiled diabolically and spoke:

> - Interesting. It seems that the Elves affinity with the Zeto Crystals makes it possible for me to charge my crystals using your life force. How delightful.

Mellron:

> - What are you talking about, you evil monster! The True Maker's benevolence charges the Zeto Crystals.

Rangda:

- The True Maker might charge your useless crystal, but she does not charge my crystals.

- Farewell, Mellron. Die knowing that your death will serve a useful purpose; making me more powerful.

Mellron:

- Please don't. The Zeto Crystal is the source of all life on Elvonia. Steal the crystal, and you'll turn our beautiful paradise into a barren wasteland.

Rangda:

- That is precisely what I intend to do, Mellron. Goodbye!

Rangda turned the power of her corrupted Zeto Crystals towards King Mellron. The Elven-king tried to resist her influence, but he couldn't. He had drained his pure Zeto Crystal when he misused it to kill the attacking Xenos. Rangda used her powers to trap Mellron in a psionic force field that stopped him from moving. She proceeded to absorb and shatter Mellron's soul to charge her crystals. Rangda decided to torment Mellron before killing him, as a punishment for resisting her. Mellron's tormented screams echoed for hours before he finally slumped headless to the ground.

After Rangda had killed Mellron, Melchior approached her.

Melchior:

- I take it your mission was successful.

Rangda:

- Yes, as I anticipated, forcing Mellron to kill our troops with his pure Zeto Crystal turned out to be his undoing. His crystal lost its power the moment he used it to take life instead of giving life.

Melchior:

 - Good, how many casualties on our side?

Rangda:

 - Less than a thousand, so inconsequential.

Melchior:

 - Good. The local population have neither the strength nor the technology to stand against us. We can conquer the whole planet within a week.

Rangda:

 - Don't bother. I know a quicker way!

Rangda picked up Mellron's staff and studied the Zeto Crystal. Its bright blue light had faded, and it looked like any regular gemstone. Rangda lit a bonfire, and she put the uncorrupted Zeto Crystal in the middle of the fire. Rangda took a knife and cut her arm, and made her blood drop down on the crystal in the blaze. She chanted curses and focused her mind on the Zeto crystal. After a while, the fire had extinguished and left in the ashes was, a corrupted Zeto Crystal. Rangda picked up the dark crystal and slotted it into her staff. As she did this the plants around her started to wither, and the decay spread at a tremendous pace.

Melchior:

 - I guess we won't be able to sell Elvonia as a tourist destination anymore.

Rangda:

 - The Elves should have surrendered their crystal and bowed to me. Now they will suffer.

- Order your men to gather as many resources as they can. We'll stay here for a while to regain our strength before we move on. The galaxy is vast, and we have plenty to do.

Melchior:

- Yes, Empress Rangda. I will do your bidding!

# Chapter 52: The True Maker Convinces Sabina to Save Mars.

A year later, in December 2879, Sabina was meditating together with the other children of Eden in her light brigade. Under Sabina's supervision, many of the children had acquired unique healing powers. The True Maker had shown Sabina how to channel the energies of the universe, to create an aura where peace and harmony reigned. Under the influence of that aura, incredible feats of healing could occur.

Sabina got visions from Elvonia where she saw how Rangda tormented the Elves on the dying planet. Rangda had locked up the Elves in cages and drained their life force to power up her crystals.

Rangda's action terrified Sabina. But instead of letting this bring down her mood, she felt inspired by how Elvonia used to be. The Elvonia of the past had been a paradise, the planet had flourished, with everything in balance. Now that the Zeto Crystal was gone all life on Elvonia suffered. This was because all life forms of the planet had evolved to live attuned to the crystal. When the crystal disappeared, none of the lifeforms could adapt to the circumstances.

Sabina heard the voice of The True Maker:

- Sabina, do you understand what happened on Elvonia?

Sabina:

- Yes, Rangda destroyed the planet.

The True Maker:

- Yes, but how could Rangda destroy a planet blessed by one of the seven primordial Zeto Crystals?

Sabina:

- With her army of monsters and evil men? The Elves of Elvonia were peace-loving creatures that hadn't trained for warfare. Thus, they stood no chance against Rangda.

The True Maker:

- Yes, on the surface, that is what it looks like. But that wasn't why Elvonia fell.

- Elvonia fell because their leader, King Mellron, gave in to his fears. Being a slave to his worries, Mellron used Elvonia's Zeto Crystal to slay the invaders. When Mellron misused the crystal, it lost its power, and he was powerless against Rangda's dark curses.

Sabina:

- But if he hadn't done anything, the Xenos would have killed him and his whole entourage?

The True Maker:

- No, they wouldn't have. The Xenos weren't always evil. They evolved on a planet with rough conditions and lifeforms. The Zeto Crystal did not govern life on Xenora. This didn't make them evil, but rugged and easy to influence. It was Rangda who turned them evil and made them a threat to the universe.

- If Mellron had tried to turn the attackers good instead of murdering them, things could have had another outcome.

Sabina:

- But Mellron tried to turn Melchior's soldiers good, and they died anyway?

The True Maker:

- Yes, the Xeno-Martian hybrid is such an abominable creation that the only thing that could keep them alive is the forces of darkness. Mellron did what he could to save them and bring them to light. But when Mellron decided to slaughter the Xenos with fire magic, he succumbed to the darkness. This drained the Zeto crystal's holy power.

Sabina:

- So, the lesson is to always try to do good, even in the face of adversity?

The True Maker:

- Yes, and to know what is right, you must first understand yourself. You have come a long way, my child. I have faith in your ability to stop Rangda and Melchior and restore peace and balance to the cosmos. But first, you must hone your skills, and to do so, you must save the Martians.

Sabina:

- But I am still a child?

The True Maker:

- Yes, but in a few years, you'll be ready. You'll know when the time has come.

Sabina:

- Okay. There is one thing that I don't understand.

- If you are the omnipotent and omniscient creator of the whole cosmos, why can't you stop Rangda?

The True Maker:

- I could stop her, but the consequences wouldn't be pleasant.

- You see, my celestial holy powers are on a Cosmological scale. Like you cannot kill a single bacterium in your body using your fist, I cannot kill an evil individual using my divine powers. My only way to kill Rangda would be to release a blast that would destroy the entire galaxy. I would do that if I had to, but I prefer not to.

- Instead, I try to use gifted individuals of light like you, to stop the forces of darkness.

Sabina:

- Thank you for telling me. This makes a lot of sense.

The True Maker:

- Yes. Now focus on your meditation and your spiritual abilities. Saving Mars is the first step to foil Rangda's evil plan.

After saying this, the True Maker disappeared from Sabina's mind. Sabina felt at peace and motivated to focus on her training.

# Chapter 53: Rangda and Melchior Prepares for Their Next Conquest

In January 2880, Melchior and Rangda were preparing for their next conquest. They planned to invade the Dwarven homeworld, Goldonia. Melchior studied his and Rangda's massive army. They had plundered Elvonia and turned it into a barren wasteland. While doing so, they had converted the planet's biomass into an army of millions of cloned Xeno-Martian hybrids. Elvonia was beyond saving, and it would soon turn into a Venusian wasteland. Global warming and volcanic activity were turning the planet into a hot and toxic hellscape.

To Melchior, the destruction of Elvonia was bitter-sweet. It had made him a lot more powerful than before, but it had been a waste. Melchior dreamt of conquering Earth, and now he had come across an even more beautiful planet, and he had destroyed it in less than a year. At some point, he would need to get rid of Rangda so he could rule his galactic empire, without destroying it. But he had still much to learn from Rangda, so he'd stay loyal for now.

Rangda entered the room, and she had brought an Elven prisoner. Melchior forgot about his rebellious plans to focus on a more critical issue, his hunger. Together they devoured the Elven prisoner and proceeded to copulate.

After their meal, Rangda spoke to Melchior:

- We need to move on. The planet is dying, and we cannot stay here any longer.

Melchior:

- I am annoyed by the wasted opportunity. Elvonia was such a beautiful planet when we first got here.

Rangda:

- Yes, but I doomed the planet when I corrupted and stole its Zeto Crystal. After that, speeding up the downfall of the planet and building our army was the right thing to do!

- No matter, we are evacuating Elvonia before it becomes uninhabitable and we need to focus on our next goal. To steal the Zeto Crystal belonging to the Dwarves on Goldonia.

Melchior:

- With our army this strong, I doubt they'll be any threat towards us?

Rangda:

- Don't underestimate them. While they are not as advanced as we are, their technology is not as obsolete as the Elves were. The Dwarves are stubborn, and they refuse to submit to overwhelming power. Conquering them would take years and cost more than it's worth.

Melchior:

- So, how do you suggest that we deal with these creatures to secure the Zeto Crystal?

Rangda:

- We make them an offer they cannot refuse. The Dwarves praise the Zeto Crystal for its beauty and uniqueness. But it has no influence on them or their planet. So, we make them a better offer.

Melchior:

- And what would that be?

Rangda:

- In the Goldonia star system, there is a colossal asteroid made of gold. We can offer to land this rock on Goldonia in exchange for their Zeto Crystal. Blinded by their greed, they will accept.

Melchior:

- But wouldn't this make the Dwarves wealthy and powerful?

Rangda:

- Quite the opposite. Gold is only valuable because of its scarcity. When it becomes abundant, it loses its value, and the Dwarven society collapses. Once we have weakened them, we can subject them to our will. But regardless, our main priority is the Zeto Crystal.

Melchior:

- You are an evil genius, Empress Rangda.

Rangda:

- I know! I am soon to be a goddess! Prepare the army to move. Goldonia is far away, so we better get going.

Melchior:

- Yes, Empress Rangda. I will do you your bidding!

# Chapter 54: Hilda Muller Faces Motherhood and Prepares an Army.

Hilda Muller felt tired but happy. She had two daughters born within a matter of days. Freya had rewarded Hilda's hospitality by fulfilling her wish to have children with her partner Melanie Weber. Freya was a master in fertility technology, and she had enabled Hilda's eggs to fertilise Melanie's eggs. Hence, they were both the biological mother to each other's children. Both the children were daughters, as a boy was not a possible outcome from merging two eggs together.

Hilda let her servants care for her children. She was the leader of a vast empire and, she didn't have time to change diapers and other demeaning duties.

Hilda studied her drone factory. House Muller had cooperated with Frey and Freya to create an army of drones suitable for fighting the Xenos. Frey had preferred an army of human soldiers, but Hilda had refused. Times had changed, and humans were no longer cannon fodder for the Zetan armies!

Accompanied by Michael Muller, Hilda met Frey and Freya, in the military drone storage outside Hansstadt. Hilda spoke:

- 100,000 military drones adapted to fighting the Xenos. We have provided you with an army, Frey!

Frey:

- Yes, but I am a bit worried about how useful these robots will be on the battlefield. Human soldiers have always been more innovative and creative than AI limited drones. Drones without AI limiters are unpredictable and difficult to control.

Michael:

- These robots will do very well on the battlefield. Our field-testing scenarios have proven this.

Frey:

- In those tests, you put the robots to fight untrained Xenos in a controlled environment. Killing those Xenos were equal to butchering civilians. Hardly a test of the robots' usefulness.

Hilda:

- That's enough. I have spent a large chunk of our fortune on these robots, and it is all we are going to provide. I am not going to send our citizens to fight aliens in a war that is no longer ours. There have been no Xeno sightings on Earth for over five years.

Freya:

- But I told you already, the Xenos will come back. They are licking their wounds and attacking weaker civilisations to regain their strength.

Hilda:

- Is that so? Then I want you to put these drones to good use, helping these other weaker civilisations to fight the Xenos.

- If you excuse me, I have some business to attend to. We will transport you and the drones to the portals tomorrow.

Frey:

- Thank you, Hilda and Michael. I hope that you are right, and that these drones are all that I need to stop Rangda. We need to save the remaining Zetans, as well as the rest of the galaxy from her tyranny.

Hilda:

- I am sure that we'll find out. Best of luck to the two of you.

Hilda left the facility. She wasn't going to do any work, but she needed an excuse for leaving. Hilda wondered whether she had done the right thing when she refused to seek the aid of the other faction leaders. Together they could have sent a sizeable force to the Divine Dimension to deal with the problem.

Hilda decided that she had made the right choice; as a matter of fact, she had been too generous. Hilda had spent a fortune providing two alien refugees with an army to fight their common enemy. What else could she do? Given their history as the deceivers on Earth, Hilda had been too generous to the Zetans.

Hilda drove her hovercraft to one of her nearby residences. It was ancient castle, where she enjoyed spending time with Melanie and her baby daughters. Screw the Zetans, time was too short to worry about intergalactic warfare when Hilda could spend time with the people that she loved. As Hilda met Melanie's smile when she got home, she forgot her troubles.

# Chapter 55: The Deception of the Dwarves

In July 2880, Rangda, Melchior, and George Smith arrived at the Dwarven homeworld of Goldonia. Rangda had advised Melchior that they were better off coming as a small group impersonating Zetan gods. While the outer layer DNA modifier couldn't change their heights, Rangda was certain that no-one would question that detail. The Zetans hadn't visited Goldonia for millennia so no-one would have seen the real Dwarven gods.

Rangda approached the palace guard and spoke:

- Greetings. I am the goddess Dumathoin, and this is Moradin and Beronnar.

- We are Zetan gods and have come to offer your master an offer he cannot refuse.

The sentry looked dumbfounded but walked off.
Melchior turned to Rangda and spoke:

- The sentry seemed clueless and not awestruck by seeing his deities. Are you sure everything is going according to plan?

Rangda:

- I must admit I had expected another reception, but we will have to improvise as we go along. Worst come to worst; we'll have to fight our way out. In that case, I will call in my Xeno horde, to keep the Dwarves busy.

The sentry came back, accompanied by one of his superiors.

Chancellor Randall:

- Greetings strange visitors. I am Chancellor Randall. May I ask your names and why you wish to speak to the King?

Rangda:

- I told your guard already. I am the goddess Dumathoin, and with me are the gods Moradin and Beronnar.

Chancellor Randall:

- We are not falling for that trick. We haven't worshipped those dead deities for thousands of years. Drop the act and tell me who you are, or I won't allow you to speak to the King.

Rangda decided to drop the act and tell the truth. Since she couldn't deceive the dwarves with her appearance, appealing to their greed was better option. She deactivated her Zetan DNA modifier and showed her real appearance. The guards stared at her in awe and Rangda spoke again:

- I am empress Rangda of the Xenos. I am accompanied by Melchior Dorevitch Emperor of Mars and his General George Smith.

Rangda signalled Melchior and George to revert to their real appearances. Rangda continued speaking:

- We are travelling the galaxy collecting the Zeto Crystals, which we are using to fight our ancient enemies, the Zetans. Your King has a primordial Zeto Crystal in his possession. We are willing to pay him more gold than there are in all his vaults in exchange for the crystal.

Chancellor Randall:

- And if the King refuses the deal?

Rangda:

- Then I will lead my huge army here and take it by force.

Chancellor Randall:

- Very well. Under those circumstances, I accept your offer.

Rangda:

- You are not the King. I wish to speak to the King.

Chancellor Randall:

- I was testing you. Everyone on Goldonia knows that the King died two years ago, and that I am the one governing this nation.

- Bring me the riches that you promised, and you can have the crystal.

Rangda:

- I will bring them. And you'll uphold your deal, or else...

Chancellor Randall:

- I am an honourable man. It wasn't I who pretended to be a long-dead deity to get my way. I'll see you when you get back, Rangda.

After the Dwarves had left, Melchior felt compelled to speak to Rangda:

- Do you think they will uphold their part of the bargain?

Rangda:

- Yes. The Dwarves and the other life forms on this planet are not attuned to the Zeto Crystals. To them, the Zeto Crystals are beautiful gemstones and nothing else. Hardly worth going to war for, especially when I am offering them a king's ransom in exchange for the crystal.

Melchior:

- I hope you are right. I would hate to go through all the effort of intercepting and landing that asteroid if it comes to fighting anyways.

Rangda:

- You would hate trying to fight the Dwarves in the tunnels below. The Dwarves are cunning and stubborn. Fighting them on their home ground would be a bloodbath.

- But as you'll find out, Melchior. I am right, as I always am.
- George Smith!

George:

- Yes, Empress Rangda,

Rangda:

- Prepare an expedition to intercept and land the golden asteroid from this star system on Goldonia.

- It is time to show the Dwarves the real consequence of greed. Hahaha!

# Chapter 56: The Consequence of Greed.

Gold is uncommon on Earth because only a supernova explosion can create it. The sizeable golden asteroid in the Goldonia star system was the result of a colossal supernova explosion. The asteroid had been a wayward passenger of the galaxy until the star of Goldonia's star system attracted it, eons ago.

In January 2881, George Smith's expedition landed the golden asteroid close to Chancellor Randall's domains on Goldonia. It turned out to be a problematic task landing the huge rock. Because of the asteroid's weight, 100 Megaton, the expedition needed to be careful. Because otherwise, the kinetic energy from the collision would cause widespread destruction.

After landing the golden asteroid, Rangda and Melchior approached Chancellor Randall. The sight of the golden asteroid mesmerised the dwarf.

Chancellor Randall:

- I thought that you were lying when you spoke about a King's ransom. Is that entire block gilded?

Rangda:

- Not gilded. The entire asteroid consists of gold.

Upon hearing this, Chancellor Randall almost fainted. In his greedy mindset, he forgot that such a massive influx of gold would render gold worthless. Seeing the gold, filled Randall with visions of his own greatness and the future. Rangda pulled him back to reality:

- Chancellor Randall. I have fulfilled my part of the bargain. Now bring me the primordial Zeto Crystal and uphold your part.

Chancellor Randall:

- Oh yes, of course, I will tell my servants to bring it at once.

One of Randall's servants brought the Zeto Crystal and gave it to Rangda. Having secured the Zeto Crystal, Rangda and Melchior, headed back to the Divine Dimension. Before entering the portals, Melchior studied the Dwarves that were flocking to the golden asteroid. Melchior spoke:

- Look at them. The gold possesses their minds.

Rangda:

- Yes, as I predicted. Dwarves only have one vice, greed, and as such, they obsess about gold.

Melchior:

- But you said that gold would be worthless if it's that plentiful?

Rangda:

- To humans, yes. You are greedy, but it's not your only vice, and humans have no intrinsic interest in gold. For humans, it only has value due to its rarity. When gold becomes abundant, you lose interest. But Dwarves are different.

- By the time that we come back, the Dwarves will have decimated each other fighting for that gold. This will make the planet easy for us to invade.

Melchior:

- So, you do plan to invade Goldonia?

Rangda:

- I plan to invade everything. But one thing, that my immortality has taught me is the value of patience. Let's head back to the Divine Dimension.

- Our next destination is the Orcs on Grashdunt.

Melchior:

- The Orcs? I bet they will be a useful ally!

Rangda:

- Yes. I will brief you before we head to Grashdunt. Now, prepare our army to move.

Rangda and Melchior entered the portal and left the dwarves to their fate.

# Chapter 57: The Pursuit of Rangda Begins.

In March 2881, Frey and Freya arrived at the battlefield where Melchior had betrayed the Zetans. The field was an eerie sight. The Xenos had gnawed off the flesh from the fallen Zetans, and all that remained of their once-proud army was piles of broken bones.

As gruesome as the scene was, Frey and Freya were here on a critical mission. They needed to gather DNA from the fallen so that they could use cloning technology and synthetic wombs to have their species reborn. Doing so, was the only way to save their species from extinction. Spending a few weeks collecting samples, they had gathered the DNA of most of the fallen.

Having collected the DNA of all the Zetans that fell on the battlefield, Frey spoke:

- That's it. Let's hope that Hilda Muller will keep her promise to give our fallen brethren life again.

Freya:

- Yes, I have my doubts, but hope is all that we have left for our species.

Frey:

- Yes, Hilda did help, but she didn't commit very much to it.

Freya:

- Well, she doesn't feel that committed to the cause. How would you react, if two aliens asked for help to stop an evil demon from the destroying the galaxy?

Frey:

- Right, I wouldn't trust those aliens either. Unfortunately, we are on the wrong side of history, and we have to be grateful for the help that she did send us.

Freya:

- Yes. Regardless of the future of our species, we need to stop Rangda before it is too late. We do not have the time to go back to Earth with the DNA samples. All we can do is to send these droids with the DNA samples to Hilda with a message hoping that she will help us.

Frey:

- Yes, sister. So, what do we do now?

Freya:

- Well, I guess that Rangda wants to corrupt the primordial Zeto Crystals and increase her own power. Do you know where we can find them?

Frey:

- The True Maker placed the seven primordial Zeto Crystals on Zetani, Zetani Nova, Xenora, Elvonia, Goldonia, Grashdunt and Earth.

- Presumably, Rangda has access to the ones from Zetani, Zetani Nova, and Xenora. Do you reckon she captured the one from Earth?

Freya:

- Well, I'd say so since she stopped attacking Earth, yet I sensed it when I was there.

- Which planet do you reckon would be her next target?

Frey:

- Elvonia. The elves live in peace and harmony without any advanced technology. They would be easy pickings for Rangda's army.

Freya:

- Well, we better hurry up then. She has a three-year head-start, so time is running out. But we cannot give up hope.

- I hope that we will come across some Zetan survivors as well. The ones that died in the battle cannot have been the only ones left of us?

Having said this, Freya and Freya gathered their drones and jumped on a hovercraft hoping to intercept Rangda's army. Rangda had a three years head start, but they were moving a lot quicker with their drone army, so there was still hope.

# Chapter 58 Rangda Prepares to Conquer Grashdunt

In October 2881, Rangda was fighting a deathmatch with some of her Xeno warriors. Melchior studied her and he saw her slaughter five Xeno warriors that were almost twice her size. Rangda signalled for the battle to be over. The remaining Xenos feasted on their fallen, while Rangda walked up to Melchior to speak:

- Are you enjoying the show,?

Melchior:

- Yes. You impressed me with your fighting. I didn't know you were such a fearsome warrior. But why, are risking your life, fighting your own soldiers in the arena?

Rangda:

- I plan to conquer Grashdunt though challenging King Gromm in single combat. Once I have claimed the Orcish throne, I'll claim the Zeto Crystal on Grashdunt. I will also have an orcish army to invade Goldonia and subject the dwarves to my rule.

Melchior:

- But why don't you kill King Gromm with powers of your corrupted Zeto Crystals?

Rangda:

- I could. But if I kill their leader using magic, the orcs will consider me a cheater. Instead of having a willing army at my disposal, my army would have to fight the Orcish Horde.

Melchior:

- Understood, but how can you be so strong, fast, and fearsome?

Rangda:

- I have always been strong and fearsome. But I have learnt to channel the energy of the corrupted Zeto Crystals into my own body. This gives me super-speed and super-strength.

Melchior:

- Very well. It seems like you know how to handle yourself.
- When are we going to Grashdunt?

Rangda:

- In a while, I need some fresh blood first. Bring one of the Elven prisoners!

Melchior:

- Of course, Empress Rangda. Anything for my lady.

Rangda:

- Hah! You have never been the one to turn down a meal! But let's get this over with. I am thirsty, and I have a planet to conquer.

After saying this, Rangda and Melchior feasted on an Elven prisoner.

# Chapter 59: Rangda Duels with King Gromm.

King Gromm felt amused. Who was this puny looking foreigner that had come through the portal to challenge him in single combat for the throne of Grashdunt? Towering at over four meters in height, and weighing almost a ton, he was twice the height of his challenger and over ten times as heavy. And on top of that, his enemy was a woman. What a fool to challenge him!

King Gromm felt relieved that Rangda chose to fight him in traditional Orcish single combat, instead of using her army to fight him. Gromm was not a dimwit, and he recognised that the alien invaders had much more advanced technology than his own people. But technology didn't matter when it came to Orcish single combat. In single combat, the duellists fought naked, wearing only a sword and a shield.

King Gromm entered the arena, and the large crowd was cheering. It had been a while since anyone had challenged him. That Orc's head hung as a trophy over the fireplace in the grand royal hall. Rangda entered from the opposite side of the arena. The spectators studied her. She was a fearsome and mysterious sight in her own way. Who was she? Where had she come from? And how could she believe that she could best King Gromm in single combat?

The Announcer yelled out the names of the contestants and that today's deathmatch was for the Grashdunt throne. "And for the primordial Zeto Crystal!" Rangda added, and King Gromm agreed. After the introductions, the fight began.

King Gromm lunged out with a mighty swing against Rangda, and she dodged it. He swung again to the same effect. A few more swings followed with the same result. On the fifth swing, Rangda blocked Gromm's swing with her shield, and Gromm realised that something was amiss. Rangda stood sturdy and unmoved from the impact of the enormous swing. Gromm felt like he had swung his sword into a large rock and his hand felt sore from the impact. Gromm forgot about his sore hand when Rangda stabbed him in his right thigh, drawing first blood. "Hah! is that all the damage you can do!" Gromm mocked Rangda, but on the inside, he felt worried. "I am just getting started," Rangda smirked at Gromm.

Gromm attacked faster than Rangda had anticipated, and in the blink of an eye, he had cut off her right hand. Rangda realised that she had underestimated Gromm and that she needed to finish him off. She dodged the next blow, and then bashed Gromm's head with her shield to him take a few steps backwards. Rangda dropped her shield, and she picked up the sword with her left hand. Attacking with supernatural speed, she slashed the giant Orc dozens of times, decapitating him with the last strike.

Rangda dropped her sword, and she held Gromm's severed head up in the air to signal her triumph to the cheering crowd.

Rangda picked up her prize, the primordial Zeto Crystal, and left the arena without saying a word.

# Chapter 60: Frey and Freya Arrives at Elvonia

Frey and Freya arrived at Elvonia a few weeks later. With their fast hover-crafts and their fission-powered robots, they could travel a lot quicker than Melchior's and Rangda's army. As they arrived in Elvonia, they realised that they had come too late. The beautiful planet that they once knew was no more. Elvonia was now a toxic hellscape with everything dead or dying.

Freya:

- Oh no! We are too late. What happened here?

Frey:

- The same thing that happens to every world that Rangda visits. Chaos and destruction.

Freya:

- But it's such a terrible loss. The Elves lived in balance with nature, and they loved each other. They never harmed anyone. They were our best creation, purer than ourselves.

Frey:

- That may be, but their purity also made them an easy target for Rangda. They didn't stand a chance against Rangda's evil army.

- But what happened here doesn't matter anymore. We must intercept Rangda and stop her from stealing the other crystals.

Freya:

- Agreed. We'd better hurry up! With a bit of luck, we can relieve the Dwarves on Goldonia from her evil-doing before it is too late.

Having said this, they headed back to the Divine Dimension, hoping to reach Goldonia on time.

# Chapter 61: Destruction by Greed.

Frey and Freya arrived at Goldonia. They were too late, and they saw a devastated planet. Goldonia reeked of death and destruction with burned houses and corpses everywhere.

Frey:

- These Dwarves were not killed by the Xenos, they still have flesh on their dead bodies. Other Dwarves must have killed them.

Freya:

- I Agree. But why so much death and destruction. What caused such madness among the Dwarves?

Frey:

- We better investigate and pray that the Zeto Crystal is still here, although I fear for the worst.

Frey and Freya kept exploring. After a while, they came across the wounded Chancellor Randall. They could tell from his eyes that the stab wound in his abdomen was not the most debilitating condition. Randall's eyes were blood-red and filled with insatiable greed and paranoia. Chancellor Randall hissed at Frey and Freya as they approached him:

- Have you also come to steal my gold? Thieves! The gold is mine, and mine alone. I deserve it. I traded for it, fair and square. In exchange for that crystal.

Chancellor Randall had to stop his tirade to cough up some blood. Frey approached the wounded Dwarf and disarmed him.
Frey:

- What happened here, pitiful dwarf? What gold? We are Zetans, and we don't care about these things.

Randall:

- So, the Zetan have also emerged from the damn portal.

- The last alien that came here gave me a lot of gold, in exchange for a puny crystal.

Freya:

- Crystal? Did you give the Zeto Crystal to Rangda?

Randall:

- Aye, Rangda was her name. Brought down a massive nugget of gold the size of a mountain from the heavens. All for me.

- But the others. Those greedy bastards didn't acknowledge my property rights, so they turned against me, and against each other. Friend fought against friend; brother fought against brother. Everyone wants to steal my dear gold.

Freya sang to Randall with a soft mesmerising voice. She wanted to help the wounded dwarf, but more so, she needed to make sense of what had happened. It worked, Randall's anger disappeared, and he fell into a deep melancholy.
Randall:

- That damn beautiful gold. It has destroyed us all. I wish it never appeared here.

Freya:

- Where is this gold, Randall? Can you show me?

Randall:

- I am too wounded to walk. without rage keeping me alive, my days are over.

Frey applied some Zetan healing gel that closed the dwarf's wound. Randall's eyes shone with relief.

- Aye, that's what I'd call magic. Although nothing compared to the magic in bringing in all that gold.

Freya:

- Can you show us where the gold is?

Randall:

- Aye, it's in the valley behind that crest.

They walked together to the top of the hill where they could see the valley below. It was a gruesome sight. Dead and wounded covered the valley with chaotic fighting still taking place. In the middle of the valley, there was a gigantic golden asteroid. Upon seeing the asteroid, Randall turned insane, and he tried to stab Freya with his sword. Frey acted instinctively, and he struck Randall with full force. Acting on instinct, Frey forgot to moderate his strength, and he killed the Dwarf with his powerful strike.

Freya tried to comfort the guilt-ridden Frey:

- Frey, it isn't your fault. You did what you had to do to save me.

Frey:

- I know. But I wish that we could do something to save them.

Freya:

- There isn't. Rangda played them. She took their crystal, and she gave them what would destroy them in return. Dwarves by nature are very sensitive to the effects of greed; especially towards the desire for gold.

- Their greed is so bad, so it infests their minds.

- This gigantic golden asteroid is useless, and yet it consumes their minds. To own it, they are willing to kill each other.

Frey:

- I know. I wish there was more of us here. We could have set things right. We could have pacified the area for long enough to use fusion to turn the gold into lead. We could have solved the Dwarves' disease.

Freya:

- Yes. But wishful thinking won't get us anywhere. We need to go. More dwarves are coming for the gold, and I'd rather avoid confrontation.

Frey:

- It seems that ship might have sailed already.

Frey pointed at the band of armed Dwarves approaching them. The leader of the Dwarves shouted:

- Hey! You there! Bloody aliens! Have you come to murder and steal our gold?

Freya:

- We are Zetans. We don't care about gold. We want peace.

Brigand:

- Aye, is that so? Then explain why there is a dead Dwarf next to your brother!

Frey:

- That Dwarf attacked my sister. We killed him in self-defence. Leave us alone, or you'll face a similar fate.

Brigand:

- We'll never let you steal our gold. Attack, fellas!

A dozen of Dwarven brigands charged the two Zetans. Frey and Freya killed their attackers with little effort. Seeing so much death and destruction, Freya got emotional, but Frey snapped her out of it.

- We don't have time to cry, sister. We need to hurry to the portal. More dwarves are coming.

In the distance, Frey saw hundreds of armed Dwarves approaching. The Zetans realised that time was short. They pulled themselves together and ran as fast as they could back to the portal. Once they had crossed the gateway to the Divine Dimension, they collapsed from exertion.

# Chapter 62: The End of the Chase

The exertion from the battle and the guilt from the lives lost caused Frey and Freya to sleep for days on end. When they woke up, Rangda's army had surrounded them. In shock and awe, Frey and Freya took up their binoculars and studied their surroundings. Rangda had gathered a large and diverse force:

- There were millions of Orcs in their steam-punk outfits, muskets and coal-powered airships.
- There were Elves enslaved and in chains serving as humanoid shields and food.
- There were millions of Xenos since Rangda had bred and cloned them on Elvonia.
- There were regular Martian human troops, dressed in 29th century Martian armour.
- The most fearsome-looking of the enemy's combatants were the Xeno/Martian hybrids, twisted and unnatural beasts. The mutants had had the intelligence of Martians but the bloodlust of the Xenos.

Against this, Frey and Freya felt helpless with their puny army of 100,000 military drones designed to fight the Xenos. Rangda appeared telepathically to mock the Zetan siblings:

- Well, well, well! Look what we have here. The Zetan siblings, the only remainders of your majestic race have come to face me. Tell me: What did you hope to achieve by coming here?

Frey:

- We have come to end to your evil reign. We saw what you did on Elvonia and Goldonia. Your tyranny ends today.

Rangda:

- That is awfully cocky considering the situation you are in. But let's discuss what happened on Elvonia and Goldonia.

Freya:

- You murdered everyone and destroyed two peaceful planets.

Rangda:

- Oh, but did I? Let's look at the evidence.

- Elvonia was an unnatural planet, and its life forms didn't deserve to exist. Nature means for life to be a struggle, favouring the survival of the fittest. On Elvonia, there was no struggle. The weak and useless species on the planet could live on due to the perverting effect of the Zeto Crystal. Without the impact of the Zeto Crystal. Elvonia's lifeforms were unsustainable. As a result, I rid Elvonia of a bunch of unnatural species.

- I killed no-one on Goldonia. I cleansed the planet of the greedy Dwarves by introducing an abundant amount of gold, to trigger their innate greed. Once the Dwarves have killed each other, the planet will be free of their filth, and other worthier lifeforms can thrive.

Frey:

- Justify your evil however you want, Rangda. We have come to end to your reign of terror.

Rangda:

- Well, that has come to a good start, hasn't it, oh great General Frey? Didn't anyone tell you to not sleep on the job? I have encircled you, and you can't escape!

Frey:

- It doesn't matter. I have seen these military drones in action. They will tear through your Xeno filth like a hot knife cuts through butter. Today will be the end of you, Rangda.

Rangda:

- Oh, is that so? Because you have seen the humans test these drones on Earth? Hilda thinks that these drones function through sending out a signal that blocks the Xeno's neural patterns. In Hilda's tests, the drones mowed down the Xenos like chaffs of wheat, right?

Frey:

- Hold on. How do you know this?

Rangda:

- I have a telepathic connection with all the Xenos cloned or captured on Earth.

- I influenced Ramun to give you all the information about me. He didn't betray me, quite the opposite, he told you exactly what I needed you to hear.

- I influenced the cloned Xenos captured in the House Muller weapon testing program, to allow the drones to butcher them. This way, I tricked the Terrans into developing weapons that are useless against my army.

- Zetans and humans are alike. You keep underestimating my Xenos and my evil mastermind. Your arrogance will be your downfall, and the new Xeno/human hybrid will emerge as the pinnacle of creation. Ha-ha-ha!

Freya:

- I have heard enough of your lies, Rangda. Prepare to face justice!

Rangda:

- Good Luck.

Rangda disconnected with the Zetan siblings, and she rained barrage of artillery and small gunfire against Frey and Freya's drone army. While the ballistic energy absorber stopped the barrage, this drained their batteries. Frey decided to abandon his defensive formation and charge against the enemy. As they charged against the enemy, the Orcs attacked them from behind, while the Xenos and Martians assaulted from the front.

As Rangda had predicted, the military drones didn't work well against the Xenos. In the end, Frey and Freya fought back to back in a melee battle against the oncoming Xeno hordes. They held up valiantly in their last stand, slaying dozens of foes. When Rangda had seen enough, she blasted the Zetan siblings out of existence with a Martian artillery shell.

Rangda walked up to the dying Frey and Freya who had their legs blown off by the artillery shell. Their blue Zetan blood covered the ground, and Rangda smirked at them.

- Impressive, you fight better than your old man Odin did. You fought for the survival of your species, to avoid extinction.

- Unfortunately, evolution is harsh. It is time for me to put your Zetan species to rest. Any last words?

Freya:

- You will never get away with this. The True Maker will come after you and stop you.

Rangda:

- Ah. The True Maker. That coward doesn't even dare to face me. But I will force her out! Once I have corrupted the last primordial Zeto Crystal, I will force her out of hiding. I will drain her as I have drained everyone else. Once I have killed the True Maker, I will become the almighty goddess of this universe. I will master the fundaments of existence. I will be the destroyer of time and matter!

Frey:

- The True Maker is not a coward. She wants to avoid collateral damage. Force her out, and you'll destroy the entire galaxy.

Rangda:

- You speak like you know it. The True Maker is a powerless clockmaker who tries to stop me, the true goddess from seizing power. I have seen through her schemes. The True Maker is putting her last hope on, the Human/Zetan hybrid, Sabina. I have had several opportunities to kill Sabina. But I will let her grow powerful and then I'll kill her and drain her energy. Only then can I show that pathetic deity, who is the true ruler of the galaxy!

Rangda realised that the Zetan siblings had almost outsmarted her. When she had her long-winded rant, they had set explosives to kill themselves and Rangda. In the last second, Rangda activated her dark Zeto Crystal shield, to avoid getting killed from the explosion.

But Rangda still got injured from the massive blast. Her shrieking of pain and hatred continued for hours on end, until she passed out from the pain.

# Chapter 63: Sabina Sets Out to Save Mars

Sabina could feel the shockwave through space/time continuum when Frey and Freya perished. Sabina realised that it was time for her to act. She walked into Metatron's office. Her appearance surprised Metatron. Sabina's essence radiated a divine light that had a calming presence and made him feel at peace.

Sabina:

- Father. The time has come. It is time for me to save the Martians from Dov's demented tyranny and restore hope for our future.

Metatron studied his daughter. It was July 2882, and Sabina was seven years old. What could she do against a demented dictator on another planet? Metatron knew that Sabina would get her way in the end, but he still decided to argue against her point:

- But Sabina darling. You are only seven years old. What can you do against the evil monster that rules Mars?

Sabina:

- Yes, I am a child. But I am destined to face Rangda, the greatest evil in the universe on the day that my adulthood starts, on my 12th birthday. How am I going to confront such an evil, if I haven't faced lesser villains before that?

Metatron studied his daughter. Sabina had the glowing blue eyes that she always had when the spirit of The True Maker filled her. But now, her body emitted a holy white light that illuminated her essence of nobility and graciousness. Metatron asked himself whether he was looking at his own daughter or a spirit. Metatron touched Sabina's hand. She was still there, and her touch soothed his worries and put his mind to ease. Feeling at ease, Metatron spoke again:

- Okay, Sabina, I will help you save the Martians.

Sabina:

- Thank you, father.

Metatron:

- But can you please tell me how you intend to save Mars from Dov's villainy and his bloodthirsty army of mutants?

Sabina:

- Yes, father. You are a good man that deserves to know every detail.
- I intend to go to Dov's capital and save Dov from himself.

Metatron:

- Save Dov from himself? The man is a monster that caused the death of millions. He is irredeemable.

Sabina:

- No. I must strive to save every soul. Besides, I do not want to taint my powers of light by using them to hurt others. The Elves on Elvonia succumbed to fear and used their powers to kill some of Rangda's Xenos. But once they did, they also destroy their own innocence. If I want to face Rangda, I need to remain innocent and pure to a stand a chance.

- Besides, I can save Dov. Fear drives Dov's actions. If I can soothe his anxiety, I can save Mars.

Metatron:

- This is crazy. There must be a better way to save Mars than to go the demon's lair and try to win him over with kindness?

Sabina:

- I am not asking you to cast aside your doubts, father. I am asking you to help me do the right thing despite your qualms.

Metatron:

- Yes. I will help you, Sabina. How can I reject the will of the True Maker, the eternal deity of the universe?

Sabina smiled at Metatron and spoke:

- You can reject the will of the True Maker. You are a human, and you have a free will. But I am happy that you choose not to. Gather my siblings and the other children in my light brigade. We are going to Nea Atina on a diplomatic mission.

After saying this, Sabina left the room and went back to her room to continue her meditation. Metatron sighed. What had he had gotten himself into? This was insane. Yet, he had to believe and hope, it was better than the alternative, to give up and live in despair.

# Chapter 64: Sabina Cleanses Dov's Soul.

Dov Dorevitch studied his strategic position on Mars. He was powerful, and he would soon be able to attack Earth to aid his brother's invasion of the planet. Dov thought about his brother, Melchior. He hadn't heard from Melchior in many years. Melchior had entered the Divine Dimension with an expeditionary force to aid Rangda against the Zetans. What had happened to his brother on the other side of the portal? Dov had no idea, and he didn't intend to spend time pondering about the subject. When Melchior had appointed Dov to rule in his stead, he had given Dov a clear goal: to build up an army capable of invading Earth in ten years.

In the first year, Dov had been hours from defeat when rebels and deserters were close to overrunning his capital. But the release of the Xeno Virus had changed everything. Those that survived the virus had become non-questioning Xeno/Martian hybrids that were loyal as long they got fed. A lot of people didn't survive the virus outbreak, and over two billion Martians had died from the Xeno mutations. This had been a necessary sacrifice. Dov needed to punish the disloyal, and besides Dov would rather rule over two billion loyal subjects than over four billion dissenters.

Dov's chief right-hand man Frank Van Stein entered the room and spoke:

- A diplomatic delegation from Eden has landed. Metatron has come. He is accompanied by a bunch of children.

Dov

- What? Is this joke? Did the leader of an insignificant colony land and expect to get an audience with me, the emperor of the Martian Dominion?

Frank:

- Dov, you are the chancellor of the Martian Dominion. Melchior is the emperor.

Dov:

- Melchior has been gone for five years, and no-one has heard from him. He is most likely dead.

- No matter, I am happy to be the chancellor of the Martian Dominion. The different title doesn't affect me!

Frank:

- Very well, Chancellor Dorevitch. Shall I send the Edenites away or punish them for their insolence?

Dov:

- Hmm. I remember Melchior obsessing about Metatron's daughter, Sabina. He was agitated when Rangda, forbade him to eat her.

- Grant an audience to Metatron and his daughter. I want to see this child.

Frank:

- Understood, chancellor.

Dov:

- Arrange a meeting in the throne room. Please join us. I am sure watching this child will be interesting for both of us.

Frank touched a tablet and allowed access to Metatron and Sabina. Sabina and Metatron entered the throne room of The Martian Dominion. Sabina walked ahead of Metatron towards Dov who had an arrogant smirk on his lips. Sabina spoke:

- Dov Dorevitch. Your days of evil are over. I have come to save your soul and the future of your people.

This bewildered Dov. He hadn't understood why Metatron had brought his daughter for a diplomatic meeting. But he had expected that the child would stand in the background while the adults were talking. Dov got up, gave Metatron a disapproving look and spoke:

- You better teach your daughter some manners. Rudeness is not appreciated at my court. You would hate to experience what happens to people that are rude to me.

- Now state your business before I lose my temper.

Sabina:

- My father has no business here. I am the one who came to talk to you, Dov.

Sabina's statement confused Dov. Was this a stupid joke? If so, they should know better and be careful around him.
Dov:

- What exactly does a seven-year-old girl from Eden want to discuss with the Chancellor of the Martian Dominion?

Sabina:

- I told you already. I am here to save you and the Martian population from your tyranny.

Dov studied Sabina. There was something eerie about her that made him very uncomfortable. Her eyes were shining blue, and her entire being was glowing with a bright white light that made her look ethereal. Dov pulled himself together; he couldn't afford to show fear in front of a young child.

Dov:

- Why would I need saving? I am the chancellor of the Martian Dominion. I have everything provided. I have every comfort at my disposal.

Sabina:

- That might be. And yet you hardly sleep at night. Self-loathing and fear fill your mind. You wander around without aim, feeling guilty over all the evil deeds you have committed.

Dov:

- You arrogant twat!

Dov lashed out, and he slapped Sabina, as hard as he could. She didn't flinch, but guilt overwhelmed Dov. He felt embarrassed over having such bad self-control. Sabina reached out with her hand and spoke:

- I forgive you, Dov. Take my hand, and you'll feel better.

Dov took Sabina's hand. As their hands met guilt and shame overwhelmed Dov over the terrible crimes that he had committed. Dov felt intense hate towards his right-hand-man Frank Van Stein. With tear-filled eyes bubbling with rage, Dov yelled at Frank:

- You! You were the one who convinced me to release the virus. I never wanted any of this to happen. All that I wanted was to make my brother happy. But he is the devil and nothing will ever satisfy him, so it was all in vain!

Before Frank had the time to respond, Dov pulled up his plasma knife and stabbed Frank several times in the head. After killing Frank, Dov ran up the stairs to the viewing platform overlooking the throne room. Sabina ran after him. When Sabina reached Dov, he was standing with his back to the ledge. Sabina shouted:

- Dov! Stop! There is still time, I can save you.

Dov, with tears running down his cheeks, smiled at Sabina, and replied:

- You already have. Thank you, Sabina!

After this, Dov looked at his bloody and glowing hot plasma knife. He aimed it towards himself, and he stabbed himself between the eyes. Dov fell backwards, and the spikes of the Martian Dominion emblem impaled him. It was a fitting end for Dov's tyranny.

Metatron walked up to Sabina on the viewing platform. Sabina was crying.

Metatron

- So, so baby girl. Everything will be okay.

Sabina:

- I couldn't save him...

Metatron:

- In a way, you did. Dov couldn't live with the guilt over what he had done.

Sabina:

- You are right, dad. I cannot save everyone. I can only do my best.

Metatron:

- Yes, that is how I have learnt to live my life.

Sabina:

- Let's release the antivirus and save as many as we can. There is a lot for us to do on this planet!

After saying this, Metatron and Sabina walked towards the wind generator. Metatron took out a vial with the antivirus, and he inserted it into the same wind generator that had spread the virus. Shortly afterwards, the cloud cover over Nea Atina dispersed, and the inhabitants could see the sun for the first time in many years!

# Chapter 65: Hilda Finds out About Dov's Death

Hilda Muller was at the Hansstadt Zoo with Melanie and their two daughters Emma and Mila. It was a beautiful day, around 22 degrees and clear skies. It was always good weather when Hilda Muller decided to have a day off. Being the ruler of House Muller, she used weather control technologies to make sure of that.

As they studied the animals at the petting zoo, Hilda felt the restlessness creeping in on her. When Hilda had found out about the Zetan technology to create babies from two eggs, the prospect had excited her. But once the surrogate mothers had given birth to her and Melanie's babies, she had realised her mistake. Children didn't interest her. Politics, ruling and management did. Besides, she was living in a unique time in human history. With the threat of a looming alien invasion, forming the next generation couldn't catch her attention. "Yes, that is a sheep, it gives wool", Hilda said with a distant voice. Her mind was elsewhere.

Hilda spotted her cousin, Michael. At first, she got annoyed, this was her day off, and Michael couldn't be slacking here with his family. But Hilda realised that Michael had come with his military aides and that he was heading towards her. He seemed relaxed and casual, so what was going on?

Michael walked up to Hilda and spoke:

- Hilda. There has been a very unexpected development in the Martian Dominion.

Hilda:

- Good or bad?

Michael:

- Good!

- During a meeting with an Edenite delegation, Dov Dorevitch lost the plot and murdered his right-hand man Frank Van Stein in front of everybody. After the murder, he ran to a viewing platform, which overlooks the throne room. He jumped off the platform and plunged to his death.

Hilda:

- Woah. This is great news! Dov was creating an invasion force to invade Earth, but we haven't dared to intervene with the dangerous virus on the Martian surface.

- Is there any hologram video of Dov suicide?

Michael:

- There is. The Martians sent this video to every news outlet.

Hilda studied the hologram video in amazement. The man from Eden was Metatron, and the young girl must have been Sabina. But what did the girl say that drove Dov insane? And why was there a strange aura surrounding the girl?

Hilda:

- Is there any way that we can hear what they are saying in the video?

Michael:

- Only if we hack the Martian Dominion mainframe. This is the video that they provided. They have filtered away the sound.

Hilda:

- What about the strange light surrounding the little girl, Sabina?

Michael:

- Hmm. It looks like a failed video manipulation.

A breaking news notification popped up in one of Hilda's bionic microchips. It read as follows:

Olympus Republic Tribune, 25th October 2882.

The Martian Dominion collapsed today when Dov Dorevitch murdered Frank Van Stein during a meeting with Jack Silver from Eden. Jack Silver has seized interim control over the Olympus Republic. Jack Silver's first move is to grant independence to all the other states subjugated by the Martian Dominion. Jack Silver, also known as Metatron, gave the following statement:

- This is a historic day for the Martian People. The tyranny of the Dorevitch brothers has come to an end. We can now focus on reversing the effect of the horrible Xeno virus that has claimed so many lives. I will be the interim president of the Olympus Republic until we have contained the outbreak. After that, we will hold free elections. I implore everyone to send humanitarian aid to help the afflicted.

May the True Maker bless you all!

Michael, who had read the same news article, spoke in amazement:

- Metatron usurped power from the Dorevitch brothers on Mars.
I can't believe it!

Hilda:

- It wasn't Metatron. He is only a figurehead.

Michael:

- So, who is behind it?

Hilda:

- Metatron's daughter, Sabina Silver.

Michael:

- I hope you are joking? Sabina Silver is seven years old. A seven-year-old play with their dolls and artificial intelligence hologram buddies. They don't stage coupes in other nations.

Hilda:

- But Sabina Silver is anything but ordinary. There is something divine about her. She is a messiah sent to save humanity during these difficult times.

Michael:

- That sounds like superstitious nonsense. But if you are right, that is excellent news.

Hilda looked at Melanie playing with their daughters Emma and Mila. She sighed:

- I am not too sure about that. What if she is meant to save humanity from us?

Michael:

- From us? We have been working tirelessly to save Earth from an alien invasion.

Hilda:

- Yet, less than eight years ago, our relatives tried to commit genocide against the Martian population.

Michael:

- Well, we are different. We are not our relatives. We can change things for the better.

Hilda:

- Yet, I have a lot of blood on my hands.

Michael:

- That is different. You did what you had to do.

Hilda paused and reflected for a moment over her past actions. She couldn't get over the murder of Emma Schindler, and her guilt made Emma's lifeless body appear in front of her eyes.

Hilda stared at the mirage of Emma's corpse for a long time until another Emma, her daughter grabbed her hand. "Are you okay, mommy?" "Yes, I am okay" Hilda mumbled and walked away.

Why had she agreed to Melanie's suggestion to name one of the children Emma? Why had Melanie picked that damn name? Did Melanie want to mess with her head or was it a coincidence? Hilda panicked with paranoia and guilt gripping her mind, and there was only one thing she could do. Hilda ran away, as fast as she could!

# Chapter 66: A Tear-Filled Confession

**"I** *killed her!"*

Hilda Muller was sitting alone with Melanie in her room, hyperventilating and shaking with remorse. Tears were running down her cheeks.

Melanie:

- I don't understand. You killed who?

Hilda:

- I killed Emma Schindler. I poisoned her with a synthetic virus to make it look like a heart attack.

Melanie studied Hilda. She had never seen her partner like this before. Hilda was usually a strong and determined woman, but now her bottled up guilt had brought Hilda to the edge of desolation.

Melanie:

- But why would you kill Emma? She was your best friend?

Hilda:

- Yes, and that is why it is killing me from the inside.

Melanie:

- Tell me what happened?

Hilda:

- Emma led a secret expedition to the Divine Dimension to kill Rangda. It failed terribly and she ended up fighting the Zetans instead. Emma abandoned her unit, and she escaped back to Earth. She was the sole survivor of that expedition.

- I realised that Emma needed to be silenced. The news of what had happened couldn't reach the public. To keep it a secret, I decided to do the dirty deed myself.

Melanie:

- But Emma died many years ago. Why haven't you shared this with me?

Hilda:

- I shared it with my partner at the time, Markus White.

- In my deluded state of mind, I shared it in the most gruesome way possible. Emma's corpse was still in my office when he came to visit.

- Markus stared at me in disgust, and he ran off. I haven't heard from him since.

Melanie:

- At least he did not drag your name in the dirt.

Hilda:

- Yes. I must be thankful about that.

Melanie:

- Is this why you are so distant to our daughter Emma? Because of her name?

Hilda:

- Perhaps. When you suggested naming her after Emma Schindler, I didn't know what to say, so I just went with it.

Melanie:

- I understand.

Melanie studied Hilda for a long time. Eventually, Melanie spoke:

- We'll have to come up with a new name for Emma. I don't want her name to serve as a reminder of what you did!

Hilda dried off her tears with a napkin and spoke:

- So, you do you forgive what I did?

Melanie:

- It is not my place to forgive what you did. You must learn to forgive yourself.

- I will stick by your side for the sake of our children. You are a good person and a good leader. One bout of insanity won't turn you into your evil uncle, Joachim.

Hilda:

- Thank you, Melanie. I will try to forgive myself.

- But one thing scares me. I need to meet with Sabina Silver as I am convinced that she is The Chosen One. But I am afraid that she'll drive me insane as she did to Dov Dorevitch.

Melanie:

- It won't happen.

- You are a good person that is honest about your crimes and try to repent.

- Dov was a psychotic mass-murderer until Sabina showed him the light. You'll be fine. I believe that you'll feel better after meeting Sabina.

Hilda:

- Thank you! I will meet with Metatron and Sabina as soon as possible.

After saying this, the burden on Hilda's chest lightened and together they drank tea watching the soothing fire, in the central fireplace of their residence.

# Chapter 67: Complications with the Antivirus

It was February 2883, and Metatron was sitting in his office in the presidential palace of the Olympus Republic. He studied the reports on hand, and he sighed. There were unforeseen complications with the airborne antivirus. Although the Xeno virus had disappeared from the population, it had done so at a steep cost. 20 per cent of the remaining population had died from the cure, bringing the Martian population down to 1.6 billion.

Metatron didn't know what to do. He had been running Eden for a decade, but that was a tiny world where he knew most of the inhabitants personally. Running a crumbling empire, while trying to avoid a complete collapse was another matter.

Unfortunately, all the helpers that Metatron had brought in from Eden faced the same predicament. In his desperation, Metatron had invited the Terran Council to come back and run the planet. The Terran Council had declined the proposal. After their total defeat in the war of Martian independence, they had lost interest in the planet, and besides, they had more pressing matters on hand than retaking a former colony, when the threat of an alien invasion was still looming.

Metatron thought of Sabina. Did his sweet and gentle daughter understand the consequences of their actions? She hadn't been out much since they released the antivirus. Her usual self would be out among the poor and inflicted, trying to help them. But since they seized control over Mars, four months earlier, Sabina had acted reclusively staying by herself for days on end.

Metatron decided to visit Sabina, and as expected she was in deep meditation when he entered her room. Sabina opened her eyes, and she smiled upon seeing him:

- Nice to see you, daddy. I am happy that you are here.

Metatron:

- I am happy to see you too, darling. But I am worried about you. You used to be out with other kids and help people back on Eden. Since we arrived here, you have sought isolation. What has changed?

Sabina:

- The other children in the light brigade are doing my work for me. And they are doing it well.

- The True Maker told me to stay in isolation and meditate. She told me that if I went out and witnessed the carnage and destruction caused by Dov and his men, I would be filled with rage. Rage would taint my soul and make me vulnerable to Rangda.

Metatron:

- Okay, I see. So, is the True Maker a girl?

Sabina:

- The True Maker is an eternal force that is older than our universe. It has no real form. To me, she is a girl my age. To you, probably a man your age. To a cat, perhaps a cat. Such is the nature of the True Maker.

Metatron:

- Well, that is an interesting idea. I have some good news. We have managed to rid the planet of the Xeno virus infection.

Sabina:

- I know. And the cost was high. Way too high. And I don't understand why.
- Why couldn't the True Maker give me an antivirus that killed no-one?

Metatron:

- Maybe there is no such thing in the world. A universal solution without drawbacks?

Sabina:

- But I wonder, why did she choose me? She could have picked anyone?

Metatron:

- Well, perhaps she did choose anyone, and you happened to be that person?

Sabina pondered what Metatron had said for a while and then she smiled and spoke:

- Thank you, dad. Can you bring my games console? We haven't played together for such a long time.

Metatron thought about his commitments for the day, and then he thought *"fuck it"* He wouldn't be useful to anyone if he kept sacrificing his alone time with his daughter to help others. Metatron spoke:

- Yes, darling. Which game would you like to play?

Sabina:

- The game with the fairy princess and the frogs, daddy.

Metatron turned on the game. During that afternoon he felt like a normal dad for once, enjoying electronic games with his seven-year-old daughter.

# Chapter 68: "It is Not My Place to Forgive You."

In March 2883, a month after Metatron had declared Mars Xeno virus-free, Hilda Muller arrived at Nea Atina. Hilda studied the city that she hadn't visited since 2872 when the Olympus Republic was a vassal state to House Muller. Back in 2872, Nea Atina was a bustling metropolis. While it had been dirt poor compared to the luxury of the House Muller capital, Hansstadt, it had still been a liveable city. Now, the city resembled a ghost town. It was clear that most of the inhabitants had died. A thick sensation of death and suffering was still covering the city.

Hilda entered the throne room where Metatron and Sabina received her. Hilda felt weak, and her legs almost buckled under her weight. But she had to atone for her sins, and what better way to do so, than confessing her sins to the Chosen One?

As Hilda was approaching, Sabina stood up and spoke:

- Hilda Muller. I know why you have come. But it is not my place to forgive you for what you have done.

Hearing this, Hilda collapsed to the floor and started crying:

- But I have travelled so far to meet you. I don't know what to do. I can't live with this pain and guilt any longer.

Sabina studied Hilda, who was lying in front of her feet, wailing. She walked up to Hilda, held her hand to comfort her and spoke:

- It isn't my place to forgive you, but I can give you the energy to pursue the righteous path and do good for humankind.

While saying this, Sabina shone with an aura of white holy light. Hilda, who held Sabina's hand, felt rejuvenated with a burden lifted off her chest. Hilda:

- Thank you for sharing your time with me, Sabina. How can I start my journey towards atonement?

Sabina:

- You can organise a relief and rebuilding program for Mars, now that the Xeno virus has disappeared and it is safe to do so.

- And I have a favour to ask of you.

Hilda:

- I will do anything you ask of me, Your Grace.

Sabina:

- Good. Somewhere on Earth, there is a primordial Zeto Crystal hidden. I need you to find it and bring to me, for safe-keeping against Rangda.

Hilda:

- Primordial Zeto Crystal? I have never heard about such an arte-fact?

Sabina:

- But you might have heard about the Holy Grail?

Hilda:

- Yes.

Sabina:

- It's the same thing.
- You better hurry up, Rangda will come to look for it.

Hilda:

- What about you, Sabina?

Sabina:

- I need to stay here. There is still so much suffering on Mars. Perfect conditions for Rangda to sway a weak mind to do her evil bidding.

Hilda:

- I understand. I will head back to Earth as soon as possible. I will assist you with the full might of House Muller.

- I hope we will meet again, Mistress Sabina.

Sabina:

- So, do I, Mistress Muller. Farewell and good luck.

After the conversation, Hilda and her delegation headed back to Earth. There was plenty to do, and time was running short.

# Chapter 69: Rangda and Melchior's Armies Approach Earth.

Two years later, In July 2885, Rangda and Melchior's massive armies had arrived close to the portals to Earth. They had spent the last years plundering Goldonia and Grashdunt to build an even bigger army, and new troops were joining them every day. They had over 30 million soldiers under their command, and together with Dov's forces attacking from orbit, the Terrans wouldn't stand a chance!

Melchior rushed into Rangda's command module. He was pale, fearful, and furious at the same time. Out of breath, he spoke:

- Dov is dead, and we won't receive any Martian help from orbit.

Rangda:

- What! Who killed that fat fool?
- Wait, don't tell. I know who did it. I can feel her presence.

Melchior:

- Spit it out! Grrrrrr!

Rangda:

- Sabina! That holier than thou lackey of the True Maker has more guts and potential than I gave her credit.

Melchior:

- We should have killed her when we had the chance!

Rangda:

- Yes! On the bright side, her shattered soul will be a worthy addition to the tormented souls that fuels my corrupted Zeto Crystals!

Melchior:

- I don't care about that! How the fuck are we going to invade Earth now that the Terran Council controls the skies?

Rangda gave Melchior an evil look and blasted him to the ground with a psionic blast. Rangda roared:

- Silence, you dog. Earth means nothing to me. I am here for the last primordial Zeto Crystal. That is all that matters.

- We will order our troops to commence with the invasion as a diversion. Meanwhile, you and I will lead a small strike force through a secret portal to steal the last Zeto Crystal.

Melchior:

- Yes, Empress Rangda. May I ask where the secret portal will take us?

Rangda:

- To the temple in Jerusalem. We will find the primordial Zeto Crystal hidden in the catacombs below.

- Assemble your best men, we are moving at once. The Terrans are looking for the crystal as well. I worry that they are close to uncovering it and give it to Sabina. This would be a monumental setback!

Melchior:

- Yes, Empress Rangda. I will alert the troops to strike at once!

Having said this, Melchior left the room to prepare his troops for the upcoming invasion of Earth.

# Chapter 70: A Confrontation in the Catacombs

Hilda Muller was at the excavation site in the catacombs under the great temple in Jerusalem. Hilda's archaeology expedition had reached a breakthrough, and her archaeologists had summoned her.

Hilda studied the blue crystal. It shone with a surreal light, and it was exciting to uncover something so magical.

Hilda received a phone call in one of her nanotechnology augmentations. It was from Michael Muller:

- Hilda! Red Alert. The Xenos have launched full-scale invasion through the portals. They are bringing other unidentified alien species as well.

Hilda:

- Okay. Send all our troops to protect the defensive perimeter. We must stop the enemy from gaining a foothold.

Michael:

- Understood. I will convey the order at once.

After hanging up on her cousin, Hilda turned towards the archaeologists and shouted.

- Hurry up.

- We are facing a full-scale alien invasion. We need to get this crystal to safety!

The workers dug as fast as they could. Half an hour later, the workers had cut away the rock that encased the crystal. Hilda picked up the crystal, and she studied it. Hilda stood mesmerised for a while, but a terrible noise brought her back to her senses. It was the noise of Xeno claws chopping her workers into pieces. Hilda turned around, and there she was, her worst nightmare, Rangda!

Rangda:

- We meet again. After over 10 years, it's time to end your life!

Hilda:

- I am not dead yet, and you'll regret stabbing my workers in the back.

Rangda:

- We'll see about that. Xenos! Charge!

Dozens of Xenos charged at Hilda, who held the Zeto Crystal in her left hand. Hilda moved with incredible speed and strength as she danced the room, killing the dozens of beasts with her plasma sword.

Rangda:

- Impressive. The Zeto Crystal is enhancing your already exceptional combat abilities.

- But you are no match for me! Check this out.

Rangda powered her own physical body using her six corrupted Zeto Crystals. Faster than the eye could see, Rangda stabbed Hilda a dozen times. Hilda collapsed to the ground, and she dropped her plasma sword and the Zeto Crystal. Rangda picked up the Zeto Crystal from the ground. She studied it for a while, and then she laughed psychotically.

- Ha-Ha-Ha-ha! The seventh and last Zeto Crystal, with this in my hand no one will able to stop me. I am on the brink of reaching godhood!

- Any last words?

Hilda:

- You talk too much.

Having said this, Hilda pulled up a pistol from her foot holster and shot Rangda six times in the face. The bullets blinded Rangda, but they didn't kill her as the corrupted Zeto Crystals powered her. Blinded and hissing, Rangda took the Zeto Crystal and rushed towards the portal where she met Melchior, who looked at her in awe:

- What happened, Empress Rangda?

Rangda:

- Nothing, you fool. I got the crystal, and these are small scratches. Let's head back, you idiot.

Screeching in pain, Rangda hurried back through the portal. Shortly afterwards, all the attacks ended. As for Hilda, she died from the blood-loss, but her faction could revive her as Rangda had failed to permanently kill her.

# Chapter 71: Rangda Corrupts the Final Zeto crystal.

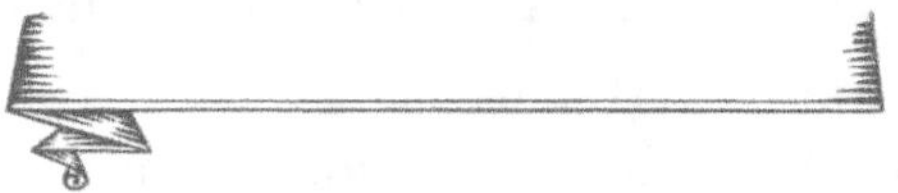

A few weeks later, Rangda's eyes and face had healed from the gunshot wounds. She had been careless but lucky. Mocking the dying Hilda, without ensuring that she wasn't a threat, was an embarrassing oversight that could have cost Rangda her life. Luckily, the power from the corrupted Zeto Crystals had filled her body with immense energy. This unholy energy had absorbed most of the power in the bullets, preventing them from penetrating into her brain.

Now that Rangda's eyesight had recovered, she was ready to perform the ritual to corrupt the seventh and last primordial Zeto Crystal. Once she had completed the ceremony, she would have close to limitless power, and no-one would be able to stand against her. As Rangda prepared for the ritual, she heard an unfamiliar voice:

- Don't do it, Rangda. If you corrupt the seventh and last crystal, you will upset the balance of the universe and the Milky Way. You'll destroy the galaxy, which you seek to enslave.

Rangda screeched at the tranquil voice:

- Is this the True Maker that I am talking to?
- If so, come out and face me! You have been hiding for long enough!

The True Maker:

- I see no reason to show myself to you. I have lived for trillions of years in hundreds of iterations of the universe. Your schemes, no matter how grand they seem to you, are insignificant to me.

Rangda:

- Grrrahhhhh! You are afraid of me. That is why you have been training your protégé girl to face me. Once I have corrupted the last Zeto Crystal, I will be more powerful than you, and I will take your place. I don't care if you have lived for trillions of years. Times are changing, and I am coming after you.

The True Maker:

- The only thing that concerns me is the immensity of my own omnipotence. Also, I prefer non-interference as I have given free will to all my creations.

- You'll face Sabina in two years. Kneel to her and seek my forgiveness. If not, I will smite you. I am done talking to you.

Rangda:

- Very well, old fool. I got things to do anyway.

Rangda performed the ritual to corrupt the seventh Zeto Crystal. After finishing the ritual, the seven crystals merged to one and became part of her body. If Rangda had felt powerful before, it was nothing compared to what she felt now. As Rangda shrieked in triumph, the entire fabric of the Milky Way trembled. Cosmic energy of hatred and malevolence radiated from Rangda and dimmed the starlight.

# Chapter 72: Hilda Wakes up from a Coma Facing the Impending Doom.

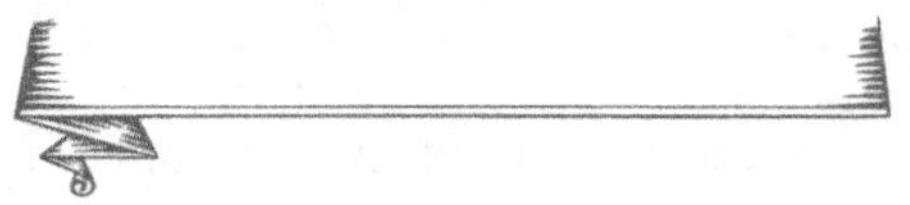

In October 2885, Hilda Muller woke up from her induced coma. Hilda felt very strange. She had experienced the dreamless sleep of cryogenic sleep in the past, but it hadn't felt like this. Had she come back from the dead? Hilda looked around in the room, and she saw the faces of her partner Melanie and her cousin Michael. Melanie tried to smile, while Michael wasn't trying to hide his worries and distressed emotional state. Hilda decided to address the situation:

- What is going on? What happened to me? Why do you guys look so worried?

Michael:

- Rangda ambushed you. You fought well and killed dozens of Xenos. Unfortunately, Rangda got the better of you, and she stole the Zeto Crystal. You succumbed to your injuries. Our men found you dead but not beyond resurrection. We have regrown your damaged body, and you are as good as new.

Hilda:

- How is the war against Rangda and Melchior going?

Michael:

- They couldn't break through our defences. They stopped attacking as soon as they had secured the Zeto Crystal.

Hilda:

- That is excellent news. If they can't defeat us, that means we can overcome them. Especially if we get the Martians to help.

Michael:

- No, we can't. They closed the portals behind them. Frey and Freya never gave us the correct sequence for opening the portals.

Melanie couldn't take it anymore. She fell into tears, and she started talking:

- War or no war. There is an even bigger problem.
- Our galaxy is dying!

Hilda:

- What do you mean, Melanie?

Melanie was too agitated to answer, so Michael replied for her:

- It started a few weeks ago. We have detected a lot of gamma-ray bursts lately, and our own Sun is acting erratically as well. Stars are dying around us, and there is nothing we can do about it. Earth's magnetic field has protected us this far. But the gamma bursts have fried some of our asteroid mining stations, killing everyone affected.

Hilda:

- Then there is only one person who can save us.

Michael:

- What do you expect Sabina to do about the cosmic gamma-ray blasts?

Hilda:

- It is not a matter of logic. It is a matter of faith. We must turn to the light when everything seems dark.

Michael:

- Very well, I will extend her an invitation.

Hilda:

- And, I will beg her to come. The True Maker needs to be on our side!

After saying this, Hilda pushed herself to get out of bed, and she sent an emergency transmission urging Sabina to come.

# Chapter 73: I am not ready yet.

Sabina and Metatron arrived on Earth to meet with Hilda and Michael. It had been a perilous trip, as the massive increase in background radiation and sun activity made space travel dangerous. The trip was essential though, as they needed to get to Earth to fulfil Sabina's purpose.

Sabina and Metatron stepped out of their spacecraft. A large group of kneeling worshippers met them and paid them respect. Hilda Muller was one of the worshippers.

- Welcome to Earth, Saint Sabina.

Sabina:

- I wish I had received the same welcome on my latest visit. How different things could have been.

- No matter, please get up. I can sense that your knees are hurting, and the last thing I want is to cause you pain.

The worshippers got up on their feet, and Sabina spoke:

- I know why you have summoned me to the home planet of humanity. Trust me, I would love to help, but I am not ready yet.

Hilda:

- But people are dying every day, from the gamma-ray bursts. A massive blast could wipe out all life in on the planet.

Sabina:

- So will the black hole that is moving towards us from Alpha Centauri. It is bound for collision in a decade. But I am not ready yet.

Hilda:

- What do you mean? Alpha Centauri is still around. We received an update from our colony there, earlier today.

Sabina:

- The radio signals from Alpha Centauri have travelled for four years and are from four years ago. By the time you'll notice what happened to Alpha Centauri, the Black Hole will be halfway to our solar system.

- But don't worry. The True Maker said I'd be ready on my 12th birthday, and that is only one and a half years away.

Hilda:

- Can't you move any faster? A lot can happen in one and a half years.

Sabina:

- I could. But it would be unwise to ignore the advice from the deity that grants me my powers.

Hilda:

- So, what can we do?

Sabina:

- You can pray, but only if this makes you feel better. I don't need your worship; I am only playing out the role that the True Maker gave me. Pray to the True Maker if you wish, but prayer doesn't affect the True Maker. Aim to live well-balanced lives in peace, harbouring hope and a desire to do good deeds.

- Now, I must meditate. The space travel upset my harmony, and I need to restore it to fulfil my purpose.

Hilda:

- Of course. Your accommodation contains a specific meditation room.

Sabina:

- Your hospitality is much appreciated.
- Farewell, and I hope to see you for dinner.

Hilda:

- It will be my pleasure. See you later, Your Grace.

After the conversation, Hilda led Sabina to a shuttle that took her to her accommodation in Hansstadt.

# Chapter 74: "You're Destroying the Galaxy that We Seek to Dominate."

Melchior felt agitated. His brother was dead, and he had lost control of his empire. All that remained was his large, but beatable, army. On top of things, it seemed like the Milky Way Galaxt was self-destructing. Every single day one or several star systems exploded. Every star that exploded sent out gamma-ray bursts with the potential to kill anything that they hit. If nothing changed, there wouldn't be anything left for him to conquer and dominate.

Melchior made his way to Rangda's new temple. It was a sight to behold. The Xenos had built it from the Dwarven gold on Goldonia. Large rubies symbolising blood covered the temple. In the temple towers, flames struck up like spectacular fire fountains. Melchior entered the building. He walked past some blood fountains, and he approached Rangda's throne. Rangda had ornamented the throne with severed heads, representing the races that she had conquered. Rangda didn't notice Melchior as she was busy torturing the unfortunate Keila Eisenstein. Rangda had kept Keila alive and had spent the last decade abusing and draining her of psionic energy.

Melchior shouted to Rangda:

- Rangda! What are you doing?

Rangda turned around and gave Melchior a dirty look:

- Is that the way to address your empress?
- Do not ever interrupt me when I am enjoying my time with Keila!

Melchior:

- I don't give a shit about Keila, but you're destroying the very galaxy, which we seek to dominate.

Melchior's attitude infuriated Rangda. She blasted him with a powerful psionic blast, which knocked him to the ground. The blast caused Melchior to bleed from all his cavities.

Rangda:

- Silence, you fool!

- I am not the one who is destroying the galaxy. It is that coward, the True Maker who doesn't dare to face me.

- But I will destroy her "Holy Prophet". As Sabina falls, the True Maker has no choice but to face me.

Melchior responded weakly:

- Forgive me, my empress. I never intended to anger you.

Rangda:

- I don't care. Crawl back to your soldiers. I am sure that they can patch you up. Do not return here unless I summon you!

After saying this, Rangda ran to her dungeons where she murdered some prisoners while she kept shouting: "Come out you coward, I will get you!"

# Chapter 75: I Am Ready.

In July 2887 Sabina woke up in the middle of the night. She felt different but at peace. She felt like her spirit was about to leave her body. Was she dying? Sabina got out of bed and realised that her body was still carrying her without a hitch. Sabina realised what it was. She would turn 12 in a couple of days, and she would reach the age of the ancient adulthood ceremony. Her body was telling her that she was ready to face Rangda. Sabina left her room, and she walked over to the private bedroom of her hostess, Hilda Muller. Sabina studied Hilda for a while, realising that Hilda was having a nightmare. She put her palm on Hilda's temple, and Hilda calmed down.

Hilda woke up and looked at Sabina. It wasn't the girl she had gotten used to seeing. Instead, it was like seeing an angel appearing in front of her.

Hilda:

- Sabina, what happened to you?

Sabina:

- I am turning 12, and I am becoming an adult. I am ready to fulfil my destiny and face Rangda.

Hilda:

- That's a great relief! Is there anything I can do to assist you?

Sabina:

- Yes. Tell your soldiers to clear a path for me to the portal at the Cheops pyramid. Tell your people that the age of darkness will soon be over.

Hilda:

- I can do that.

Sabina:

- You'd better hurry. Time is short, and I need to fulfil my destiny.

Hilda:

- Got it. I will assemble the full might of House Muller to help you at once!

Having said this, Hilda got up, and she hurried to contact her army to put everyone on full alert.

# Chapter 76: Sabina Faces Rangda

A week later, Sabina; Hilda and Metatron visited the military base that secured the portal at the Cheops Pyramid. Sabina double-checked the date. Today was her 12th birthday, and it was time to face the destroyer of the universe, Rangda. Sabina picked her clothes: a simple white dress, sandals and a walking stick. Hilda had offered her a high-technology battle armour, but Sabina had rejected the notion. The key to defeating Rangda lay in her mind, and in her faith, not in her technology. Using modern technology would weaken her spirituality, and it would be suicide to approach Rangda's hordes with force.

Sabina travelled in an open car towards the pyramid. Along the road, thousands of worshippers had lined up, all dressed in white clothes to honour her. They reached the perimeter to the pyramid, and the car drove to the base of the Cheops pyramid. Sabina, Hilda and Metatron got out of the car.

Sabina:

- This is it. My time has come.

Hilda:

- I wish that I could do more...

Sabina

- You have played your part. I couldn't have done any of this without your support.

- Now you must leave. Once I open the portal, the enemy might choose to invade.

Metatron:

- I am coming with you.

Sabina:

- Father, this isn't your fight.

Metatron:

- It doesn't matter. You are my daughter, and if you are the Chosen One, I will stand by you to the end.

Sabina:

- I cannot deny you that wish, father. Hilda, please return to your people. They need you.

Having said this, Sabina and Metatron started climbing the Cheops Pyramid. A myriad of drones filmed them, and broadcasted the event to population. As they reached the top, Sabina started chanting a verse in an ancient language. Energy in the form of white light flowed from her hands and powered up the portal. The portal lit up, bluer than ever.
Sabina:

- This is it. If you enter this portal, you'll see Keila one last time, but you'll never return to see Jasmine, Jordan or Melissa.

Metatron:

- So, will I die if I enter this portal?

Sabina:

- The only certainty in life is death. Melissa needs you; Jordan and Jasmine need their father. The only reason you are clinging on to me is the hope to see Keila again. But what you hope for will never be.

Hearing this made Metatron emotional, and he started crying:

- But you said you'd let me come with you. I want to stay by your
side until the end.

Sabina:

- I am happy that you do father, but some sacrifices are not meant
to be. Now sleep, father.

Sabina grabbed Metatron's hand. And she used her powers to put her father to sleep. After that, she entered the portal, and then she closed it from
the other side.

Sabina walked towards the enormous golden temple that Rangda had
built to honour herself. In front of the temple, Rangda had stationed a large
army. The army attacked Sabina, but to no avail. A sphere of bright light, surrounded Sabina, and it stopped every attack that Rangda's minions threw at
her. The sphere stopped bullets mid-air. Anyone who tried to attack Sabina
from close range got pacified by her divine powers, and ended up bowing to
her instead.

Sabina entered Rangda's temple. Rangda was sitting on her throne, and
Melchior was sitting on a chair below her. Keila was also in the room, and
she was locked her up in a psionic force-field. Sabina walked towards Rangda. When she was ten metres away, she spoke:

- Rangda Kaliankan! On behalf of the True Maker, I request that
you surrender to me, and repent for your many crimes.

Rangda:

- Kaliankan, the daughter of Kalianka? So, your master told you
to use my Zetan family name. To what purpose may I ask? I made
it my life goal to exterminate the Zetans, and I have succeeded.
The Zetans are no more.

Sabina:

- The Zetans and your mother still live on within you. I know what happened to your mother. But you misguided your anger. You can't hate an entire species for what one individual once did.

Rangda:

- Ah, joy. I realised a long time ago that vengeance was a stupid motivation. But I also understood something else about myself. That I enjoy increasing my own power and causing suffering towards others.

Sabina:

- Well, your reign of terror is over. You will yield to the power and the mercy of the True Maker, or she'll smite you.

Rangda:

- Ah, The True Maker. That snivelling coward sending a little girl, instead of facing me herself! This is my answer!

- Melchior!

Melchior:

- Yes, Empress Rangda.

Rangda:

- Slay that insolent girl and bring me her head!!

Melchior did as Rangda commanded, and he rushed towards Sabina with a drawn plasma-sword. When he was about to strike her, Sabina grabbed Melchior's hand and spoke:

- Melchior, it is okay. By the powers of The True Maker, I forgive your sins and cleanse your soul. May you find the ability to forgive yourself.

The influx of light into Melchior's dark soul caused him great agony, and he fell to the ground screaming from pain. Inner conflict tore Melchior apart. After a few seconds, he found his resolve. He would kill Rangda, who had caused him to do all these evil things. Melchior lifted his sword and ran towards her, but he didn't get far. Rangda used the powers of the corrupted crystals to disintegrate Melchior's body.

Rangda scoffed at Sabina:

- Ah! Bless. The pure Sabina Eisenstein, "The Chosen One", using her magic to drive a man insane causing his death. Are we that different after all?

Sabina:

- I gave him a chance to return to the light. I couldn't affect how he would react. The True Maker gave us free will, after all.

Rangda:

- A distinction without a difference. You knew exactly how he would react. Thus, you caused his death, regardless whether you'd admit it or not.

- And now I will cause your death!

Sabina:

- I am protected by the light of the True Maker. There is nothing you can do to me. Your army couldn't touch me; your champion couldn't affect me. And you can't touch me either.

Rangda:

- True as that may be, the same doesn't apply to your poor old mother, Keila. It is time to wake her up so she can see her lost daughter!

Rangda blasted Keila with a psionic blast. This woke up the weak and old Keila from the suspended animation that she had been in. Rangda deactivated the force-field that surrounded Keila, and Keila collapsed to the floor.

Sabina was crying and said:

- Mother. I have come to save you.

Rangda:

- Yes. Keila, your dear old mother. Why don't you comfort her and tell her that everything is going to be okay?

Sabina didn't respond. Instead she ran towards her dying biological mother. When Sabina was close to Keila, Rangda blasted Keila with a psionic blast that caused Keila to bleed from every orifice in her body. Keila looked at Sabina with a terrified look, before passing out from the pain. Rangda laughed hysterically:

- Oh, your poor mother! Who would have thought that finally seeing you would cause her so much pain?

Sabina:

- You were the one causing her pain. Seeing me, ignited hope in her soul. Now she can die in peace.

Rangda:

- Oh, but she is not dying. I have perfected the art of torturing her. I will resuscitate her again and again. Only endless pain awaits your poor old mum in this timeless place.

Sabina:

- But why would you treat my mum so horribly? What did she ever do to you?

Rangda:

- Oh, little girl, you don't know me very well. I do it because I can, and because it amuses me. I have free will, after all! Hee-hee-hee!

Sabina lost her cool and yelled out:

- Rangda, you are an evil monster!! I will end you once and for all.

After saying this, Sabina smote Rangda with an intense flash of pure light. The blast was insanely powerful, and it scorched Rangda. Rangda fell, burning and screaming to the floor, and Sabina collapsed from exhaustion. Sabina crawled to her dying mother. Sabina held Keila's hand to ensure that her soul could move on to the afterlife, escaping from the evil curse that Rangda had cast on her. Sabina felt drained, but she also felt a sense of optimism. Had she fulfilled her destiny?

Deep despair struck Sabina, when she realised that she had failed to kill Rangda. Rangda arose, with third-degree burns all over her body. Rangda hissed towards Sabina:

- You pitiful girl. I defeated you like I defeated the Elves. The True Maker's light protected you, and you threw it away. How does it feel knowing that your death is approaching?

Sabina:

- I feel at peace knowing that my mother's soul has been able to move on. If I die because of my love for my mother, I might have failed, but at least I didn't fail for the wrong reasons.

Rangda hissed and spoke:

- Very well. Prepare to die!

Rangda rushed towards Sabina. Sabina tried to defend herself, but she stood no chance without her divine assistance. After a short fight, Sabina lay lifeless on the floor as Rangda tore her body to shreds. Rangda laughed diabolically and called out:

- True Maker. Your Chosen One has failed. Now face me, you coward!

A flash of bright light appeared and shook the foundation of the temple.

# Chapter 77: The True Maker Destroys the Milky Way Galaxy

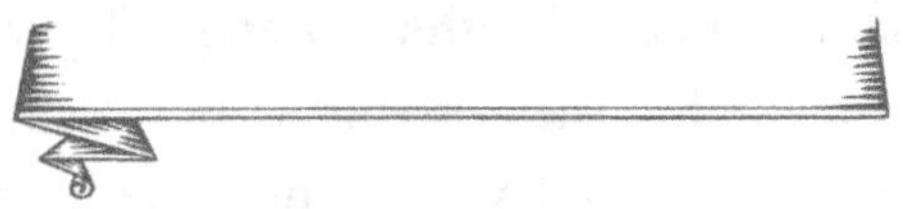

Rangda stared in disbelief. In front of her, was the mirage of her dead mother, Kalianka, accompanied by the spirit of the fallen Sabina. In shock, Rangda stuttered:

- Mother?!

The True Maker:

- Your mother was one of my septillion forms in this galaxy, and the one I found the most suitable to use communicating with you.

Rangda:

- I don't understand!

The True Maker:

- I am the creator of the universe, but I also am the universe. In this universe, I am everyone and no-one. That's why I don't have an ego and a body of my own.

Rangda:

- Bullshit. You sent that kid to fight me. You have your own agen-da.

The True Maker:

- Harmony and balance. Although I am the universe, my celestial power can't regulate something as large as the universe. Thus, I divided my essence into Zeto crystals and spread them out. I placed seven crystals in each galaxy to keep the cosmos balanced and full of life.

- The unbalancing happened with the Zetans. The Zetans discovered the potential within the Zeto Crystals, which was the starting point for the abnormal development. "Intelligent life" as you call it, is not the natural state of the universe, as intelligent life always destroys the ecosystems that they live in.

- The vanity of the Zetans caused them to alter species in their image. The Zetans altered Humans, Xenos, Dwarves, Elves, Orcs and many other species. They are all unnatural creations, but in the grand scheme of things, insignificant.

- The real issue is you, Rangda. When you corrupted the Zeto Crystals, you disrupted the harmony of the Cosmos. When you corrupted the last Zeto Crystal in the Milky Way Galaxy, you destroyed the balance, and you doomed the galaxy.

Rangda:

- Thank you for exposing the truth. Now that I know that there are seven Zeto Crystals in each galaxy, I know that I can become even more powerful if I conquer all galaxies!

The True Maker:

- But you'll not. Because I will stop you.

Rangda:

- You fool. I am not scared of you. I killed your pawn, and I will kill you! Take this!

Rangda blasted the True Maker with the full force of her seven corrupted Zeto Crystals. This didn't affect The True Maker, as they were only seven out of billions of Zeto Crystals that existed in the universe. The True Maker realised that Rangda would never stop. She would have to sacrifice the Milky Way galaxy to save the universe.

The True Maker:

- I wish to say sorry to all living beings of the Milky Way Galaxy. I have chosen to cease your existence.

The True Maker released a gargantuan burst of energy that destroyed the Milky Way Galaxy.

After an extended hiatus, The True Maker studied what remained of the Milky Way. There was nothing but darkness and dead stars. "I'm still here", The True Maker heard a familiar voice and, she turned around. There she was, the spirit of Sabina, who was the sole survivor of the destroyed Milky Way Galaxy.

# Chapter 78: Sabina Pleads the True Maker to Turn Back Time.

The True Maker heard the voice of Sabina and spoke:

- How can you still be around? How did you survive the blast that destroyed your galaxy? This is beyond my divine knowledge.

Sabina:

- Change your form to one more relatable to me, and I will explain. Please change to a young version of my mother, Keila Eisenstein.

The True Maker did as Sabina requested, and Sabina spoke again:

- I thought I failed when I lashed out against Rangda and lost your protection.

The True Maker:

- Yes, that was the fate that befell the Elves of Elvonia. You cannot misuse the Zeto Crystals to kill living beings.

Sabina:

- Yes. But as Rangda tore my body into shreds, I realised something. That I didn't feel any pain or fear. My death was a transition to my natural state. The state of a spirit.

- I also realised something else. That I was never at fault for using the power of light to smite Rangda. I was lashing out to save my mother from more suffering. It was an act of love.

The True Maker:

- Yes, but a reckless one at that. It forced me to destroy the entire galaxy to stop Rangda's evil from spreading throughout the universe.

Sabina:

- Yes, but what if it was inevitable? How would I ever defeat Rangda by being pure good? Melchior and the other villains were suffering from their evil deeds deep inside, but Rangda didn't experience those feelings.

The True Maker:

- Yes, you are right; it was inevitable. I foresaw it, but I mourned the loss of life that would follow if I confronted Rangda myself. I guess I put my 'hope' in you when everything else failed.

Sabina:

- But what if this is not the end?

The True Maker:

- What do you mean?

Sabina:

- Well, you have told me that you have reset universe many times and that you are trillions of years old...

The True Maker:

- I am not sure I follow you.

Sabina:

- What if, we could turn back time?

The True Maker:

- In theory, it's a good plan, but in practice, no. If we turn back time, we might save this galaxy, but we might condemn ten others. Even for me, the Almighty Creator of the universe, it's impossible to foresee the consequences of such an action.

Sabina:

- But if we settle for turning back time in this galaxy, we won't affect the other galaxies.

The True Maker:

- But I cannot reverse time in individual galaxies. They are all connected, and so are my time-reversing capabilities.

Sabina:

- But what if I can do it for you? I am a lesser spirit, and I would have a smaller scope for your abilities.

The True Maker:

- Hmm. It's a blatant violation of the physics of the universe. But I am the physics of the universe, and I am willing to give it a try. Enter my soul, Sabina.

Sabina entered the True Maker's soul, and it was an exhilarating and magical experience. She experienced memories of the septillions of life forms, which had lived throughout the history of the Milky Way. Sabina snapped out of it. She had a mission, and she would make sure that things turned out good this time.

The year 2868 came up in Sabina's mind. It was the year when Rangda escaped from her Zetan prison and set out on her evil quest. "Here goes nothing," Sabina thought. Sabina activated the time reversing capability. She turned back time to the year 2868, when her mother was 18 years old.

# Chapter 79: Remembering an Old Friend

Rear Admiral Bjorn Muller was staring at the calendar in his office on the Phobos base. The date was the 12th of February 2868, and it triggered terrible memories. 18 years earlier, his best friend in exile, Mahmoud Rashid, had succumbed to the harsh living conditions on Mars. Mahmoud had been stripped him of his Terran citizenship, due to his love to Susanna, an Edenite woman.

The episode had shocked Bjorn. The fact that his friend had married a non-Terran woman against his families wishes, flabbergasted Bjorn. The harsh punishment of Mahmoud also surprised Bjorn. Mahmoud got dumped off on Mars without money or ability to sustain himself. Mahmoud's only crime was to fall in love with someone against his grandfather's wishes.

Losing Mahmoud had been hard for Bjorn. Despite coming from rivalling families, they had grown close, as they came from similar circumstances. Bjorn and Mahmoud had frosty relationships with their families, which had urged them to leave Earth and serve in the army. While they received high ranks in the Terran Council Security Forces, they knew why they were in the military. Their families wanted to keep them as far away as possible.

Bjorn had tried to keep his best friend alive throughout the decade that had followed. Bjorn couldn't support Mahmoud Rashid directly due to a Terran Council decree. So, Bjorn instructed the puppet president of The Olympus Republic to support Mahmoud and Susanna. Mahmoud and Susanna changed their family name to Susana's family name, Eisenstein, to blend in. After many years of marriage, Susanna became pregnant with Keila. Unfortunately, Susanna's pregnancy coincided with Mahmoud falling ill.

Mahmoud's sickness and death created a permanent scar in Bjorn Muller. The fact that Mahmoud's condition was treatable with Terran technology plagued Bjorn. He had failed his friend as he could not give Mahmoud the treatment he needed.

After Mahmoud's death, Bjorn lost interest in Susanna and Mahmoud's daughter, Keila. He instructed the puppet president to give them enough money to lead a good life, but apart from that, he played no part in their lives.

# Chapter 80: Dreaming about Earth

Keila woke up with a smile. She had the same recurring dream that she had experienced a lot lately. In the vision, Keila was on Earth, together with her handsome prince and their beautiful children. She closed her eyes again, and the images continued. Mars was no longer a dry and cold dust-bowl filled with poverty and suffering. Instead, the planet had turned into a paradise full of flora and fauna, where people lived in harmony and peace. Keila sighed. If only these dreams could come true!

Keila had grown up in a well-off home raised by her mother, Susanna. Her father had been from a prominent Terran bloodline who died before she was born. This had brought the advantage that she had a secret benefactor, ensuring that she would never go hungry. All in all, Keila's life in Pamshal was pretty good. Pamshal was a wealthy city-state and its massive city walls, as well as Pamshal's alliance with The Olympus Republic, kept the city safe.

Despite her young age, Keila had seen a lot of Earth. Her mother, Susanna, was an activist who smuggled supplies to help the starving regions of Mars. While appreciating the importance of her mother's work, Keila did not want to go in her footsteps. Instead, she wanted to move to Earth and live a good life there. Keila was turning 18 in a month, and she had looked into getting a Terran citizenship. If she got it, she would be able to leave Mars and live on humanity's beautiful home planet instead.

Susanna had shunned Keila's plans as unrealistic dreaming. The Terrans were very oppressive to Martians, and entry permits were rarely given out. Keila had ignored her mother's objections. She wanted to live the future that her visions showed her every night. She wanted to live on Earth with Bjorn Muller, the prince charming that often popped up in her dreams.

Although Keila had never met Bjorn, she was confident that he was the one from her visions. Bjorn was a famous figure, so he featured often in the Terran and Martian news broadcasts. Bjorn was also the spitting image of the man from her visions and dreams. Although Bjorn was way too old for Keila, he had charm, charisma, looks, and wealth. So Bjorn was everything that Keila wanted in a man. Besides, Bjorn seemed healthy, and he was better looking than most Martians.

Keila made up her mind. When she turned 18, she would board a shuttle to the interplanetary transfer terminals orbiting Mars. From there, she would find a way to meet her prince charming!

# Chapter 81: Another Round of Matchmaking

Bjorn Muller was back in Hansstadt. He was waiting for his father, Joachim Muller, in one of his father's many residences. This residence was a reconstruction of an 18th-century castle. Although Bjorn didn't understand why anyone would want to live in such an archaic building, it was nice to be home and see his family. Spending his time on a military base was not that stimulating, so Bjorn hoped that this could be his chance to leave the army and return home.

Joachim approached Bjorn and spoke.

- Welcome back, Bjorn. I suppose you understand why you are back this time?

Bjorn:

- Yes. I am summoned for another round of matchmaking. It's a shame you are so adamant on marrying me off for political reasons, instead of letting me look for 'the one' myself.

Joachim:

- Bjorn, we have been over this. You are way too old to be a bachelor. You are past your youth. I could overlook your addiction to prostitutes and drugs when you were younger, but not anymore. It's time to be more like your brother, Michael, and settle down with an obedient wife and children.

Bjorn:

- I suppose that you tell Michael that he needs to be ambitious and work hard, like Benjamin and I?

Joachim:

- Yes, but we are not here to talk about your brother's shortcomings.

- I am giving you a chance to come back to Earth and get what you want. All that you need to do, is to marry a member of House White for political reasons.

Bjorn:

- But I already know who I want to marry. I have seen 'her' in my dreams. But I haven't found this woman that appears in my dreams yet.

Joachim slapped Bjorn, and replied.

- Enough of this silly talk! I don't care about your dreams about a woman you haven't even met. I need you to step up and produce an heir to the family empire. An official heir, born within wedlock!

Bjorn:

- Alright. I'll meet with her. I hope that she'll be less dull than the other ones!

Joachim:

- Dull? The other ones were genetically engineered pre-conception to be good future wives to you, and yet you turn them away.

- But I can guarantee you that you won't find Alicia White dull!

Bjorn:

- Alicia White?

Joachim:

- The daughter of John White and a perfect match to strengthen the Muller – White Alliance!

Bjorn:

- Why have I never heard about this woman before?

Joachim shrugged his shoulders and spoke:

- You have been orbiting Mars for the last decades and missed out on most of the official gatherings. Besides, Alicia is only 21 years old, and she rarely attends formal conventions.

Bjorn:

- Is it because she is an outcast, shunned by her own family, like I am?

Joachim:

- Yes.
- But like I said. I can guarantee that you won't find Alicia dull!

Bjorn:

- Very well. When will I meet this woman?

Joachim:

- You'll meet her tomorrow morning. If everything goes well, you will marry her tomorrow night!

Bjorn:

- What? How are you going to make it a formal affair in such a short timespan?

Joachim:

- Neither John White nor I want this wedding to be a formal affair.
- Now get your beauty treatments so you'll look good on your wedding day!

After this, a servant entered the room to lead Bjorn to his beauty therapy appointment.

# Chapter 82: Not Exactly Love at First Sight!

Bjorn Muller woke up in the morning, and he didn't know what to feel. Getting married was his ticket back to a luxurious life on Earth. But what kind of cruel joke was his father playing on him? Bjorn understood the need to marry someone in House White for political reasons. But why in such a hurry and why was there so much hush-hush about his bride-to-be? Alicia White was the youngest daughter of John White, and yet Bjorn had never seen her. She was also a staggering 45 years younger than he was. While Bjorn could understand why a poor woman would marry someone older for money and status, he could not understand why Alicia wanted him.

Bjorn assumed that Alicia was in a similar situation as him. In that case, the marriage would be for show, and they would live their own individual lives. This arrangement suited Bjorn, and he wasn't even bothered if she turned out to be ugly, which was very likely.

Bjorn got dressed and he met up Joachim.

Joachim:

- Good morning, Bjorn.
- You look presentable for once! Excited for your wedding day?

Bjorn:

- About as excited as I am before a dental appointment! But it will be great to leave the army and get to enjoy my birthright.

Joachim:

- Glad you finally came to your senses and listened to my wishes.

- Anyways. Alicia is a very special woman, but I am sure that you'll get along, despite your 'differences'.

Bjorn:

- Despite our 'differences'?
- You are not exactly talking up my wife-to-be, how special is she?

Joachim:

- You'll be alright. Besides, from the bright side, you are getting away from the army!

Bjorn:

- Yes. Let's go meet this mysterious wife-to-be.

They walked to the grand dining hall of the mansion. Alicia White and John White were sitting by the end of the dining table. Bjorn and Joachim sat down opposite them, and joined them for breakfast. Joachim and John were busy talking, while Bjorn checked out Alicia. Alicia didn't look that bad, but Bjorn could tell that she was wearing a thick layer of makeup. This wasn't a good sign, as most Terran women had optimised genetics for good looks and should not need make-up. Bjorn reflected over why Alicia was wearing tinted contact lenses. If this was his bride to be, didn't he deserve to see her real appearance, without attempts at concealing it?

Bjorn decided to break the ice, and he tried talking to Alicia. It wasn't easy, as she kept covering her mouth with her hands every time she spoke. Furthermore, her voice sounded like she had received large quantities of sedatives.

Bjorn:

- So, Alicia, tell me about yourself?

Alicia:

- Uhm.... I am Alicia, daughter of John White.... I am 21 years old.

Bjorn:

  - Okay, so what do you like to do in your spare time?

Alicia:

  - Uhm... I like... anything that you want me to like...

Bjorn:

  - So, you are the submissive type?

Alicia:

  - Uhm... I can be if you know how to handle me.

  - Excuse me, but I must take my leave. While the food you are providing looks delicious, it is not compatible with my special dietary needs...

John:

  - Please, my darling Alicia, stay and get to know our hosts better, will you?

Alicia:

  - No dad, I am not feeling well, and I need to rest for tonight!

John:

  - Okay, my dear. You are free to go. I will meet with you shortly.

Alicia got up, and she reversed out of the room, keeping her front towards Bjorn and Joachim. After she had left John spoke.

  - Alicia is feeling sick today, but she is usually a joy to deal with. She is energetic, loyal, quirky and spontaneous. She is my favourite child, and if you can love her as much as I do Bjorn, I can guarantee you a long and happy marriage.

- I must look after Alicia now. She is nervous about the evening as you can imagine. She is so young, and this is such a big day.

After John had left the room, Bjorn turned towards his father:
Bjorn:

- What is the matter with that woman? Is she retarded? Why is her father so eager to marry her off? She is only 21, there is plenty of time for her.

Joachim:

- I have seen Alicia's IQ score. While she is not as intelligent as you are, she is by no means stupid. Alicia's flaw is the same as yours; her elevated sexual drive and degeneracy.

- Thus, while your initial connection was lacking, you will complement each other well.

Bjorn:

- Sexual degeneracy? What did she do?

Joachim:

- Well, rumour has it that she is very pushy when it comes to convincing her servants to satisfy her sexual urges. We have had similar issues with you. Hence you are a good match!

Bjorn:

- I see. So, she is more than meets the eye? But it would have helped if she wasn't all covered up in that ugly make-up!

Joachim:

- It would also have helped if you weren't a drug-abusing sexual degenerate! But now things are the way they are!

Bjorn:

- Noted.
- Well, I better get ready for tonight.

Bjorn left the room, and he returned to his private quarters. Unbeknownst to Bjorn, John White and his father had conned him when it came to Alicia. John had sedated Alicia to hide her personality, as Alicia was mutant. Alicia was a failed experiment by House White's science-lab to co-mingle her Terran's DNA with that of a crocodile, a bull and a tiger. Alicia had applied a thick layer of make-up and inserted tinted lenses to hide her yellow predator eyes. Finally, John had told her to cover her mouth when she spoke to avoid showing her fangs. Alicia had reversed out of the room to make sure that Bjorn didn't see the small lump on her back, that was her tail!

# Chapter 83: A Failed Hunt.

Alicia White woke up a few hours later, feeling very hungry and strange. Unbeknownst to her, her father had spiked her previous meal of raw meat with sedatives to make her calmer, and more suitable for marriage. John White planned to sedate and marry Alicia to someone influential. Whoever married her would then have to deal with her true self when the effects of the sedatives wore off.

Alicia looked out through the window. It was midday, and it was a beautiful day. A great opportunity to go for a forest walk and catch some prey for lunch.

Alicia remembered her father's instructions. That she should stay in the mansion and not go out on her own. The instructions annoyed her, and Alicia would not obey them! After all, Alicia was a good girl, and she had agreed to marry the man he had picked for her. So, she should have the opportunity to do what she loved the most, to catch and eat animals! The man that her father had picked for her, Bjorn Muller, was old but attractive, and Alicia purred in anticipation of the wedding night. But more than she wanted sex, she wanted to hunt and kill prey!

Alicia realised that she hadn't brought any weapons with her. It didn't matter, as it was more fun to kill her prey in a proper fight with her claws and fangs than it was using guns. Alicia snuck out in the woods that surrounded the mansion. It was a lovely day, and with her beastlike super senses, she soon found a suitable target, a medium-sized Red Deer Stag! Alicia snuck up on the animal, and she leapt at it. Alicia was ready to tear its arteries when she realised something, that she had blunted her claws for the damn wedding! Instead of splitting the animal's arteries with her razor-sharp claws, she only scratched it a bit. And now she had angered a hundred kilo's animal with large horns!

The stag charged at Alicia, and it hit her head. This led to a concussion and caused a big open wound on her cheek. The stag charged at her again. For a split second, Alicia thought of running away. But then she remembered that she was her father's warrior princess and as such, she did not run. Alicia leapt at the stag, and she ended up in a wrestling bout with the animal until she managed to bite its throat with her sharp teeth. Alicia joyfully drank the stag's warm blood, while it was still pumping.

Once Alicia had satisfied her bloodlust, she realised that her wounds wouldn't heal in time for the wedding. Her father wouldn't be happy, but what could she do, she was who she was.

# Chapter 84: A Runaway Groom

Bjorn Muller stood at the altar. He was restless, and his "love", or rather, ticket away from the army, was late. Bjorn could hear the wedding guests gossiping. It had already been a 15 minutes delay and what was Alicia doing?! Bjorn closed his eyes. Yet again, he saw the same vision that had been haunting him for the last years. The vision was of him and a beautiful woman and their daughters. Together they were bringing peace and prosperity to the solar system and ending the tyranny. Bjorn was not a do-gooder, but somewhere within him laid an urge to change for the better, to repent, and to correct past shortcomings.

But who was this mystery woman that kept appearing in his dreams? She was not Alicia; of that, he was certain. So, what would he do? Would he settle for Alicia, his ticket away from the army? Bjorn needed to get away from the military. Bjorn had seen so much suffering and so many atrocities, during his years of service.

Bjorn wanted a comfortable life like his relatives had, and Alicia was his ticket to that life. But if he settled for Alicia, he would never find the woman from his dreams, the one who could bring him true happiness.

Bjorn heard the door open, and he turned around. Alicia and her father entered the room. What had happened to her cheek? And why were her eyes glowing yellow? Alicia smiled at him, and he could see that she had sharp fangs, instead of regular teeth. Alicia approached Bjorn.

Bjorn stared at her in disbelief and spoke.

- Alicia, what happened to you?

Alicia:

- I had a hunting accident. A staghorn pierced my cheek. But at least I got the bastard in the end!

Bjorn:

- Hunting accident? How can stag's horn pierce your cheek when you are hunting deer? They run away from you if you miss the shot!

Alicia:

- It is a lot more fun, killing the prey with your bare hands.

Bjorn:

- That's insane! And what is the deal with the glowing yellow eyes and the fangs? This is a wedding, not a Halloween party!

Alicia:

- That is my real looks.

- During our breakfast meeting, I wore makeup and tinted lenses. But then I woke up, and I realised that my real looks make me who I am. It makes me unique, and it makes me beautiful!

Bjorn was lost for words. He would have settled for the caked-up woman that he had met for breakfast. It would have been worth it to get out of the army. But the absolute freak in front of him was too much. Bjorn would rather stay in the army rather than spending the rest of his life with such a creature! Lost for words, Bjorn decided to make a run for it. "Fuck this, I am out!" Bjorn yelled, and then he ran as fast as he could away from the wedding.

The aftermath of the abandoned wedding was that Bjorn returned to his post as Rear-Admiral on the Phobos base. Meanwhile, John White realised that he couldn't marry Alicia for political gains. Thus, he opted to enrol her into House White Special Operations, where she excelled. Unfortunately,

Alicia's tenure transformed her from a naïve huntress to a mass-murdering psychopath.

# Chapter 85: Au Revoir, Red Planet.

Keila was on a shuttle to the closest interplanetary passenger terminal orbiting Mars. Her ticket stated that she was heading for the underwater colonies on the Europa moon, but that wasn't the actual story. Instead, Keila was heading to Europe on Earth, to Hansstadt to be exact. Keila's visions had told her that she would meet her prince charming there, and together they would reform the solar system for the better. It was a risky move, as Martians were not allowed to travel Earth. If the border control officer caught her, they could send her to the infamous Kaguya Detention Centre on the Moon. Fortunately, Keila looked like a Terran rather than a Martian, so there was a chance that she would get through unnoticed.

It was peacetime, and there was no passport control to get on the ship to Earth. Keila thought that she was in the clear when she had found an untaken cabin for the one-week trip to Earth. As it turned out, she was mistaken. The reason there was no passport control was to test people's willingness to follow the law, something Keila had overlooked. As the terminal was full of security cameras, border officials knew that she had entered a spaceship heading for Earth. The border officials detained Keila and a few others. The guards took Keila to an interrogation room.

Security Officer:

- Miss Eisenstein, why were you on a vessel set to travel to Earth? You are not allowed to travel to Earth without special permission. Are you aware of the punishments associated with going to Earth illegally?

Keila:

- I bought a ticket for Europe, and I am travelling to Europe. I don't see the problem. If I wasn't allowed to travel to Europe, why sell me a ticket there in the first place?

Security Officer:

- Your ticket is for the Europa Moon orbiting Jupiter, not Europe on Earth. Don't play games with us, miss Eisenstein!

Keila:

- But I am a half Terran. My father was a prominent Terran, Mahmoud Rashid. Doesn't that count for something?

Security Officer:

- Your kinship with Mahmoud Rashid doesn't matter. You are not a Terran citizen, and you have boarded a spacecraft without permission.

- We will detain you here while we establish your background to assess your threat level. If we consider you to be safe, we'll transport you back to Mars and ban you from interplanetary travel for 5 years. If we assess you to be dangerous, we'll send you to the Kaguya Fetention Centre. Pray to your Martian gods that we don't consider you to be a threat!

The security officer left, and Keila was stuck in the interrogation room. What a mess she was in. Where was her knight in shining armour, now that she needed him?!

# Chapter 86: An Interesting Prisoner Report

Bjorn Muller was back in his office on the Phobos base. He felt depressed. Bjorn hated everything about his job, orbiting and supervising the cold red desert below him. Now that he had eloped from his arranged marriage, he was unlikely to go back back to Earth anytime soon. Bjorn considered quitting the army, against his father's wishes. He didn't need his family's wealth, he could get a small cottage in the Alps, spending his time mountaineering and writing poetry. Bjorn would have to quit his sex and substance abuse, and he would age quickly if he lost access to his family's wealth and DNA regeneration therapies. But on the flip side, he would find peace at last. Bjorn closed his eyes, and he visualised the concept of finding inner peace!

Bjorn opened his eyes and fear struck him. If he went against his family's wishes, they would expose him to the same fate that befell Mahmoud Rashid. Being a famous Terran Rear Admiral, Bjorn wouldn't last long on Mars, and the best he could hope for in that scenario was a swift death. Bjorn bit his lip, and he felt resignation to his predicament. Captain Adal Schneider entered Bjorn's office.

Adal:

- Greetings, Bjorn. Here is the list of illegal Martian migrants that have tried to go to Earth in the last week. The list also states which prisoners that we will send to the Kaguya Detention Centre, and which prisoners we will send back to Mars.

Bjorn:

- I know what the list says! It's the same damn lists every week, and my answer is still the same. Follow the recommendations set out

by the immigration security officers. I don't like reading these bor-
ing lists!

Adal:

- Yes, sir. This week, however, there is something that might interest you. One of the prisoners is Keila Eisenstein, daughter of your
late friend, Mahmoud Rashid.

Bjorn:

- Oh! That is interesting! Thank you for sifting through the reports for me. Now bring up Keila's file.

Bjorn looked at Keila's file. What stunned him the most was how familiar
she looked. It was as if he knew her, but as far as Bjorn could tell, they had
never met. The files summary read:

*"Medium to High Threat Level. Miss Eisenstein is obstinate and adamant
that she has the right to go to Earth due to her heritage. Observation of Keila
has also revealed that she seems to experience seizures and hallucinations. The
recommended course of action is to lock her up on the Kaguya Detention Centre
for further observation."*

Bjorn put down the file and spoke:

- Come with me Adal, I'll better meet with this woman myself.

Having said this, Bjorn and Adal left the office, and they took a shuttle
to the Interplanetary passenger terminal.

# Chapter 87: Love and Guilt.

**20** minutes later, Bjorn and Adal arrived at the interplanetary passenger terminal. Bjorn sent his bodyguards and Adal on a lunch break, as he wanted to talk to Keila himself. He also deactivated the security camera in the room before entering. Bjorn entered the room and saw Keila.

Bjorn realised that Keila was the woman from his dreams. But how was this possible? And why did he meet his supposed future wife, while she was being locked up like a criminal? Bjorn's head spun as he sat down opposite to Keila. Before he had the time to talk, Keila spoke.

- You are Bjorn Muller, aren't you? So, it was really you! I have seen you in a lot of my dreams. Together, we shall bring peace, prosperity and equality to the solar system.

Bjorn was struggling for words. How could Keila have the exact same dreams as him? He managed to maintain a professional approach.
Bjorn:

- Keila Eisenstein, we detained you because you tried to travel to Earth illegally. What's your position on the accusation?

Keila:

- I am guilty.

Bjorn:

- Are you aware that the penalty for illegal travel, ranges from a five-year travel ban to indefinite detention at The Kaguya Detention Centre?

Keila:

- Yes, I am aware of that.

Bjorn:

- So, why did you do it?

Keila:

- Because I needed to meet you. Together we can help the downtrodden and set things right.

Keila's words triggered Bjorn's emotions, but he tried hard to not show it:

- You could have requested an audience with me.

Keila:

- Yes, but do you grant audiences to average Martian citizens?

Bjorn:

- Of course not. But I don't interrogate illegal aliens either. So, you were fortunate.

Keila:

- Yet, here we are.

Bjorn:

- Yes... Here we are.

- If you excuse me, I need to discuss your situation with my colleagues.

Keila sighed and replied:

- Okay, I am not going anywhere.

Bjorn got out of the interrogation room. He was panicking and hyperventilating. Confusion blurred his mind, and he did not know what to do. How could the woman from his dreams be the daughter of his late friend, Mahmoud Rashid? How could Keila have the exact same visions as he had? And how was he going to act? Bjorn had three options:

1.  To follow his subordinate's recommendation and condemn Keila to detention at the horrible Kaguya Detention Centre.
2.  To show leniency and send Keila back to Mars with a five-year travel ban.
3.  To risk everything for the woman of his dreams. To run away with her, like his friend Mahmoud Rashid had done in the past. Things had not ended well for Mahmoud, and Bjorn believed that his grandfather, Hans Muller, would act the same way against him.

Crippled by his predicament, Bjorn went to a bar and started drinking. Meanwhile, Rangda was studying Bjorn from the Divine Dimension. Rangda had recently dug herself out from her Zetan prison cell.

Rangda knew that Bjorn's and Keila's premonitions came from Brahma, her former Zetan lover. Brahma wanted Bjorn and Keila to fall in love and have plenty of descendants. Rangda didn't like Brahma's plan and she wanted to ruin his divine intervention. Rangda would give Bjorn fourth option; an option she had foreseen would cause a chain reaction of events that would aid her cause. If Bjorn kidnapped Keila, and used her as his sex slave, he could satisfy his sexual desires without worrying about his father's reaction. Rangda planned to help Keila escaping the sex slavery and fill her mind with vengeance. In Rangda's plan, Keila would cause a massive violent uprising against the Terran Council.

Rangda tried to connect with Bjorn's mind, to intercede with his soul. But she couldn't reach him. How could this be? Bjorn had plenty of Zetan DNA, and given that he was a human, he should be easy to influence. Rangda tried again and again to connect but to no avail. On the fifth attempt, a silhouette of Sabina, garbed in a white robe, appeared and spoke. "You shall not corrupt this man's soul, Rangda. I bid you goodnight." After that, Sabina knocked Rangda unconscious with a psionic blast.

After Sabina's intervention, Bjorn's mind reached clarity, and he felt no fear anymore. He would stand up for the one he loved and had dreamt about. He walked into the interrogation room, and he shocked Adal, as he unchained Keila and spoke. "I'm sorry for the treatment that you have received, Keila. I will escort you to Earth. I will take your hand if you wish to marry me."

Flabbergasted, Adal and the guards watched Bjorn escort Keila to the shuttle that would take them back to his command ship.

# Chapter 88: Bjorn and Keila arrive at Europeum Tower.

Joachim Muller was sitting in the CEO's office of the Europeum Tower. Joachim's office was a few levels below the chairman's penthouse, which belonged to his father, Hans Muller. Joachim resented his father. Despite Joachim being over 120 years old, Hans treated him like an ignorant child, as an errand boy.

Joachim feared that Hans might be correct about his lack of ability. Joachim saw no talent or skill in his own three sons, and there was a possibility that he was equally useless. The feeling of inadequacy had tormented Joachim for most of his life. It had started on a Terran Council meeting back in 2785 when Joachim had suggested that the Terran Council should focus on helping the Martians. This suggestion had severed ties with everyone in Joachim's family. After a few decades of bullying, Joachim was a broken man, who blamed the Martians for all his troubles. Hans treatment had converted Joachim from being an advocate for Martian rights to one of the worst oppressors.

Joachim looked at a picture of Bjorn and sighed. What we would he do with his eldest son? Joachim meant for Bjorn to succeed him one day, but Bjorn had turned out to be such an abject failure. When Bjorn was born, House Muller scientists had described Bjorn's genes as perfect. 66 years later, the 'perfect' specimen Bjorn was a whore-mongering drug addict, who was an incompetent Rear-Admiral. Joachim sighed. Bjorn had humiliated House White when he ran away from Alicia at the altar and it would take ages to repair the damage that Bjorn had caused.

Joachim had a sip of coffee, looked up, and speaking of the devil; Bjorn had arrived with an unknown woman in tow. Joachim spat out his coffee in shock. Why had Bjorn come all the way from Mars unannounced? Joachim was about to find out as Bjorn started to speak.

- Father, I realised that you were right. It is time for me to settle down and to get married. Meet my future wife, Miss Keila Eisenstein.

Joachim stared at Bjorn in amazement and disbelief. This was too much even by Bjorn's standards. Showing up unannounced and declaring that he wanted to marry an unknown woman, who appeared to be a Martian! Eventually, Joachim spoke.

- Marriage? What are you talking about, Bjorn? You are a high-ranking member of the solar system's most prominent family. You can't marry someone on a whim! Who is this woman? She looks like a Martian!

Joachim scowled at Bjorn with resentment. Bjorn was going to answer him, but Keila beat him to it:

- Mr Muller, while my origin shouldn't matter as we are all humans, I will answer your question. I was born on Mars, but my parents were not Martians. My father was the prominent Terran, Mahmoud Rashid, and my mother was an Edenite woman named Susanna Eisenstein.

Joachim:

- You better learn some manners around here! Give me a good reason why I should let my son marry you instead of shipping you off to the Kaguya Detention Centre.

Keila:

- Because we both want the same thing. I know about your youth, Joachim. I know how you once wanted peace and equality in the solar system. It's time to pursue that goal now.

Joachim freaked out when he heard Keila say these words. How could she know about his youthful indiscretions, almost 80 years earlier? The Terran Council controlled all the media in the solar system, this episode should have been a well-kept secret.

Joachim acted decisively to hide his weakness. He pressed a button under his desk to alert security. A short while later, the guards arrived. Joachim corrected his tie and spoke:

- Guards, arrest my son and this insolent Martian woman! Put Bjorn under house arrest and transfer Miss Eisenstein to the Kaguya Detention Centre!

Bjorn:

- Please, father, don't do this. I love her!

Joachim walked up to Bjorn and slapped him. Then he spoke:

- Love? You do this to humiliate me.

Keila shouted at Joachim as the guards dragged her out.:

- Joachim! You are making a great mistake. The union of Bjorn and I is the will of the True Maker.

Joachim:

- Then have him smite me, you religious fool!

When the guards had dragged Keila away, Joachim assaulted Bjorn, with a flurry of kicks and punches.

Once Joachim had ended his assault, the guards helped the injured Bjorn to a medical ward. Joachim remained alone in his office to wallow in his bitterness and hatred.

# Chapter 89: A Guilt-Ridden Epiphany.

Joachim Muller was lying sleepless, getting flashbacks from his tortured youth. The crucial mistake to invite his dear friend Agnes Bojaxhiu to speak at the Terran Council meeting, back in 2785, had cost him everything. Agnes' tirade had infuriated the rest of the Terran Council. Joachim's father, Hans Muller, had ordered for Joachim to be "re-educated," i.e. tortured and indoctrinated.

After many months of psychological torture, Hans gave Joachim a test to secure his release. Joachim had to kill a dozen of chained Martian prisoners with his bare hands if he wanted to achieve his freedom. Among the prisoners were women and children, but Joachim was so desperate for his torture to end, that he complied with everything.

A gruelling 30 minutes later, Joachim had finished with his task. The Martian prisoners lay dead in the room, and Joachim was blood-soaked and psychologically scarred. After completion, Hans walked up to him and congratulated him upon passing his test. Joachim had asked Hans why they had murdered the prisoners. Hans had answered that the prisoners were innocent, but their deaths were necessary to punish Joachim.

Joachim got up. Why was he thinking about his youth now? It happened so many years ago. He realised that it was because he had treated Bjorn as bad as his father had treated him.

The ethereal mirage of Sabina materialised in front of Joachim. The illusion was the spitting image of Keila Eisenstein, the love interest of his son. Fumbling in fear, Joachim stepped back and fell over. Sabina whispered gently to Joachim.

- Do not fear, Joachim. I am here to help you do the right thing.

Joachim stuttered back:

- Keila? is that you? What is happening!

Sabina:

- I am Keila's daughter, Sabina. I'm speaking to you from the future, by the powers granted by the True Maker.

Joachim:

- What are you talking about? Did someone drug me? Why am I hallucinating?

Sabina:

- Humans will always fear what they do not understand. Realise this! You can either allow the love between Keila and Bjorn to change destiny and build a more harmonious solar system. Or you can stop them, which will lead to the downfall of your entire species and the rest of the Milky Way Galaxy.

- The choice is yours. But remember, darkness is coming.

Sabina granted Joachim a vision of Rangda and the Xenos. After that, she broke the connection with Joachim, leaving him dumbfounded on the floor. Joachim did not understand what had happened, but he did know one thing. He needed to see his father and set things right!

# Chapter 90: The End of Hans Muller's Tyranny.

An hour later, the aging Hans Muller, sat at his desk with several body-guards' present. Joachim had shocked Hans when called him in the middle of the night and required an urgent meeting. The two leaders of House Muller hardly spoke to each other, and when they did, it was always about business matters, with other people present.

Hans disliked Joachim, and he never spent time with him alone. Hans knew that the treatment he had exposed Joachim to would cause a scar between them that would never heal. But what other options did Hans have, being the rightful leader of House Muller and the Terran Council? He couldn't endorse his son's farfetched demands about equality on Mars. Hans couldn't tear down everything his ancestors had stood for in the last 500 years. That was out of the question!

Hans had loved Joachim back then, but things had to be the way they were. Breaking Joachim's rebellious attitude was his only option.

Hans watched the lift as it opened. Hans spotted his son, Joachim, his useless grandson Bjorn, and a Martian who could only be Keila Eisenstein! Hans was uncertain how to react, but he did not want to show weakness. Hans spoke with a commanding and stern voice as he had done during his entire almost 160-years long life.

- What is the meaning of this? A little happy family reunion? I don't allow Martian filth on this level!

Joachim spoke back with a ferocity that shocked Hans:

- This Martian woman has a name. Her name is Keila Eisenstein, and she is a prophet sent by the True Maker to end the hatred and mistrust that have kept humankind divided for too long.

Hans:

- The True Maker? Who gives a fuck about that religion!

- And didn't you order the deportation of this Martian convict less than 12 hours ago?

- You know what? Screw this. I will deal with her myself. Permanently!

After saying this, Hans pulled up a pistol that he had hidden under his desk. He took aim and fired the gun in Keila's direction, but due to divine intervention, the bullet missed. Instead, the bullet ricocheted and hit Hans Muller in the eye, severely wounding him in the process. One of the guards ran up to the injured Hans to stop the bleeding, but Joachim told him off:

- Stop it. As you can see, Hans has lost his mind, firing a pistol against his own family members.

- Dying by his own hand is a well-deserved fate for a man like him.

Since Hans was unconscious, and no-one wanted to argue with Joachim, Hans bled out in his own office, dying by his own hand. Thus, Joachim finally got his revenge on his abusive father and became the leader of his faction.

# Chapter 91: Joachim Muller Makes New Plans

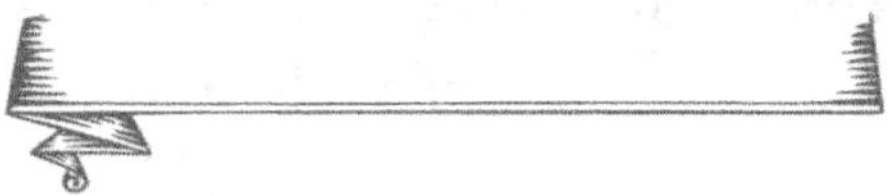

A few weeks later, Joachim had buried Hans Muller, and he became the chairman of House Muller. On Joachim's request, the funeral was a private affair. Joachim didn't want the details regarding Hans' death to become public. Neither did he want to explain why he had refused to revive Hans.

After Joachim had finished with the formalities, he met with Bjorn and Keila in his office.

Joachim:

- Dear Bjorn, my son, and Keila, my daughter-in-law to be. Sorry for being busy the last few weeks. But as you can appreciate, the death of my father has caused upheaval within House Muller.

Keila:

- That is okay, Chairman Muller; we understand that you are a busy man.

Joachim:

- Yes, but now that I am the Chairman of House Muller, I have resources to help you.

Bjorn:

- Great. Are these House Muller resources, or help from the entire Terran Council?

Joachim:

- Only secret House Muller resources, I am afraid. While I know what threat Rangda poses to us, the other factions don't know. I don't dare to risk my credibility by seeming insane to the others.

- If you want a better world, I need to change the Terran Council from within. Seeming insane wouldn't help us.

Bjorn:

- So, what help can we expect?

Joachim:

- Well, there is a portal to the Divine Dimension located in House Rashid territory. It's hidden inside the Cheops Pyramid, and the Rashid's are not exactly our friends. I guess I could send a few special operations soldiers posing as regular bodyguards.

Bjorn:

- Just a few? But we will be up against a dangerous monster. We need to end her life before she causes this apocalyptic catastrophe.

Joachim:

- That is why I am sending another important person, a very capable one, with her own bodyguards.

Bjorn:

- Dad...? You didn't?!

Joachim:

- Well, actually, I did. Keila, meet Alicia White.

Joachim flipped a switch, and the door opened. Alicia entered the room wearing a full combat outfit, smiling a crazed and witty smile, licking her lips and staring at Keila:

- So, this is the woman that Bjorn chose instead of me. What a beauty!

Keila stared at Alicia in disbelief, she had never seen anyone like Alicia. With fangs of a wolf, razor-sharp tiger claws and glowing yellow eyes of a crocodile, Alicia was a sight to behold. While she wasn't pretty, she was most definitely unique. Keila spoke:

- So, how do you guys know each other?

Alicia:

- Our father's betrothed us in an arranged marriage. Unfortunately, a minor hiccup caused us to miss the wedding night.

- I have heard, that you want to open a portal, and fight an evil demon queen in another dimension. And I thought I was the crazy one! Yeah!

Bjorn:

- Father! Why did you bring Alicia here?

Joachim:

- I told you already. I can't send you an army to escort you into House Rashid territory.

- Alicia is the best warrior there is, and besides, she provides an excellent cover-up story for your visit to Rashidium. You'll need to activate four portals, spread across the world, to travel to the Divine Dimension.

Bjorn:

- And what is your cover story?

Joachim:

- The cover is that you you have decided to travel the world together, to get to know each other after the failed arranged marriage.

Keila:

- But Bjorn and I love each other. Why do you want to break us
apart?

Joachim:

- You won't be apart. You'll be posing as one of Bjorn's bodyguards.
It doesn't make sense to make Alicia, the daughter of John White,
appear to be a bodyguard.

- What you do at night, when no-one is watching, is none of my
concern.

Bjorn:

- My father is right. It will take us weeks to travel the world and
clear the paths to the activation switches. Making it look like a
honeymoon is the best way to divert attention from what we are
doing.

Keila:

- I don't like this!

Bjorn:

- Neither do I. But sometimes you must look past your own feelings and focus on the greater good. The future of mankind is dependent on our success.

Keila:

- I guess.

Joachim:

- Great then we are all sorted. Sabina has spoken to me, and she ordered that you head to the Sun Pyramid in Central America.

- Jurgen!

Jurgen the bodyguard:

- Yes, sir.

Joachim:

- Show Miss Eisenstein to our armoury and commission her with House Muller bodyguard uniforms and equipment. Make sure to finalise her employment details in our system. I have already given executive permission to allow this Martian to work with our military.

Jurgen:

- Yes, sir. Come with me, Miss Eisenstein.

After that, Keila followed Jurgen to the armoury, trying out body armours and getting weapons training. As Keila weighed the pistol in her hand, she reflected over how familiar the setting was. She remembered training with weapons and wearing body armour, and yet she had never been in the army before.

# Chapter 92: Jealousy in Central America.

Keila, Jurgen and a few other House Muller operatives were digging in the Sun Pyramid in Mexico. They needed to clear a path to the activation switch. It was tiring work, and they weren't used to such hard labour. Because of the secrecy of the mission, they hadn't brought robots to do the digging for them, so they had to clear the path themselves.

They needed to keep the path to the chamber clear so that they could move quickly. They needed to flip the activation switches at four different locations at noon local time. The only way to do so was to travel fast between the locations. While Bjorn had suggested that they could station one person at each site to activate the switches at local noontime, this wasn't an option. Keila was the only one who could understand the switches, due to her unique genetic makeup.

Bjorn entered the tunnels and spoke:

- Alicia and I have been invited to House Bolivar's fundraising dinner. Keila and Melanie, I need the two of you to come with us as our personal bodyguards.

Keila:

- But why me? And what do I need to do?

Bjorn:

- I will bring you and Melanie to be my bodyguards. Jurgen and others are not very presentable for a fancy fundraising event.

- As for your job, stay in the background and don't say much. I don't expect any threats at the event, and House Bolivar has their own security.

Keila:

- Okay. And you'll be posing with Alicia and speak about your engagement to the press?

Bjorn:

- Yes. We agreed this was the only way. There must be a legitimate reason for me to spend all this time around the pyramids. A reconciliation tour, where we are talking about our love for ancient buildings is a reason that everyone will accept.

Keila:

- I don't like it. It should be you and I together.

Bjorn:

- Look. My father was going to send you to a detention centre on the Moon when he first met you. Although he cannot accept you as my partner, this is a lot better than detention.

Keila:

- You are right. Let's go.

A while later, Keila, Melanie, Bjorn and Alicia arrived at the event centre where the fundraising dinner took place. The venue was beautiful, Bjorn was dashing, and Keila was head over heels for him. It was everything that she had ever wanted. Except that she wasn't his date for the event, she was his bodyguard. Keila felt bursting with jealousy, but there was nothing that she could do. Besides, if her visions were correct, there were more pressing matters on stake than her love life. She needed to stop Rangda, before the universe was in grave danger.

Keila watched Bjorn and Alicia speaking to the press about their renewed engagement. Keila reflected that whoever had done Alicia's make-up had done a fantastic job at hiding her beastly features. Alicia wore contacts to conceal her yellow eyes, she had retracted her claws, and her dress hid her tiny tail. Wearing the makeup, Alicia was a beautiful young woman, unlike the beast Keila had got used to seeing.

A reporter interrupted Keila.

- Wow, you are an exotic one!

Keila:

- I beg your pardon?

Reporter:

- A half Martian, employed by House Muller, as a personal bodyguard to Bjorn Muller. What are the odds?

Keila:

- I don't know. I don't calculate odds. I do my job.

Reporter:

- There is a rumour that your Terran father was Mahmoud Rashid. He was a prominent Terran that Ibrahim Rashid expelled. Do you have any comment on this?

Keila:

- No. My employment contract doesn't allow me to comment on politics.

Reporter:

- But this wasn't a question about politics.

Bjorn noticed Keila's predicament, and he intervened:

- Please don't disturb my bodyguards. They have an essential job to do.

Reporter:

- But this bodyguard, wow! She is a half-Martian. How does that fit in with House Muller's racial policies?

Bjorn:

- My father, Joachim, has relaxed our racial policies after the death of Hans Muller.

- Miss Keila Eisenstein is an exceptional bodyguard who has saved my life on several occasions.

Reporter:

- What about Miss Eisenstein's family ties with House Rashid?

Bjorn:

- Miss Eisenstein's father was my good friend, Mahmoud Rashid. But House Rashid had expelled him before he fathered Keila.

- Now we must proceed to the gala dinner. No more questions!

Bjorn grabbed Keila by the arm, and they entered the event centre; far away from the prying eyes of the press. Once they were in a secluded room, Keila spoke with an agitated voice:

- Why didn't you mention that you knew my father?

Bjorn:

- I didn't know how to bring it up. How do you bring up someone's long-dead dad when you first meet them?

Keila:

- I never knew my father. How was he?

Bjorn:

- Mahmoud Rashid was energetic. He was an idealist that went
his own way and believed more in love than anything else. That's
why he ran off with your mum, Susanna, against the wishes of his
grandfather, Ibrahim Rashid.

- But he never knew that he would get banished from Earth. I
helped him and your mother with money, but there wasn't much
else I could do.

Keila:

- I see. So, the mysterious donations that my mother received,
were from you?

Bjorn:

- Yes. I had no idea what to do when the woman from my dreams
turned out to be the daughter of my dead friend. But, there are
more important things at stake than our own lives.

Keila:

- Yes.

Bjorn:

- So, let's play the roles that Joachim has assigned to us. If we get
out of this alive, we can worry about our relationship later. Please
don't talk to the press. Walk off when they try to interview you.

Keila:

- Yes, sir!

Keila and Bjorn returned to the fundraiser event where Keila had to play the role of Bjorn's loyal bodyguard.

# Chapter 93: Involvement in House Rashid Affairs

A few weeks later, Keila's group were in Egypt to reach the activation switch in the gilded Cheops Pyramid. It was the hardest one to map as it was a famous tourist destination. Besides, House Rashid was unlikely to provide them with a digging permit. Bjorn and Keila had decided to activate the switch in the Cheops Pyramid first. This way, they would have plenty of time to outpace Earth's rotation speed, to activate the switch in the Sun pyramid.

Before they had the time to set their plan in motion; a group of armed men, led by Khaleel Rashid surrounded them. The prominent House Rashid member walked up to Keila and spoke:

- Keila Eisenstein, or should I say, Keila Rashid. Why have you come to our territory? We banished your father from Earth. You are not welcome here.

Keila:

- I prefer that you to call me by my mother's surname, Eisenstein. My father's banishment has nothing to do with me. I am here as an employee of House Muller, to guard Bjorn Muller and Alicia White while they are on their honeymoon.

Khaleel Rashid:

- Bjorn Muller, why are you insulting us by bringing one of our traitors as your bodyguard?

Bjorn:

- Cut the crap, Khaleel! Keila is my bodyguard, and our business here is our own's. If I intended to use her to claim her father's inheritance, I would have done so over a decade ago. Now go back to your father and don't bother me unless you have something important to say!

Khaleel Rashid gave Bjorn and Keila an ice-cold murderous gaze, and he took off in anger. After the interrupters had left, Alicia spoke:

- They'll be back, and it won't be pretty. We'd better activate the switch at Cheops Pyramid today and get the hell out of here before all hell breaks loose.

Bjorn:

- Agreed. Let's hurry up and go.

Keila:

- But who was that guy and why is he after me?

Bjorn:

- That was Khaleel Rashid. He was the one who inherited your father's share of the family fortune when your father died. He is worried that you will make a claim to your inheritance.

Keila:

- So, I am meant to be a wealthy and prominent person on Earth?

Alicia:

- Only in theory. House Rashid's members are infamous for killing each other to elevate their own positions. A consequence of the many progenies that Ibrahim Rashid's harem has produced throughout the years. As an outsider and a half-Martian, they would kill you if tried to make any claims.

Keila:

- Very well. Let's activate this portal and get the hell out of here.

Having said this, Keila rushed to the room with the activation switch. At noontime, she deciphered the portal switch with the correct sequence of codes, and she activated the switch. They rushed back to their spaceship to outrun Earth's rotation speed so that they would arrive in Central America on time.

# Chapter 94: Entering the Divine Dimension.

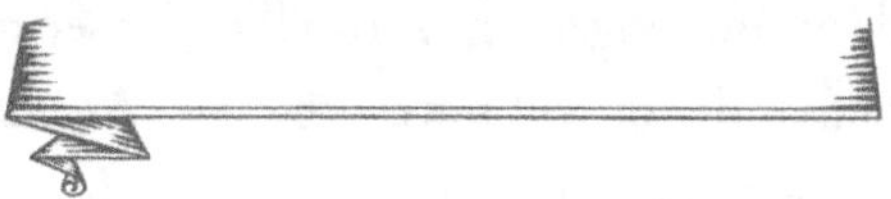

16 hours later, Keila activated the Zetan portal switch in the Great Pyramid of China, located near the city of Xian.

The Great Pyramid of China was the last of the four pyramids that they needed to activate. To Keila's disappointment, nothing seemed to happen when she activated the switch. Confused and bewildered, she walked up to Bjorn and spoke:

- I don't understand. We all heard Sabina, my supposed future daughter, who warned us of a galactical apocalypse. I have done everything that she has asked me to do. Why is nothing happening?

Bjorn:

- Yes. But she never told us that the portals would open straight away. Let's have dinner and enjoy a well-deserved break. The Xian region is famous for its cured mutton.

Alicia:

- While cured mutton sounds delicious, I will take my leave. Keila is the one you love, and I have plenty of other things to do. With no evil alien demon queen to fight, I don't want to stand in your way anymore.

Bjorn:

- Don't be like that, Alicia. Please stay for another day. There might be a delay on the portals.

Alicia:

- I have waited for too long already. You'll never see me as anything else than a freak, and you will never love me. As will no-one else. But I didn't choose to be born this way. I never decided to have my embryo imbued with predatory DNA.

- But it happened, didn't it? And now I might as well live out my life as the fearsome monster that my father created me to be.

Keila:

- Well, I would be sad if you chose to be that way. The Alicia that I know; is kind and has a beautiful soul. It would be a shame if your father's choices become your destiny.

Alicia:

- Thanks, Keila. I guess it wouldn't hurt to travel to Xian and enjoy an evening of sightseeing and a lot of cured mutton.

Melanie Weber joined in on the conversation:

- Then it's settled. The three of you go to the city for dinner, while I stay here and observe the pyramids. I'll let you know if anything changes.

Bjorn:

- Thank you, Melanie. Let's go, Alicia and Keila.

Having said this, they flew to the nearby city of Xian and they ate the delicious cured meat, topped with a heap of hot steaming rice. As Alicia was helping herself to a fifth plate to satiate her hunger, Bjorn received a message from Melanie. "The top of The Great Pyramid is glowing blue, come as soon as possible!"

The group flew back to the pyramid. As they arrived, it was glowing with a bright blue light, and it had a neon blue laser beam coming out of the tip of the pyramid. It was a magnificent sight, and some of the locals had gathered to stare at it in awe. Keila looked at Bjorn and spoke:

- The portal has opened, what do you reckon is on the other side?

Bjorn:

- I have no idea, but I know one thing. House Cheng's security forces are on their way, so we better move quickly.

- I'll pick up Melanie and Jurgen, and we'll fly straight into it.

Alicia:

- Finally, some excitement!

Bjorn landed the spaceship and picked up Melanie and Jurgen. He noticed that House Cheng's troops were approaching, and he realised there was no time to lose. Bjorn flew straight into the portal at The Great Pyramid of China. Zoom! There was a bright flash of light, and the spacecraft disappeared from the onlookers' sights into thin air.

# Chapter 95: Meeting Brahma.

Bjorn opened his eyes as the spaceship hovered over the dusky and featureless plane that was the Divine Dimension. Apart from the shimmering mist of galactical debris in the background, there wasn't much to see.

To Bjorn's surprise, the spaceship's dashboard picked up objects 50,000 kilometres away. It was as if he was on an infinite flat plane. Bjorn saw how planet Earth, as well as the entire Milky Way Galaxy, was zooming out from his peripheral view. It was getting smaller and smaller, as they were leaving the normal dimension. Bjorn turned to Keila, and she opened her eyes.

Bjorn:

- We made it through alive!

Keila:

- Yes, we are alive. Although there is no way to be sure. Then again, is there any way to ever know whether one is alive?

Bjorn:

- That's a philosophical question, and we didn't come here for a mind-boggling debate. What is our next step?

Keila:

- I have seen a kind and old gentleman, the Zetan Brahma, in my visions. Finding Brahma would be our priority.

Bjorn:

- Okay. The ship's sensors are picking up the heat signature from a group of creatures not far away. Can it be them?

Keila:

- It must be. Let's go there and communicate with them.

Alicia:

- Excellent. You do the talking, while I stand ready to save the day if it comes to violence.

Bjorn:

- Keep calm, Alicia; we didn't come to this mysterious place to pick unnecessary fights.

Having said this, Bjorn navigated the spacecraft towards the group of Zetans and he landed close to them. As they approached the Zetans, Odin spoke confidence:

- Greetings, humans. I see that you have finally solved the riddle within the portal in the pyramids, and opened them from your end. Have you brought us any offerings?

Keila:

- We are not here to offer you any gifts. We need to find Brahma and warn him of the apocalypse. Rangda has escaped, and we need to stop her.

Odin's face lost its colour, and he spoke again:

- Rangda? But we locked her up in an inescapable prison, how could she escape? And who are you guys? I sense strong Zetan abilities in you.

Keila:

- I am Keila Eisenstein. I am accompanied by Bjorn Muller, Alicia White, Jurgen Kessler and Melanie Weber. We need to find Brahma at once.

- As for Zetan abilities, I have had strange dreams and visions of Brahma and my future daughter Sabina. Does that count?

Odin:

- I don't know anyone called Sabina, but if Brahma is calling for you, you'd better go see him. He is at the Uluwatu Temple two hundred kilometres that way.

Bjorn:

- Thank you, my good sir. I am looking forward to making your acquaintance when we get back. Now we must hurry.

Bjorn and the others got into the spaceship. A short while later, they arrived at the Uluwatu Temple, where Brahma was expecting them. He nodded as they approached them, and he spoke:

- My premonitions were correct. Pairing the two of you together would open the portals to Earth and free us Zetans from this prison. Have you come to worship us?

Keila:

- Your premonitions are not as good as you think they are. Your ex-lover, Rangda, has escaped. We must stop her before she gathers and corrupts the Zeto Crystals and becomes unstoppable.

Brahma:

- What are you talking about? How do you know?

Keila:

- My daughter from the future, Sabina, told me everything. How you Zetans fooled ancient humans that you were our gods, to make us fight the Xenos.

Brahma:

- You insolent girl. We altered your intelligence to make you what you've become. Without us, you'd be primitive apes and not the "crown of evolution" as you perceive yourselves! For all intent and purposes, we are your gods.

Keila:

- That might be, but that discussion is irrelevant. I need to know where Rangda is so we can stop her.

Brahma froze, and he realised what he had done. The engagement ring he had once given to Rangda, had contained a tiny stone made of a replicated Zeto Crystal. As Zeto Crystals were the hardest material in the universe, Rangda could have used that tiny stone to dig herself out from her prison cell. Brahma had forgotten about this important detail when he sealed Rangda's prison cell. Worse yet, once Rangda was out of her cell, she could have used the Zeto Crystal in her ring to power the portal to her home planet, Xenora. On Xenora, Rangda could find one of the powerful primordial Zeto Crystals.

Brahma:

- Xenora. She must have travelled to Xenora and visited her home planet!

Keila:

- Well, what are we waiting for? Get in the spaceship and lead us to Xenora at once. We got a score to settle and a future to save.

# Chapter 96: Travelling to Xenora

Keila, Brahma and the others arrived outside the portal to Xenora. Distances were a lot shorter in the Divine Dimension. Although Xenora was thousands of light-years away from Earth in the regular universe, the trip was quick in the Divine Dimension. They got out of the shuttle and much to their dismay, Rangda had closed the portal behind her, and they had no means of powering it up.

Brahma sighed and spoke:

- So close, and yet so far. I can feel Rangda's presence on the other side of that portal, but we have no way of powering it up.

- I assume none of you brought a Zeto Crystal?

Keila:

- Well to be fair, the word doesn't exist on Earth, so we have no idea what it is?

Brahma:

- In the human language, it would be a sapphire. It's a rare and valuable form of a sapphire.

Keila:

- So, all we need to do, is to go back to Earth and pick up some sapphires?

Brahma:

- In theory, yes. But I can sense unspeakable evil from the other end of the portal. Rangda might be corrupting the Zeto Crystal as we speak, and time is of the essence.

Alicia pulled up a heart-shaped amulet, with a bright blue sapphire.

- Will this work?

Bjorn:

- Alicia! I have travelled with you for weeks, and you have never shown it to me. It's beautiful, where did you get it?

Alicia:

- I got it from my mother before she passed away. After the death of my mother, my father turned insane and deleted all the records of her. The amulet is all that I have left of her.

Keila:

- Your father seems like a complete dickhead. Why would he do such a thing?

Before Alicia had time to answer, Brahma interrupted:

- Look, humans. As intriguing as Alicia's paternal relationship might be to you, we are in a hurry! That amulet is the key to powering the portal. Give it to me now, Alicia.

Alicia had a look at the amulet. For the first time in her life, she shed a tear, and then she handed the charm to Brahma. Alicia spoke:

- Take it; this is what my mother would have wanted.

Brahma took the crystal, and he put it in a slot next to the portal. The portal lit up the door with a sparkling blue light. Brahma shouted out:

- Hurry up. Run into the entrance. We need to stop Rangda.

Bjorn:

- What about the spaceship?

Brahma:

- It won't fit. Hurry up. Run into the portal now!

They all did as Brahma commanded and they ended up in Rangda's temple on Xenora!

# Chapter 97: An Unlikely Hero Saves the Day

Keila opened her eyes, and she saw the black orb in the centre of the room. The orb radiated with such darkness, so it looks like a black hole, which almost absorbed all the light in the hall. Rangda held the sphere with her hand, and she laughed hysterically. Brahma rushed towards Rangda, and the others followed him. Brahma stopped a dozen metres away from Rangda, and he shouted out:

- Rangda! What are you doing? Stop this madness at once!

Rangda:

- Brahma, we meet again. Earlier than I had planned, but it doesn't matter.

- I was giving this primordial Zeto Crystal its true colour, and the other crystals will follow.

Brahma:

- True colour? You are corrupting it. The crystals are blue: like the sky, like freedom, like life.

Rangda:

- Bah. The air can get polluted, freedom is an illusion and life is only temporary. None of those things last. Black, on the other hand, is the only real colour. It's the colour of the universe and the colour of death. It is the very essence of life.

Brahma:

- Talk all you want Rangda. I am here to stop you, and you won't
be a prisoner this time. I will kill you!

Rangda:

- Indeed, I won't be. You have arrived too late, and you will be the
one to die today.

Having said this, Rangda blasted Brahma with a psionic blast, powered
by her corrupted Zeto Crystal. Brahma tried to resist, but he wasn't strong
enough, and he collapsed to the floor. Seeing this, Jurgen ran up towards
Rangda and started firing at her with a submachine gun. Rangda's ballistic
energy absorbers stopped the bullets. Shortly afterwards Jurgen's head was on
the floor, decapitated by Rangda's sharp claws. Rangda licked her claws and
spoke:

- Pathetic! But delicious. I don't have time for you now humans, I
got to deal with Brahma first.

Having said this, Rangda sent out a psionic shockwave in a circular pat-
tern around her. The shockwave knocked Keila, Bjorn and Melanie to the
ground. Keila tried to get up, but she was too wounded, and she could only watch as Rangda turned her attention to Brahma. Rangda pushed Brahma
against a wall while draining him with the corrupted Zeto Crystal. Rangda
had a long rant:

- I have been waiting to do this for thousands of years. You have
disgusted me ever since you first laid your eyes on my "beautiful"
Zetan appearance. I was beautiful back then, wasn't I?

- You thought that I loved you and you never saw through my intentions. I guess you couldn't read me as I was only half Zetan. I
hated you from the start, but I needed you. You were my tool to

advancement within the Zetan society so I could destroy it from within.

- How does it feel knowing that your death is imminent and that your death will power my efforts to take over the galaxy and become its god-queen?

Brahma was powerless and in immense pain, as Rangda was shattering his soul using the unholy powers of the corrupted Zeto Crystal. The pain stopped and what he saw amazed him. Alicia had intervened.

Rangda was feeling immense pain when the sharp claws of Alicia White pierced her back:

Rangda:

- Aarrgh! How did you resist my psionic blast, you feeble human?

Alicia:

- I guess I am not human enough for your magic to affect me! Take this!

Alicia pushed her pistol into Rangda wounds, and she filled Rangda's chest with a dozen bullets. The bullets tore Rangda's organs into shreds but powered by the corrupted Zeto Crystals she didn't die. Instead, she punched Alicia hard enough to send her flying into a wall knocking her unconscious.

Brahma got up, and he chopped off Rangda's arm with his plasma sword causing her to drop the corrupted Zeto Crystal. The Zeto Crystal rolled over to Keila who grabbed it. As she grabbed it, the silhouette of Sabina appeared, and she whispered. "Dear mother, this may be the last time that I will ever speak to you again. Through the power of The True Maker, I will bless this crystal back to its original purity". Thus, Sabina purified the Zeto Crystal, using Keila's body as a vessel.

Once Sabina had purified the Zeto Crystal, Rangda lost her powers, and her wounds became mortal. As she dropped to the ground, she hissed:

- I lost, but I will live on. There will always be evil in the world.

Brahma looked at Rangda and spoke:

- Yes, there will always be good and bad in people. But your evil
ends today. Goodbye, Rangda!

Brahma channelled his powers into his fist, and he struck Rangda in
the head. The strike crushed her skull and ended her evil ambitions for the
galaxy.

Brahma took out some Zetan healing serum, and he resuscitated Bjorn,
Alicia, Keila and Melanie. "Come back with me to the Divine Dimension,"
Brahma said. Wounded but alive, the group made their way back through the
portal.

# Chapter 98: Alicia gets Rewarded, and Brahma Tells the Truth.

Brahma studied the bright blue light emitting from the primordial Zeto Crystal. Its beauty mesmerised him. Brahma felt relieved that the Zetans had found a new Zeto Crystal to unite their species. But he still mourned the loss of Zetani and Zetani Nova and the end of Zetan civilisation. Unbeknownst to Brahma, primordial Zeto Crystals were indestructible. Thus, they were still floating in space where Zetani and Zetani Nova had existed. That was how Rangda had acquired them in the original timeline.

Brahma turned to Alicia and spoke:

- Alicia, when I first met you, I would never have guessed that you would be the one to save us. How did you do that? How did you withstand the psionic blast?

Alicia:

- It came naturally to me. I didn't feel it much at all, but I pretended that the blast wounded me to convince Rangda that I wasn't a threat.

- I knew that I needed to attack her from behind and take her by surprise. She showed immense speed and power when she killed Jurgen, and there was no way I could fight her in a head to head battle.

- I thought I had defeated her when I unleashed a dozen pistol shots straight into her abdomen. But instead, she knocked me unconscious. What happened afterwards?

Brahma:

- You killed her physical body, but powered by the immense malicious power of the corrupted Zeto Crystal, she wouldn't die. Rangda died when I chopped off her hand, and she lost the crystal to Keila, who cleansed it through the benign powers of The True Maker.

Alicia:

- Cool. It feels good to be the hero for once.

Brahma:

- And for your bravery, I will reward you. What do you want most of everything in the world?

Alicia:

- I want to be normal. To be free of my mutations, I want to love and find someone who loves me back.

Brahma:

- But you are an extraordinary specimen with unique capabilities?

Alicia:

- So was Rangda, and that didn't end too well.

- Being extraordinary is good, but condemnation to a life in solitude drives the mind crazy.

Brahma:

- I will speak to my fellow Zetans. We will cure your ailment turning you into a regular Terran human.

Alicia:

- Thank you, Brahma. I can't tell you how thrilled I am.

Brahma turned towards Keila:

- As for you, Keila, I could sense that you were a Terran/Zetan hybrid with extraordinary abilities. But I could never foresee that you would be this great. You cleansed the Zeto Crystal from Rangda's evil prowess, and you saved us all.

Keila:

- It wasn't me. I was only vessel for Sabina's and the True Maker's holy powers and divine will.

Brahma:

- Well, that kind of humility serves a future queen. I hope that humans will appreciate you as such when you get back home.

Keila:

- Yes. I am so excited knowing that I am to mother the future messiah of humankind with my handsome Bjorn.

Hearing this, Brahma felt deep shame. He blushed and looked away. Keila noticed that something was wrong, and she spoke again:

- What is the matter Brahma? Did I say something wrong?

Brahma:

- I am feeling guilty. You see, you and Bjorn are not meant to be together. I influenced your minds to make you fall in love, because I needed the two of you to be together to open the portal.

Keila:

- Why are you saying these things? Bjorn and I are a great match.

Brahma:

- Tell me, Keila. Except for your dreams and your instant infatuation with Bjorn, what do the two of you have in common?

Keila:

- I... I don't know.

Brahma:

- Well, that because you have nothing in common. You are still young Keila, and Bjorn is old and lonely. Bjorn needs to find love more than you do, and luckily his love is right in front of his eyes.

Bjorn:

- Alicia?

Brahma:

- Yes. The two of you complement each other. You are both outcasts, you both come from prominent families, and together you can change things for the better.

Keila realised that Brahma was correct. She felt heartbroken, and she started crying. How could things end like this for her? How could she lose her hopes and dreams after saving the world? Brahma came up to her and comforted her.

- It might not feel like it now, but there will come a day in the future when you'll realise that this will be for the best.

Keila:

- But can you tell me when that day will be?

Brahma:

- Our destined paths together have come to an end. I can provide you with emotional support, but I can no longer foresee your future. But I know that you'll one day meet Sabina's father and you'll be happy together.

Keila:

- Thank you, Brahma. I guess not everything in life can be perfect.

Brahma:

- No, it cannot. You'll have to deal with what life gives you. Let's head to Earth. There is a lot for you to do.

Having said this, the group set their course towards Earth, and a few days later they were back home.

# Chapter 99: Bjorn and Alicia get married and unite humanity.

The following months, came with a lot of upheaval for the future of humanity. Finding out about the Zetans, who were a lot more advanced than humankind, came both as a shock and a blessing. Initially, there was a lot of fear. But as the Zetans brought clarity and peace with their primordial Zeto Crystals, most people relaxed. The Zetans sent an expedition to find humanity's primordial Zeto Crystal, also known as the Holy Grail.

While the Holy Grail didn't end all evil, it stopped most of it. Under its influence most people followed ideals such as unity and peace, instead of pursuing greed, lust, and hunger.

Alicia's father, John White, couldn't handle the change. John blamed the Zetans for taking his daughter away from him. Brahma had turned Alicia from a mutated warrior princess, to a kind-hearted and beautiful young woman. Filled with feelings such a rage, desperation and guilt John took a big leap from his penthouse office to end his life. Alicia succeeded John and became the leader of House White. Everyone respected Alicia, as she had saved the galaxy from the vicious Rangda. Once she was in command, she reversed many of the former House White policies. Alicia's first objective was to send a massive aid package to Mars, to help end the Martian suffering and poverty.

Meanwhile, Joachim Muller, seeing the man that Bjorn had become, gave up leadership of House Muller to Bjorn.

A year later, Bjorn and Alicia got married. Together they united House White and House Muller to improve the solar system under their new doctrines. Bjorn invited Keila to the wedding, but she didn't attend.

Instead, Keila returned to Mars as a House Muller official coordinating the rebuilding effort of Mars. Despite the progress for her home planet, Keila felt heartbroken, and she never wanted to see Alicia or Bjorn again.

# Chapter 100: It's Time to Save Eden.

Two years later, in the year 2871, Keila was living in a fancy mansion in her home city on Mars, Pamshal. Keila was a successful official who had reversed the Terran Council's policies towards Mars. Under Keila's supervision, Mars was starting to flourish.

Due to the advanced technologies of the 29th century, the rebuilding process was swift. What was once a toxic and overpopulated wasteland had become a flourishing and peaceful planet, where everyone could get by in peace.

Despite her success, Keila felt broken on the inside. Her visions had shown her a future with Bjorn; and it had all been a lie. Although she had set herself up for life financially, she felt like a failure. It had been years, and she couldn't get her heart mended. Keila's mother, Susanna, who stayed with her, knocked on her door and entered her bedroom. Susanna gave Keila a worried look and spoke:

- Keila darling, are you feeling down again?

Keila:

- It's not fair, mother. My visions showed me the oncoming doom. I set out, and I saved everyone. Yet I am the one feeling lonely, crying myself to sleep at night.

Susanna:

- Life isn't fair, my sweetheart. And besides, everyone loves you. If you stop thinking about what could have been and start enjoying the moment, you'll be happier.

Keila:

- I am doing that every day, and it helps me with my mission to make Mars a better place. But while working for House Muller puts me in a position where I can help others, it also serves as a constant reminder of what could have been.

Susanna:

- Except nothing good would happen if you had married Bjorn. Bjorn's marriage with Alicia worked out for everyone. The marriage united House White and House Muller and gave them the power to advance the solar system. If you had married Bjorn, there wouldn't have been a combined power improving the everyday lives of the people. Besides, Bjorn would face a lot more resistance from his relatives.

Keila:

- Huh. How come?

Susanna:

- Bjorn and Alicia are prominent members of their factions, and together they strengthen each other's positions. But you are the bastard daughter of the exiled Mahmoud Rashid. Your presence would weaken Bjorn's position on Earth.

Keila:

- I guess you are right. But what can I do with my life? I am desperate for change.

Susanna:

- Well, there is one long-overdue thing...

Keila:

- And that is?

Susanna:

- My homeworld, Eden, is still oppressed by the tyrant Abraham Goldstein.

Keila:

- Mum! We have spoken about this. Abraham has a perpetual agreement with the Houses of Earth that gives him immunity. This agreement prevents them from intervening in his business if he poses no threat to them.

Susanna:

- I know. But does Abraham Goldstein have an agreement with you or me?

Keila:

- It doesn't matter. I am an employee of House Muller, and I cannot go on a rogue mission to Eden, to overthrow Abraham.

Susanna:

- Well. You could end your employment. Then you are not bound to follow House Muller's treaties.

Keila:

- But how would we attack Abraham's battle station without any help?

Susanna:

- We don't need to. Your friend Brahma, can give us stealth technology to approach the colony undetected. If we kill Abraham, we can pose as Eden's new rulers and carry out a peaceful transition of power.

Keila:

- I guess you are right. So, what do I need to do?

Susanna:

- Contact Bjorn and tell him about your resignation. Then contact Brahma and get the Zetan technology schematics that we need, to rule over Eden.

Keila:

- I can do that!

Susanna:

- That's the spirit. It's time to save the Edenites at last!

# Chapter 101: Infiltrating the Divine Control Centre.

Susanna and Keila were sitting in a small Zetan stealth shuttle. They were observing Abraham's headquarter orbiting Eden. Keila studied a scan of the base. It seemed like the entire crew were in suspended animation, and that the AI ran all the daily operations.

Keila looked at Susanna and spoke:

- Are you sure this is the place? It is so eerie, and everyone seems to be in cryogenic sleep.

Susanna pondered the matter for a few seconds and spoke:

- Well, the cryogenic sleep explains something that I never quite got my head around.

Keila:

- What is that?

Susanna:

- When I grew up on Eden, Abraham's goons, the angels, never aged. I have been thinking about how that could be the case, but extended periods of cryogenic sleep explain it. If they are only awake a couple of days a year, they never have the time to age.

- But this is excellent news. If no one is watching, it will be easier for us to enter the base and dispose of Abraham.

Keila:

- Well. We still must enter the base unnoticed and reach Abraham. Any suggestions?

Susanna:

- Yes. We'll use the Zetan Quantum Computer to hack and reprogram the AI to make it identify us as friendly visitors, and give us full access.

Keila:

- How about reprogramming the AI to kill Abraham for us?

Susanna:

- Too risky. To get the AI to kill someone, you must deactivate Asimov's three laws for robotics. It works for a military application robot with a limited AI. But altering the Artificial Intelligence on Eden might cause it to go homicidal, killing everyone, including us.

Keila:

- Agreed. I'll start the AI Hacking Quantum Computer.

A few minutes later, the Zetan AI hacking device had infiltrated the Divine Control Centre, and Keila's ship was ready to dock. Keila docked with the base, to find Abraham and end his reign of terror over the Edenites.

# Chapter 102: The End of Abraham.

Keila and Susanna snuck around inside the Divine Control Centre. They had never seen an installation quite like it. It was a mixture of a top modern research facility and a Bronze-age temple. Passages from Abraham's holy book, the Abrahameon, filled the walls. While walking in the corridor, Keila came across a cryogenic tank and she saw Metatron stuck in suspended animation. Seeing Metatron shocked Keila. She felt like they had met before, and yet she had never been to Eden.

Keila heard the voice of Sabina speaking in her head. "That man is Metatron. He will be my future father. But for now, you must move on."

Keila moved on. Since the breakup with Bjorn, she had felt empty and depressed, but seeing Metatron made her feel better. Keila wanted to study her partner-to-be more closely, but she remembered what Sabina had said, and she carried on.

Keila and Susanna entered the throne room where the robotic body of Abraham Goldstein greeted them:

- Susanna, you came back at last. I must say that I am impressed with you. Altering the AI and sneaking into my base undetected.

Susanna:

- If you saw us coming, why didn't you try to stop us?

Abraham:

- Good question, and one that I cannot answer I am afraid.

- You have fascinated me for many years Susanna; ever since you volunteered for the Edenites selection to get away from here.

- Do you know how lucky you were? Most child brides sold to Ibrahim Rashid didn't survive for long. He didn't want to leave any loose end.

Susanna:

- I never met Ibrahim. Instead, I met with his grandson, Mahmoud Rashid, and together we had Keila before he passed away due to sickness.

Abraham:

- I know. I follow the Terran news.

- From your unlikely relationship with Mahmoud Rashid, sprung your daughter Keila, who turned out to be the saviour of humanity. It is so poetic and improbable that I almost start believing in 'the goodness of love'.

Susanna:

- So you didn't believe in kindness and love?

Abraham:

- Exactly. Humans are animals that need to be controlled

- When I funded the Divine Detector machine, I felt excited. I would achieve what no man had done before. I would be talking directly with God. But once I reached the Divine Dimension, I found out that Yahweh was a Zetan imposter. I stole his Zetan schematics, and I used them to deceive and manipulate my Edenite population to obedience.

- I realised that I could become a god to my people, the god of the Edenites. So, I made a deal with Terran Council. I invested my fortune in buying this asteroid that I call Eden. The Zetan technology enabled me to control the Edenites and smite the unbelievers of the Abrahameon, the dogmata that I envisioned.

Susanna:

- So, do you feel guilty over your atrocities towards the Edenite population?

Abraham:

- What atrocities? I created a safe and enjoyable world for the Edenites to live in. I provided them with the ultimate law and a framework for a happy life.

Susanna:

- You murdered and maimed a lot of Edenite civilians for breaching your immoral laws. You sold innocent children as slaves to fund your madness!

Abraham:

- Those people knew that they were sinning. Those who disobeyed the Abrahameon laws deserved punishment.

- Selling the children was not my original intention, but I was desperate for funding the maintenance of Eden. Sometimes, one must sacrifice a few for the common good.

Susanna:

- But you never considered sacrificing your own power and your self-inflated Godhood for the common good. It was all to satisfy your egoistic hunger for oppression and power!

Abraham:

- I don't claim to be without fault. But I am hoping that you'll realise that I am not the bad guy that you think I was, and that you will spare my life. I am old, and I am nothing without the protection of my super-soldiers, who are now sleeping in their cryogenic tanks.

Susanna:

- You are missing one critical part in your argumentation.

Abraham:

- What would that be?

Susanna:

- That you have been dead for decades. Your kindness left your body when you died. The only thing that's left of you is your wicked brain, and whatever signals your brain receives inside that gigantic android glass cocoon. Your existence is blasphemy on all living beings. Goodbye, Abraham!

Susanna pulled up her pistol and she unleashed a dozen bullets into Abraham's brain. The shots broke the glass cocoon and splashed the clear liquid that contained Abraham's brain. Abraham died within seconds.

# Chapter 103: Finding Love at Last.

Metatron opened his eyes, and he looked at Keila. He felt something that he had never felt before. He felt attraction, excitement and passion the moment he saw her. But how could this be? Metatron knew that he was a genetically engineered super-soldier born out of an artificial womb, to serve Abraham. As such, he had never experienced strong human emotions before, as he only knew the dedication to work duties. Unbeknownst to Metatron, Sabina had used her powers to awaken his dormant soul. Metatron studied Keila, the most beautiful woman he had ever seen, and he spoke:

- You freed me. You freed me from my servitude to the evil dictator, Abraham.

Keila:

- You freed yourself. There is nothing that I could have done if you had chosen to take vengeance for your fallen master.

Metatron:

- Abraham's death was long overdue. As a matter of fact, he died decades ago.

Keila:

- So why did you bring him back?

Metatron:

- It was fear of the unknown. We lived to serve Abraham, and we didn't know what to do with ourselves when he was gone. Anyways, I didn't have any say in the matter, but Lucifer wanted to bring our master back. Ironically, Abraham murdered Lucifer for loving a woman more than he loved Abraham.

Keila:

- So, what will happen now?

Metatron:

- I must take my leave. There is no place for me here anymore. I served a villain for decades. I need a fresh start and a new goal for the remainders of my years.

Keila bit her lip. Should she make the leap of faith and proclaim her love for Metatron? It was insane, but her daughter from the future told her that Metatron was the one, so she could not let him go. She cleared her throat and spoke:

- How about coming with me to Mars? I have a lovely house there and influential Terran friends. We could help rebuild the planet together.

Metatron smiled at Keila. Her words filled him with joy and relief. Metatron replied:

- I would like that very much. If nothing else, for the excellent company.

Keila smiled at him and spoke:

- Oh, I am not always this nice. I can be quite a handful when I have my bad days.

Metatron:

- I wouldn't want you any other way.

Keila:

- Good. I'll let my mother know that we are heading back to Mars. We'll have so much fun ahead of us.

Metatron smiled as he watched Keila run off with youthful enthusiasm to tell her mother the good news. Although he was physically only a decade older than Keila, due to extended periods of cryogenic sleep, his soul was that of an old man.

Later the same day, Keila was watching Metatron's naked body in bed. She felt relieved that she had finally got over Bjorn, and she could imagine a bright future for herself and for her people.

Finding peace after several heartbroken years, Keila fell asleep in Metatron's arms.

# Chapter 104: Sabina Says Farewell to the True Maker.

Nine months later, Sabina felt a funny feeling she had never experienced before. She felt like she was about to be born again. While Sabina had been born during the previous timeline, before the True Maker had turned back time, it was different this time. This time, she was going to be born as a sentient being instead of as a baby. Sabina summoned the True Maker to say goodbye.

- I am about to be born again, and I want to thank you for giving humanity and the other sentient species of the Milky Way Galaxy another chance at life.

The True Maker:

- It is I who should thank you. I wanted to save everyone, but the scope of my powers inhibited me from doing so. Only through you, could I set things right.

Sabina:

- I guess we should be grateful that things turned out the way they did.

The True Maker:

- I couldn't agree with you more.

Sabina:

- So, will I see you again?

The True Maker:

- I am the essence of the universe. I am everyone and no-one.

Sabina:

- I'll take that as a yes.

- You have never told me what will happen to my soul when I die. Will we meet in the afterlife?

The True Maker:

- Once you die, the universe will absorb your life force and you'll become part of the universe. Thus, you'll cease to exist and yet you'll live on.

Sabina:

- Wow. I guess I will experience it eventually.
- Farewell, my friend, and thanks again.

Sabina's mind blackened, and she felt a strange feeling overwhelming her. Sabina felt how her mind warped and distorted through space and time. As she opened her eyes, she was in a medical room, naked and covered in slime. After a few seconds, Sabina realised that she had been reborn. Sabina looked at her mother, Keila, who had given birth to her. Sabina's body cried while her heart whispered:

- Thank you, mother. Thank you for giving birth to me.

# Chapter 105: The Official Ending

Sabina Eisenstein was a blessed child that turned out to be the Messiah of mankind. Sabina became the Supreme Leader of the solar system, and she utilised the powers of the Zeto Crystals to create a world devoid of suffering and greed. Leading humanity and the Zetans, Sabina initiated widespread space colonisation. Together, humans and Zetans spread across the Milky Way Galaxy, influenced by the benign Zeto Crystals. Having learnt from their previous mistakes, the Zetans left inhabited planets alone. They also stopped playing gods by altering the genome of other organisms.

Sabina refused to use DNA regeneration technology, and she died at the age of 112. When she died, there was nothing left of her body as she evaporated into pure light. Sabina's birthplace on Mars and place of death on Proxima II, orbiting Alpha Centauri, became places for pilgrimage for millennia to come.

Alicia and Bjorn spent a large chunk of their families' fortunes on improving the conditions in the solar system. Due to their wealth and influence, they managed to reduce poverty, war and disease in the entire solar system by 95%, in a couple of decades. When Sabina came of age, Bjorn and Alicia replaced the Terran Council with the Human/Zetan Interplanetary Alliance. Under Sabina's leadership the organisation put an end to war, disease and suffering. The organisation became a great success, and after a few millennia, most star systems of the Milky Way Galaxy was part of the alliance.

Keila and Metatron lived happily together on Mars for many years. They occupied themselves with philanthropy and Martian politics. They were proud of Sabina, although life wasn't always easy being the parents of the Messiah for humankind. Eventually, they moved back to Eden where they could live out their lives away from the press and the social media. Keila died on Eden in 2984 at the age of 134. She died on the exact same day as her daughter did, as the True Maker wanted them to meet in the afterlife.

# Chapter 106: Ending 2: Rangda Wins and Conquers the Universe.

(The following event takes place on the same timeline as chapter 76) During the apocalyptic battle, Rangda blasted the True Maker with the full force of her seven corrupted Zeto Crystals. This caused her to feel something that she had never felt before. The True Maker felt pain and fear.

The True Maker's physical form manifested in the Divine Dimension, and she was unable to make herself ethereal again. She coughed up some blood and spoke weakly:

- How is this possible...? How can you hurt me when I am the universe? I have created the seven Zeto Crystals in every galaxy, yours are only a fraction of the total.

Rangda:

- You fool. You have underestimated my wrath! Those seven Zeto crystals are the only ones that influence this galaxy. The crystals that you have spread out in the other galaxies won't save you now.

- Any last words?

The True Maker:

- Please spare me. If you kill me, there won't be anyone to reset the universe when it reaches the end of its lifespan. Eventually, darkness and death will replace everything!

Rangda:

- And that is precisely what I want. Ha-ha-ha-ha!

After saying this, Rangda blasted the True Maker with the corrupted Zeto Crystals. The blast caused the True Maker to explode, in an intense explosion of pure light.

Rangda opened her eyes, which were recovering from the intensely bright light. As her vision returned, Rangda felt better than ever. Her powers had increased by several magnitudes, and there was no reason for her to ever stop accumulating power. Rangda saw Sabina, who without the blessing of the True Maker, was just a frightened young girl.

Since Rangda was a sadistic monster, Sabina became her favourite torture victim. Rangda kept Sabina alive for eternity, to fulfil her sadistic desires. Rangda's ravenous hunger for power led her to travel from galaxy to galaxy in a never-ending quest to conquer everything. A few years later, Rangda invaded Earth again. This time she enslaved humanity, turned them into Xeno/human hybrids, and condemned them to forever serve her. Rangda enlisted every human into her army and left before a black hole swallowed the solar system.

Rangda kept increasing her arsenal of corrupted Zeto crystals, which unbalanced the universe. Eventually, the unbalancing, caused by Rangda's endless appetite for Zeto Crystals, reached a critical point. Fuelled by the pure darkness within them, The Corrupted Zeto Crystals collapsed into a Black Hole. The black hole was so large so that it destroyed both the universe and the Divine Dimension. With the True Maker no longer left to reset the timeline, this event led to the end of all life in the universe.

# Chapter 107: Ending 3 Time is reset to 10172 B.C. (Preventing the birth of Rangda)

(This ending follows chapter 77)

Sabina was inside the True Maker's mind, and she could turn back time to make things right. But the options were endless and what time should she pick? An idea flashed in her head. What if she could prevent Rangda from ever being born? This way, she would save the Zetan galactic civilisation, and she would avoid all the suffering caused by the multi-millennial war.

Sabina entered the mind of Yahweh who was on research expedition on the Xeno home planet of Xenora. Sabina could feel Yahweh's anger boiling in his head, driving him insane. Kalianka had publicly rejected Yahweh. Yahweh felt humiliated, and he wanted to get his revenge. If Sabina didn't intervene, Yahweh would assault Kalianka, and leave her for dead. The Xenos would find Kalianka and she would eventually give birth to Rangda. The key to saving the future was to stop that from happening. Sabina spoke to Yahweh:

- Yahweh. I know that you are angry, but it's not the right way. Don't do it!

Hearing Sabina's voice shocked Yahweh. He had hidden his intentions to the other Zetan, and he didn't recognise her voice. Panicking, Yahweh yelled out:

- Who are you? Show yourself.

Sabina did as Yahweh requested, and he stared at her mirage in disbelief. Eventually, he spoke:

- A human girl? Utilising telepathy? In a star system very far away from Earth? How is this possible?

Sabina:

- I am a human saint from the future. My soul merged with the True Maker when she destroyed the Milky Way Galaxy to stop Rangda from destroying the entire universe.

After saying this, Sabina showed Yahweh how the Xenos would invade and destroy the Zetans. Sabina showed Yahweh how Rangda was drinking the blood of his fallen Zetan peers. Seeing this gripped Yahweh with panic and he shouted with a desperate voice:

- So, this will happen because I put Kalianka in place for rejecting me?

Sabina:

- Yes. You are in the wrong. You can never force someone to love you. Avenging a rejection makes you a pitiful creature.

At the same moment, Kalianka arrived at Yahweh's location on Xenora.:

- You wanted to speak with me, Master Yahweh?

Seeing Kalianka overwhelmed Yahweh with guilt. During a bout of insanity, he ran up to the top of a cliff. Yahweh jumped off the cliff, and he landed headfirst onto a stalagmite, piercing straight through his brain. This killed him straight away and made his body impossible to resurrect. Shocked over Yahweh's suicide, the Zetan researchers abandoned Xenora and left the Xenos to live as they had always done.

Without the emergence of Rangda and the Xeno hordes, the Zetan galactic empire lasted a lot longer. It was still going strong by the year of 2887 when the timeline of the plot ends.

Without the need for soldiers, the Zetans left humanity alone to fend for themselves. Because of this, humanity never invented civilisation and organised religion. Instead, humans lived as they had always done, as hunters and gatherers, in harmony with nature. Eventually, Sabina was reborn within an Amazonian tribe. She decided to not share her knowledge, and instead, she let humanity live as they had always lived. Humanity lived in innocence and harmony with nature, as the True Maker had intended her creation to be.

# Chapter 108 Ending 4: The True Maker Refuses to Reset Time.

(This ending follows after chapter 76)
Sabina cried as the True Maker shouted:

- No, I will not turn back time to save your species. Things happen for a reason, and I am responsible for all the life in the universe, not only the small fraction of it that resided in the Milky Way galaxy.

After that, The True Maker disappeared. She was still there, but she refused to acknowledge Sabina's attempts to communicate.

Sabina sat devastated, and she was crying for eons. Everyone in her galaxy was dead, and the Divine Dimension was also an empty wasteland with nothing living in it. Sabina felt like the loneliest soul in the universe.

But then, Sabina realised something. That the universe was a lot larger than the Milky Way Galaxy. If she kept walking, she would reach other galaxies, and she could study the lifeforms there. The distances in the Divine Dimension was a lot shorter than in the outside world, so she could walk to the Andromeda Galaxy, in a few decades. Sabina studied the lifeforms in the Andromeda Galaxy for thousands of years until she made a depressing realisation. Sabina realised that all the lifeforms in the Andromeda Galaxy were silica-based. Since they weren't carbon-based, she would never be able to connect with them as they ran on completely different wavelengths. While this insight made her depressed, another idea made her happier. Somewhere in the universe, there would exist humanoid creatures, which had evolved independently from those in the Milky Way.

With this insight in mind, Sabina travelled the universe for millions of years until she found humans in a very distant galaxy. There she was born, and less than a cosmic blink of an eye later she was dead. That was her fate, having lived for millions of years, human life was so short to her so she could not even conceive it. On the bright side, once Sabina had been reborn and died, her travels were finally over.

# Chapter 109: Ending 5: Time is reset to 2019 AD

(This ending follows chapter 76)

Looking through all the potential timelines, Sabina found 2019 to be fascinating. It had all that she needed to achieve her objectives. There were ancestors to both Metatron and Keila that had very similar genetics to their very distant descendants. If Sabina could get these ancestors to copulate, she could ensure that she was reborn. Once she had been born in the 21st century she could find the primordial Zeto Crystal and stop Rangda who was still in prison at the time.

But first, she needed to be born, and there were a few problems. Her potential parents already had partners and they lived at different ends of the world. Also, her potential father, Marvin Orchard, had a hidden condition that would turn into a very aggressive cancer in a couple of months. The cancer was incurable and Sabina wouldn't be born and able to save him with her divine powers until he had already died. But it was what it was. She would have to deal with the unfortunate loss of her biological father.

For her conception to happen, Sabina had to make her parents meet. The easiest way would be for them to meet on holiday away from their partners. Thus, having fewer interruptions to deal with. But where would she send them? Her mother Ellen Himes was from South Africa, and her father Marvin Orchard was from Australia. The answer came up as a flash for her. She would make them meet in Egypt during a tour to the pyramids.

But time was short, as her father would get his diagnosis in less than two months. Using her powers to influence, Sabina managed to convince both Ellen and Marvin that they were bound to go on a holiday to Egypt straight away. Unfortunately, she couldn't get their partners out of the way, so Ellen and Marvin brought their respective partners to Egypt. While this was a complication, it was also for the best. It would have been difficult for her mother to explain to her partner John, how she got pregnant during a holiday if he wasn't present!

Eventually, the opportunity for Sabina's conception arose. Both Ellen and Marvin were at the same restaurant. Sabina caused their eyes to meet, and she filled them with insurmountable amounts of carnal desire. Marvin and Ellen excused themselves from their partners, and they met up in the bathroom, where they had a tryst. After that, Sabina released them from her spell, and they returned to their respective tables, confused over what had happened.

A few months later, Marvin became very ill, and he died soon after. But this wasn't Sabina's most significant concern. While it would have been nicer to grow up with her biological parents, it was not achievable in this timeline. Sabina needed to convince Ellen to not have an abortion. Sabina was successful, and some months later she was born. One of the first things Sabina did, once she was born, was to tell her mother the truth. That she shouldn't feel ashamed over the tryst, as it had to happen.

Many years later, when Sabina was an adult, she set out to find Earth's primordial Zeto Crystal, i.e. the Holy Grail. She intended to use it to open the portal to the Divine Dimension and confront Rangda.

You can read about Sabina's adventures during the 21st Century in the **Sabina's Saves the Future Trilogy**.

The End!

# Don't miss out!

Visit the website below and you can sign up to receive emails whenever Martin Lundqvist publishes a new book. There's no charge and no obligation.

https://books2read.com/r/B-A-QIOG-OMVY

# Also by Martin Lundqvist

Money Laundering in the Laundromat
James Locker: The Duality of Fate (Second Edition)
Pyramidportalen
Matts Fantastiska Vecka
Divine Space Gods Trilogy
Diez Historias Aleatorias y Muy Cortas
Ten Random and Very Short Stories
Dieci Storie Casuali e Molto Brevi
Dix Histoires Aléatoires et Très Courtes
Zehn Zufällige und Sehr Kurze Geschichten


Watch for more at martinlundqvist.com.